Fade *to* Gray

OTHER TITLES
BY MANDI TUCKER SLACK:

Tide Ever Rising
The Alias

Fade *to* Gray

a novel by

Mandi Tucker Slack

Sage Springs Press

Cover design by Valdas Miskinis.

Published by Sage Springs Press

Printed in the United States of America.
First Edition

23 22 21 20 19 18 17 16   10 9 8 7 6 5 4 3 2 1

ISBN: 978-0692630716

For my husband,
for always believing in me,
even when I didn't believe
in myself.

CHAPTER *One*

I collect the rent on the fifth of every month. If it is late, I charge twenty-five extra for every week you're overdue. If you go over by more than three weeks, out you go!"

Tarrin's gaze traveled across the small living room one last time before she turned to face the elderly woman. She realized she had forgotten the woman's name so she smiled, then nodded.

"It'll be perfect. I'll have the rent in on time. How much did you say the deposit was?" she asked.

The older woman's eyes narrowed. "Twelve-hundred-dollars, and if you want the place, then I'll need it immediately," the landlady continued. "I have two other people interested in this house. It'll go fast in this city, so you need to let me know now if you want it. I will *not* hold it. It's a year contract. No exceptions."

Tarrin Grace nodded to show she understood. Was this really what she wanted? She'd never considered raising her children in the middle of the city. She enjoyed small towns—safe communities—and the run-down neighborhood in Seattle seemed to be neither, but what choice did she have? She was quickly running out of time and options. She *was* looking for a change, and living in the middle of Seattle would certainly be a change.

"Miss Grace?" the landlady's gravelly voice prompted.

"Uh . . ." Tarrin suddenly remembered the elderly woman's name. *Cope—Edna Cope*, she reminded herself. "Miss Cope, I'll take it. I . . ." She exhaled. "I do want the place. Will you take a personal check for the deposit?"

Edna nodded. "Long as it's good. If it doesn't clear—out you go. I can't make exceptions, you understand?"

Tarrin nodded somberly. "It will clear."

"Good. Sign here." Edna shoved a worn clipboard into

Tarrin's hand.

Tarrin scanned the legal jargon before she scrawled her name across the bottom of the lease agreement. *Well, this is it.* She handed the form back to Edna with a wary smile. She wondered once again if she was doing the right thing. Could she make the dilapidated old house a home?

"No drugs. No smoking. No parties. Initial here. Break the rules and out you go. No exceptions."

"Oh, no. Of course not. That won't be a problem."

Edna eyed Tarrin with a frown, but Tarrin smiled, trying to reassure the woman as she signed the check for the deposit. She handed it to Edna. "We won't be a problem," she repeated.

"I'll need your sister's signature as soon as she arrives. I live across the street, two houses down. That red one—just as you turn up the street. Send her over so I can explain the rules."

Tarrin nodded. "I will."

"Good," Edna declared with the first hint of a smile. "I hope you and your little ones will be happy here."

Surprised, Tarrin replied, "Thank you, Miss Cope."

The smile disappeared from Edna's craggy face. "Keys." She thrust two bronze keys into Tarrin's hand. "And don't forget the rules!"

The elderly woman nodded brusquely and turned to leave just as Tarrin's son, Jake, burst through the front door, followed quickly by his five-year-old sister, Lexie.

"Mom! Mom, guess what?" Jake called when he passed Edna. He brushed a lock of dusty-brown hair out of his eyes. "There's a forest in the backyard. It's *so* cool." He grinned.

"There's a lot of ants," Lexie interjected quietly, following her brother. Lexie glanced shyly at Edna before she wrapped her skinny arms around Tarrin's leg.

"Can you guys say 'hello'?" Tarrin asked her children.

"Hi," they repeated in unison.

"This is Miss Cope. She owns the house," Tarrin continued.

Jake's face brightened. "So we're going to live here?" he asked. "Cool."

Tarrin nodded.

"Awesome. I like it. Can I go pick out our room?" Jake turned to face his mom with an eager expression.

"In a minute," Tarrin replied. "We'll take good care of this house, won't we?" she addressed her children.

Jake nodded seriously and then glanced toward his sister, who still clung tightly to Tarrin's leg. "Umm-hmm," Lexie murmured, her response barely audible.

"Thank you again, Miss Cope. I'll send my sister over as soon as she comes," Tarrin told her.

Edna cleared her throat then nodded. "Good afternoon." She turned and disappeared out the front door.

After a brief moment's hesitation, Tarrin's gaze fell toward her daughter. "Well," she spoke. "That's it, I guess," she said.

"We're really going to live here?" Lexie whispered.

"I think it's cool. I like it," Jake added, slamming the front door.

Tarrin's gaze traveled around the room one more time before she untangled Lexie's arms from around her leg. With a sigh, she knelt to face her daughter. She gently grasped Lexie's shoulders and smiled into the girl's hazel eyes. "Yes, I think we'll be very happy here, don't you?"

Lexie shrugged. "I like the forest. Can we go for a walk in it?"

"Of course we will, but later. Aunt Erin will be here soon, and we need to move our stuff in today. Maybe tomorrow?"

"I'm going to pick out our room. Come on, you slow pokes." Jake raced toward the narrow staircase situated between the small living-area and the even smaller kitchen.

"Well, what do you say? Should we go pick out our room?" Tarrin forced a smile.

Lexie nodded.

"Good." Tarrin kissed her daughter's brow. "Give me just a minute to call Aunt Erin, so she knows where to come, okay?"

03

Upstairs, Tarrin moved from one room to the next, while Jake and Lexie argued over their choice for a bedroom. There were only two bedrooms, and she cringed a little. She would need to share a room with her children. She knew her sister wouldn't mind sharing a room with her, but Erin had sacrificed so much for her already; ever since her divorce from Travis the year before. She felt the least she could do was allow Erin some semblance of solitude. *Besides,* she mused, *privacy in a house this tiny is going to be hard to come by.*

"Mom," Jake's voice pulled Tarrin from her thoughts and she turned to face her ten-year old son as he entered through the door of the south-facing bedroom. "We want the forest room," he informed her.

"The forest room?" Tarrin chuckled a little. "Alright, then. That's a good choice."

She turned back to the window, and gazed down at the cramped, narrow road that ran parallel to the house. She had to admit, she liked the view, and she smiled as she watched a car slowly make its way up the fairly steep hillside. The residential street was lined with nearly identical homes, all in various states of disrepair. She could hear the sounds of the city below. Cars honked, and a siren sounded in the distance. The noise of a bustling metropolis was definitely something that would take a while to get used to. She would miss the sound of the wind sighing through the tall desert grass. She would miss the murmur of crickets and bright, star-filled skies. She closed her eyes and again wondered, *have I made the right choice?*

"Mom," Jake's voice interjected impatiently. "Come look, okay?"

4

He darted from the room, and Tarrin breathed out as she turned from the window. She could hear the children laughing in the second bedroom, and she moved down the hall to join them.

"So," Tarrin stepped into the bedroom, "this is it?"

She eyed the sickly green walls with distaste and shrugged. The paint was peeling in the corners, and the shag, orange carpet was frayed and stained. The room smelled old and musty.

"This is the forest room," Lexie ran to Tarrin's side and grasped her hand. She pulled her mother toward the wide window. "See? You can see the forest. Maybe we'll see a bear."

"Bears don't live in the city, *stupid,*" Jake spoke.

"I'm not stupid! Y*ou* are," Lexie frowned and turned from the window to shove her brother.

Jake laughed, and Tarrin groaned. "Hey! No fighting." Then she added, "I mean it!" when Lexie stuck her tongue out toward her brother.

"Hey, did you see that? *Brat*!" Jake yelled. "She pushed me."

"Don't call me stupid!" Lexie ducked behind Tarrin. She wrapped her arms around her mother's leg, and poked her head around to stick her tongue out toward Jake once again.

"See? Did you see that?" Jake scowled

"Enough!" Tarrin admonished. "I said stop fighting. Jake, you're too old to fight with Lexie the way you do."

"But she pushed me," he protested, glaring at Tarrin.

Tarrin pinched the bridge of her nose. "Stop. Please?" she begged. "I'm going downstairs to wait for Aunt Erin. Just stay up here and play. And I mean it! No more fighting!"

"You're *stupid*. Bears live in the woods," Tarrin heard Lexie whisper as she turned toward the stairs.

Tarrin frowned. She descended the stairs and walked into the kitchen, taking a moment to gaze around the tiny room. The cupboards and counters were worn; the appliances outdated. However, despite its 1960's vintage-look, the kitchen felt comfortable—cozy. She stepped toward the refrigerator and opened the almond-colored door. A cool burst of rank air brushed across her face and she wrinkled her nose. The fridge definitely needed a good scrubbing. With a frown, she shut the door before she moved to the sliding glass entrance that led to the wooded backyard.

A thin strip of grass separated the house from a patch of dense trees. Feeling the need for fresh air, Tarrin slid the glass door open with a bit of effort. The runners needed cleaning and probably a good oil treatment. Her list of to-do's was growing longer with every passing minute. She sighed and walked out into the yard. The ground was soft, covered in a carpet of thick grass and patches of moss. It was almost sponge-like in texture. Even the air felt different than in the dry, arid climate of western Colorado.

The sound of birds echoed from within the tiny forest and she ambled closer to the edge of trees. She brushed her hand along the almost impenetrable wall of ferns growing on the border of her lawn. The soft fronds kissed the tips of her fingers, and Tarrin breathed in the heavily scented air before she gazed toward the darkened, cloud-covered sky. *I'm going to miss the sun.*

She turned to face their new home and peered up toward the bedroom window situated just below the vaulted roof. The little green house seemed to blend in with the forest, untamed box hedges, and bloom-less rhododendrons surrounding the yard. A short, leaning fence divided their plot from the neighbors', and the little houses sat close together, with barely enough space to separate one from the other.

Still, it was a suitable upgrade from an apartment. The house was a place they could call their own, despite its run-down appearance. It was a comfortable little place, although, definitely different than what they were used to. But, change was good. *We need change,* she reminded herself, *and since we have to start over, why not here?*

Tarrin had never lived anywhere besides Colorado. She had lived in a quiet, comfortable town, surrounded by family, friends, and neighbors she'd known her entire life. She led a calm, secure existence, and she and Travis had known one another since childhood. They lived in the same neighborhood—attended the same schools. They were best friends as children, and later, high school sweethearts. They married quite young, but despite that, she always believed her future with him was safe. Their life had been comfortable—idyllic—and never in her wildest dreams had she ever considered that her world would change so drastically.

Her divorce left her vulnerable, and the events that transpired before seemed surreal. Leaving Travis was one of the hardest choices she ever had to make. She inhaled when she turned back toward the patch of trees and gazed through the maze of foliage. Moss clung to some of the branches and everything looked—green. *I like green*, she mused.

"This is good. We need this," she spoke out loud.

In the months following her divorce, Tarrin felt as if she were drowning. She knew it was time to start living again—*really* living. She needed to surrender her grief and pain. She needed to embrace forgiveness in order to let herself heal completely, and for the first time in nearly a year, she felt the first inklings of hope. Perhaps this house, in the middle of the city, would be just the place she needed to start over; a place to rebuild her little family.

Her children needed the change. Travis's family had been difficult to deal with after the divorce, especially his brother, Brandon. Brandon and his wife were more than antagonist toward her, and Tarrin knew the turmoil between the two families was not good for her children to witness or endure. When she first mentioned the idea of moving to Seattle, Jake had—without any hesitation—agreed.

He'd spent his free hours before their move researching the city and all the surrounding areas. He'd been excited by the new sights they encountered on the drive from Colorado, and he was more conversational than Tarrin had seen him in months. His enthusiasm was contagious and it left her feeling ever more hopeful. The loss of his father was terrifying and confusing, so she enjoyed seeing him embrace this new adventure so whole-heartedly.

Lexie, not fully understanding the complexities the divorce brought into her life, was less enthusiastic about relocating, but she seemed to handle the change better than Tarrin expected. This move would be good for her children. She felt certain of that. Too many painful memories of a life that was forever lost lingered in Colorado. A new town, a new home, new friends, a fresh start—it was just what they needed and she could only hope she and her children would be able to progress and heal.

"Hey, Mom." Jake suddenly appeared in the open doorway, startling Tarrin.

Pulled from her thoughts, she faced her son. "What?"

"Aunt Erin's here," he informed her and disappeared again.

She glanced back at the small patch of woods one last time before turning toward the house. She was glad Erin had made it safely through the busy city in the moving truck. She and her younger sister had separated earlier in the morning. Erin stayed back at the motel with the moving truck, while Tarrin ventured out into the city to find a place to live. She and her children spent several hours visiting a multitude of apartments and condos that fit within her meager budget; none were suitable. Feeling tired and cranky, they had stopped at McDonald's for lunch, and by a stroke of luck, she'd stumbled on the advertisement for the house.

Tarrin snorted quietly when she stepped into the kitchen. *More like blessed*, she thought with a laugh. After the *affordable* apartments they toured, the little house seemed like a place in the Hamptons. The run-down house wasn't what they were used to, but it was better than what she had expected, especially considering her inadequate savings. She hoped Erin would approve, but there was no backing out now.

"This is the beginning of my new life", she murmured with a smile, and with that thought in mind, she walked quickly through the house and out onto the front porch.

Erin, catching sight of Tarrin, waved enthusiastically from across the narrow street. Tarrin smiled and waved her hand in greeting while she walked across the strip of grass in the front yard. She paused at the sidewalk and waited as her sister crossed toward the house.

"Wow, what a place. I wasn't sure the truck would make it up this hill." Erin grinned and then eyed their new home appraisingly. "When you said you found a house, I thought you meant a *house*," she laughed.

Tarrin grimaced. "If you'd seen our other choices, you'd understand."

"Do you like it?"

Tarrin shrugged just as Jake rushed over. "Hey, we have our own forest. Come and see it!"

"We do?" Erin sounded skeptical, and Tarrin nodded.

"It's just a little spot of trees behind the house," she explained.

"Yep, it's great. Mom said we can go exploring as soon as we unpack," Jake answered while Lexie suddenly appeared behind Tarrin.

The little girl's arms wrapped around Tarrin's leg, and she peered up at her aunt with wide eyes. "Jake says there aren't any bears, but I saw a deer from my bedroom window. It was watching Mom."

Tarrin laughed. "It was? I didn't see it."

Lexie nodded. "It was standing behind a tree," she added.

Tarrin turned her attention back to Erin. "It's . . . well, you know. It's not exactly what we're used to, but it'll do, don't you think?"

Erin nodded. "It'll do. Well, come on, Jakers. Give me the grand tour." She winked when she brushed past Tarrin and followed Jake into the house.

Erin and Jake's voices faded as they disappeared inside,

and Tarrin glanced down at Lexie with a smile. "Will you sit on the porch while I start unloading the truck?" She untangled Lexie's arms from around her leg once again.

"Can I help?" the little girl asked. Her thumb strayed to her mouth.

Tarrin's smile faded. Sucking her thumb was a habit Lexie had adopted following the divorce, and a sharp pain twisted against Tarrin's heart. She frowned. "Don't suck your thumb, sweetheart," she admonished gently. "Why don't you just watch from the stairs? There are a lot of cars on this street and you could get hurt."

Lexie nodded solemnly and sat on the crumbling, stone staircase, and Tarrin forced an encouraging smile before she walked across the busy road and moved toward the truck. It wouldn't take long to unpack, and for that she felt grateful. She was beginning to feel the physical exhaustion of packing and then spending days on the road. She struggled for a moment with the stiff latch, then slid the door open. They had only brought a few beds, a handful of boxes, and Lexie's rocking horse—a toy Travis had purchased just a few months before their divorce. Lexie had developed a strong attachment to the horse, and Tarrin eyed the little wooden animal with a slight scowl.

She'd sold most of their furniture to help finance the trip, and with the meager funds she retained, she hoped to buy a second-hand couch and a small kitchen table to furnish their new home. With determination she pulled herself inside the truck then gazed around, trying to evaluate where to begin. She stooped to grab a box labeled *'Erin's junk'* then gasped when Jake suddenly jumped into the truck with a nerve-jarring bang.

"Oh!" She turned. "Jake! What are you doing?"

Her son's face creased in confusion. "Helping," he stated matter-of-factly.

"Well, I really don't like you crossing that street by yourself. You should have stayed with Lexie."

Jake bent to retrieve a smaller box. "I'm not a baby," he reminded her with a scowl.

"I know, but this isn't like home. This is a city—a big city. There are too many cars, and . . . and it's just not safe," she reasoned.

"Aunt Erin's right. You worry too much. I can cross a street. Geeze, Mom." He rolled his eyes before he jumped from the truck with his box in hand.

Flustered, Tarrin stepped from the vehicle. She paused to wait for a few cars before she followed him toward the house. He turned when he reached the sidewalk to give her a mischievous grin, and she rolled her eyes before returning his smile. She noticed how tall he was getting. When had he grown so tall? He waited near the sidewalk and watched her approach with a lazy grin. It felt good to see him smiling again.

"So," Erin's voice cut across the yard. "Jake says you're going to share a room with them. What gives?" She sauntered onto the front lawn to stand next to Jake while Tarrin crossed the street.

Tarrin frowned when she met her sister's eyes. "You need some space," she defended. "Once school starts, you're going to need a place to relax and study."

"Here, I'll take that." Erin reached for the box in Tarrin's hand with a scowl. "Those are mine. So I thought having a *roomy* was what college was all about."

Tarrin laughed. "I would hardly call your sister and her children ideal college roommates."

Erin rolled her eyes and gave her older sister a disparaging look across the top of the box. "I'm putting my stuff in our room, *roomy*." she replied before turning back into the house.

"Erin?" Tarrin called after her sister. Ignoring her, Erin stomped up the stairs toward the bedrooms. Tarrin groaned before glancing down at Lexie. "Hmm," she murmured. "Well, how do you feel about all this?"

Lexie shrugged and lifted her thumb to her mouth. "I

dunno."

"Will you feel bad if I share a room with Aunt Erin instead of you and Jake?" Tarrin asked.

Lexie shook her head, her blond curls swung from side-to-side. "Uh-uh."

"No?" Tarrin's brow rose.

"Nope," the little girl replied. A small smile touched her mouth.

Tarrin reached down to touch her daughter's curls. She let Lexie's soft hair run through her fingers. "Then, I guess I'll share a room with Aunt Erin."

"Hey!" Erin appeared once again in the doorway. "Let's get the mattresses in now."

"Good idea." Tarrin turned to Lexie. "Why don't you and Jake play in our new backyard while Aunt Erin and I finish unloading? We don't want to step on you."

"Well, I want to step on her," Erin teased. She nudged Lexie with her foot.

"No, no," Lexie giggled, shoving Erin's foot away. Erin laughed again before she bounded down the stairs. "Where's Jake, Mama?" The little girl asked. She stood and wrapped her arms around Tarrin's leg.

"I'm right here. What d'ya want?" Jake called from inside the house.

Tarrin turned toward her son when he appeared in the doorframe. He eyed his mother and Lexie with a slight frown.

"Why don't you take Lexie out back for a bit?"

His frown deepened. "But I wanted to help."

"You will be helping. I need someone to watch Lexie. You can go into the backyard," she suggested.

"Can we go into the woods?" his voice rose, hopeful.

"No," Tarrin answered slowly, "not right now."

"Why not?" Jake challenged. "I won't get lost. I'm not a baby."

"I know, Jake, but wait. Please?"

"But, why?" he pressed. "It's not fair!"

Tarrin groaned. "Just—Jake! I said to wait. Don't argue with me," she answered.

"Fine." he conceded. He glared at his sister. "Come on, Lexie."

Without waiting, Jake stomped through the house. Tarrin heard the grating metal as he jerked the sliding glass door open, and she bent to unwind Lexie's arms from around her leg.

"Go with Jake," she instructed.

"Okay," Lexie mumbled.

She raised her thumb to her mouth, and Tarrin watched despondently as her daughter walked through the kitchen and out into the backyard. With a weary sigh, she turned to help Erin finish unloading the truck.

CHAPTER *Two*

The man stared out the window, studying the trees below. The wind brushed through the top of several conifers causing them to sway gently back and forth. A breeze whispered through the open window, and he breathed in deeply. He could hear his date giggling in the bathroom down the hall, and the grating sound jerked up his spine. He grimaced, but forced a dazzling smile when she suddenly appeared before him wearing a rather alluring black dress. Her hair was piled high on her head, exposing her slender neck. She had an attractive neckline. He sighed.

"You're beautiful," he spoke.

She giggled again and he closed his eyes. That sound set his nerves on edge.

"Give me just a minute to grab my purse, and then I'm all yours, baby," she crooned.

His forced smile felt stiff. "I can't wait," he murmured.

She skipped down the hall, and he waited quietly for her return. He glanced about her cramped apartment. Her décor was classless to say the least, but the apartment was nice, especially for this area of the city. It was too bad she'd never return. He smiled again. She was right—she was all his.

ೞ

Tarrin flipped the newspaper open and laid it next to her plate of pizza. She, Erin, and Jake sat cross-legged on the floor while they shared their picnic-style dinner. She was looking forward to purchasing a table and a couch. Their current arrangement was far from comfortable, but Tarrin tried not to dwell on her aching backside.

"I'll pick up some groceries after I stop in at a few places tomorrow," Tarrin murmured, scanning the job listings.

"Sounds great," her sister spoke between mouthfuls of pepperoni pizza.

Tarrin used her index finger to sort through another job listing and she groaned glumly. "Wow, this one says you *only* need a bachelor's degree to apply." She suddenly wished she hadn't quit school so soon.

She had attained an associate's degree in business, but she realized trying to find a job in the recent market required a lot more schooling than that. She had been certain in a city as large as Seattle, she would quickly secure a job, but her expectations were quickly fading. Jobs were hard to come by in her small hometown, and Tarrin had spent the past year working at a local grocery store, barely making enough to scrape by. Would they be in the same financial situation here? She turned the page and scowled again. She desperately wished she had thought to call about internet hookup sooner, but it would have to wait until the morning as well.

"Don't worry. Something will work out," Erin encouraged.

"So far all I've found are places who are hiring MBA's and people with bachelor's degrees," Tarrin complained.

"Nobody puts ads in the paper anymore," Erin encouraged. "There will be plenty of companies to check out."

Tarrin groaned. "I'm sure you're right, but maybe I'll stop in at a few of these companies anyway," Tarrin muttered more to herself than to Erin.

"Great. You should." Her sister grinned and shoved another large bite of pizza into her mouth.

Tarrin smiled wryly, and her brows creased. She was beginning to wonder whether or not she would be able to make ends meet after all. Once she had to start paying for daycare, she knew her funds would deplete rapidly. She rubbed the aching muscles along the back of her neck.

"What time did you say you need to leave for campus tomorrow?" she asked.

"Two-thirty. I have to meet with my guidance counselor and then sign some paperwork for the rest of my student loans. It shouldn't take too long. Only a couple of hours at the most," Erin replied.

"Good. I'll leave at eight-o'clock, and I can be back around one-thirty."

"Mom?" Jake's voice cut into Tarrin's thoughts.

"Hmm?"

"When are we going to see our new school?" he asked.

Tarrin knew she would need to find time to get Jake and Lexie registered for school, and soon. Lexie would attend kindergarten. Jake would start the fourth grade, and Tarrin hoped attending a new school would help her son's attitude and grades improve. He barely passed the third grade.

Following the divorce, school hadn't been easy for her son. His grades plummeted, and he was suspended for fighting more than once. He lost many friends. Rumors about Travis and their family circulated quickly around the small town, and Tarrin and her children had learned just how cruel some people's tongues could be.

Jake had not handled the rumors well, and in a way Tarrin couldn't blame him. She could easily understand his frustration. She worried about him attending an inner-city school, but she needed to trust that with a new start, he would succeed once more.

"Mom?" Jake pressed.

"Hmm?" She glanced up. "Oh, yeah. We'll check into your new school as soon as we can. Maybe tomorrow. We also need to check into daycare," she mumbled.

She was beginning to feel a little overwhelmed. Her jaw tensed as she ran her hand through Lexie's hair. Her daughter lay in her lap, and the little girl sighed softly in her sleep.

"I don't want to go to daycare. I'm ten," Jake reminded her with a frown.

Erin's brow rose, and she glanced at her sister. "The kid has a point," she spoke.

Tarrin shook her head. "This isn't like home, Jake. And it would be good if you'd remember that too," she directed toward Erin. "This is a big city. Things are different than what we're used to. You and Lexie are not staying alone, and once I find a job, we are going to look into daycare," she finished.

"I'm not a baby," Jake grumbled and folded his arms across his chest.

Tarrin reached for another slice of pizza without comment. She chewed on a bite of warm pepperoni and cheese before she spoke. "We have a lot to do tomorrow. We should go to bed soon." She forced a smile for Jake's sake, and then added, "Things will work out, Jakers. I think we're going to like it here, don't you?"

His pout slowly faded. He shrugged. "Yeah, I guess," he replied with a bit more enthusiasm.

ଓଃ

Tarrin's eyes grew large when she gazed up at the towering skyscraper. She moaned wearily and checked the address on her phone one last time. This was the right place, and it was also her last stop for the day. She had been out, actively looking for employment, since eight-o'clock that morning. The time was nearing one in the afternoon and she still needed to find a grocery store before she headed home. She glanced at her watch face and groaned when her stomach gurgled noisily. She felt exhausted, and her stomach ached with hunger. She skipped breakfast because stale, left-over pizza had been her only option, and she didn't want to break for lunch considering her time restriction.

Looking for work in Seattle was proving to be much more

difficult than she first imagined. Just parking in the city was a feat in itself. She'd paid ten dollars for a spot nearly four blocks away from the towering building, and she was forced to stop and ask strangers for directions more than once. She hadn't had any luck with her previous attempts to find work earlier in the morning, and even though she left applications with various businesses, she hadn't been able to secure any type of interview. The thought left her feeling discouraged as she gazed up toward the top of the high building.

"Here we go again," Tarrin murmured.

She paused when she caught sight of her reflection in the building's tall, glass-front door. Her shoulder length, brown hair was slightly disheveled, and her wide, hazel eyes stared back jadedly. She took a moment to smooth her knee-length, black skirt over narrow hips, and she straightened her sagging shoulders. Her feet ached, and she wiggled her toes in her flat pumps. She was once again grateful her tall frame made wearing high heels nearly impossible. She would have given up on the job hunt hours ago had she been wearing heels. As it was, she was seriously considering wearing tennis shoes for future job searches. If the amount of walking she'd had to do in just one short afternoon was indicative of what she would face in the future, she would gladly sacrifice fashion for comfort.

With a determined nod Tarrin threw her worn, leather purse over her shoulder and entered the massive building. She glanced around, curious, as she walked across the expansive foyer. An impressive modern-style chandelier hung from the ceiling and ornate paintings decorated the walls. A security guard greeted her with a curt nod, and Tarrin smiled.

She approached the desk and asked, "I'm trying to find the office for J.C. Accounting and Law Firm. I'm not certain which way to go." She laughed a little self-consciously.

"Twelfth floor. Down the hall and to your left," he answered, bored.

She smiled her thanks and moved toward the elevators then waited patiently for the lift to reach the twelfth floor. The doors slid open soundlessly and she stepped into the hall. She chewed the inside of her cheek as she walked into the office then smiled when a black-haired, pale-skinned receptionist greeted her indifferently.

"Can I help you?" the woman asked tersely.

Tarrin fixed the smile on her face and addressed the woman with forced cheerfulness. "Hi, I'm Tarrin Grace. I saw that you had a position open for hire. I've brought my resume, and—"

"Have you filled out an application online?"

"Well, no. We just moved in, and—"

"You'll need to go online," the receptionist told her in an abrupt tone.

"Well, I was hoping you had an application here, in the office. Like I was saying, we just moved in, and I don't have access to a computer at the moment, and . . . and I don't have a data plan," Tarrin rushed to explain.

The receptionist puffed out her cheeks and rolled her eyes before reaching into a folder on her desk. "Here." She tossed Tarrin a worn clipboard and a pen.

Tarrin took the clipboard, crestfallen. She sat on a hard office chair and began the arduous task of filling out yet another paper application. When she finished several moments later, she stood, and handed the application to the receptionist.

"Here's a copy of my resume. I was hoping to speak with management."

"Not here today," the woman replied.

The crass secretary took Tarrin's application and resume, and without another glance, shoved the papers into a drawer at the bottom of her desk.

"Will you make sure—?"

"That the boss gets them? Sure thing." The ill-mannered woman gave her a sardonic smile and Tarrin bit her tongue.

"Thank you," she replied curtly and with a groan, she strode out of the office and back into the hall.

Her shoulders fell, and she slogged toward the elevator. She hit the button for ground-level and forced back a wave of emotion. *Don't give up. It's only the first day,* she reminded herself. She had enough savings to last for a few more weeks if they lived tight—really tight. She stumbled off the elevator and into the foyer.

Grasping her empty, queasy stomach, she hurried toward the wide, double doors then jumped slightly when the big security guard spoke. His voice echoed in the empty lobby. "You lookin' for work, ma'am?" he asked.

Tarrin paused before she spun around. "Yes," she replied. She walked closer.

A slow grin spread across the older man's face. "Didn't mean to scare you."

Tarrin laughed a little breathlessly. "No, you're fine. You just caught me off guard."

The man nodded. "Why don't you try Sloan's? Tell 'em Todd sent you. Twenty-third floor."

Tarrin felt her spirit lift just a little. "They're hiring?"

"Last I heard," he spoke, his voice deep and rich.

"Thank you," she whispered and laughed as she took a step toward the large man. She shook his hand firmly before she walked back to the line of elevators.

"Good luck," he called as the doors slid shut.

It took much longer to reach the twenty-third floor, and Tarrin held her queasy stomach as she watched the flashing red numbers increase. She hadn't spent any significant time in large cities, and the towering skyscrapers were baffling. Once to the correct floor, the elevator slowed, and she entered a wide hallway. Glancing around, she quickly located the offices of Sloan International.

With a deep breath and a prayer in her heart, Tarrin walked into the main office. An elderly receptionist glanced up and smiled kindly. Her day had been so hectic; it was nice to finally see a genuine smile, and Tarrin returned the woman's greeting.

"Hello," she spoke, approaching the receptionist's desk. "My name is Tarrin Grace. I'm looking . . . well, to be honest, I'm looking for a job. Todd, the security guard, suggested I check here."

The woman's expression reflected her surprise, but her smile remained intact. "Is that so? Well, we just may have an opening. Why—don't—you . . ." The receptionist spoke as she rummaged through a few drawers. "Ah-hah! Here it is. Why don't you fill this out, and I'll see if Mr. Sloan can meet with you."

Tarrin's countenance brightened, and she nodded. "Yes! That would be great. Thank you." she replied, reaching for the application.

"I'll be right back." The secretary bustled from the room, and Tarrin crossed her fingers before she set about filling out the paperwork.

It didn't take long to complete the forms, especially considering her lack of work experience. Her mouth twisted. She hoped Sloan International could offer her some sort of position. She laid the clipboard on her lap, and her eyes suddenly narrowed. She glanced about the office. What sort of company was Sloan International anyway? Had she been thinking more clearly, she would have asked the security guard. Nothing in the spacious, modern office gave any indication regarding what sort of business Sloan International conducted.

Tarrin bit the inside of her cheek once again when the receptionist returned to her desk. "Mr. Sloan has a minute to meet with you, Miss Grace."

"Oh, really? That's great," Tarrin replied. Her eyes widened when a tall man appeared in the hallway and made his way toward the front. His eyes caught Tarrin's as he approached, and she swallowed nervously.

He wore expensive business attire, and his broad shoulders and dark hair did little to calm Tarrin's suddenly frazzled nerves.

He nodded politely. "Miss Grace?" he asked, his voice deep and authoritative.

"Yes. Tarrin Grace." She stood as he came around the desk. "Todd sent you up?"

He reached for her application and resume, and Tarrin handed him the clipboard with a conscious smile. "He did. He mentioned you might be hiring," she replied.

"Hmm." The man scanned her application and resume briefly.

He frowned, and Tarrin bit her bottom lip in vexation. She swallowed hard before his deep, brown eyes shot back toward hers. A slight smile touched his lips.

"I'm Calum Sloan, by the way," he introduced himself.

"Tarrin Grace," Tarrin replied then stammered, "I-I mean . . . You know that already." She shook her head, embarrassed.

Calum Sloan's right eyebrow shot up quizzically, but his mouth twitched with restrained humor. He finally chuckled. "Why don't you come on back to my office where we can discuss your resume further? We can see what our options are. Mary, hold my calls," he directed toward the receptionist before he turned and led the way across the spacious workplace.

He entered an office with a wide window, and Tarrin's lips parted when she caught sight of the scenic cityscape and the panoramic view of the Puget Sound below.

"Wow. The view is beautiful," she murmured as Calum Sloan moved behind an immense, mahogany desk.

"It is," he acknowledged. "Please, have a seat." He indicated a black leather sofa with a gracious wave of his hand, and Tarrin sat down, feeling apprehensive.

She smoothed the front of her skirt when Calum Sloan took his seat in a matching leather office chair. He leaned forward, his elbows resting on the desk. He remained silent for a moment while he read through her resume once again.

"So," he began, "let's start by being—honest. You don't

have much work experience." His eyes shot to hers.

Tarrin's breath caught in her throat, and her spirits plummeted. "No, I don't. However, I was top of my class—" she paused and her shoulders fell, "fifteen years ago. I realize it doesn't look good, but I learn fast, and I work even harder."

Calum regarded Tarrin for a brief moment. His brow furrowed, and he ran a hand across the stubble growing along his square jaw. "Tell me," he spoke. "What do you know about Sloan International?"

"Oh—" Her hands fluttered and her palms grew clammy. "Well, to be perfectly honest, I . . . I really don't know. Actually, I came in to apply with J.C. Law Firm. I met Todd downstairs, and he said to try here. So, here I am. I'm sorry. I don't mean to waste your time, but I just moved to the city, and . . ." She paused and blushed deeply. "I need a job."

Calum nodded when Tarrin finished, and he chuckled a little. "I admire honesty," he replied, and his gaze lowered toward her application once again. After a brief moment, he asked, "You live on Third Avenue?"

"I do. We moved in yesterday," she was quick to reply.

"Really?"

Tarrin went on, "I was lucky enough to stumble on a rent ad yesterday afternoon, and we—my sister and I, and my children—leased a little house."

"Hmm." Calum's eyebrows rose. "I see. How do you like Washington so far? Are the neighbors friendly?"

Confused, Tarrin shrugged. "Yes, I guess. We really haven't met anyone yet. Our neighbors probably weren't home, and our landlady seemed . . ." She frowned. "She seemed . . . uh . . . *nice*?"

She glanced toward Calum, and he studied her with a curious expression. His lips twitched. Tarrin wondered what he found so humorous, but he said, "Why don't I start by telling you a bit about Sloan International."

"Yes. Please." She breathed a sigh of relief, and he grinned knowingly.

"Our specialty is solar and wind energy products. This company is small, but successful. In the last two years, we've opened factories here in Seattle, as well as in India, but our corporate office is here.

"Our products are sold worldwide, but the majority of our customer service and sales take place right here in this office. We take care of shipping and online orders at our production factory near Kent."

"Okay," Tarrin spoke. "I see. It sounds great."

Calum continued, "What I'm looking for, mainly, is customer service representatives and sales representatives. Would you be interested in either position?"

Tarrin's brow furrowed. "I'm not so sure I would succeed with sales," she admitted.

Calum nodded. "You would be interested in customer service then?"

"Yes, I would," she affirmed.

"Alright, let me ask you a few more questions."

૦ઝ

"I did it! I found a job," Tarrin spoke into her cell phone as she left the crowded grocery store. She pushed her cart full of groceries toward her vehicle, then exclaimed, "Oh!" when she suddenly fumbled the phone, nearly dropping it. "Erin?" she said, righting her cell phone and adjusting it against her ear. "Are you there?"

"I'm here," her sister replied.

"I almost dropped the phone," Tarrin laughed a little. "Did you hear me? I found a job."

"I heard. Great! That was fast," Erin replied. "Where is it? Tell me all about it."

Tarrin struggled to hear Erin's voice over the clamor of

vehicles and the noise of the busy shopping center.

"Are you still there?" Erin called into the phone when Tarrin didn't answer right away.

"Yes. Just a minute." She reached her car and grinned as she replied, "I'm still here. I was hired on at a company called Sloan International. You're speaking to their newest customer service rep. I'll tell you all about it when I get home. I'm on my way back now. I just had to stop at the grocery store. How are the kids?"

"They're just fine. Be careful coming home," Erin called.

"I will. See ya," Tarrin ended the conversation, and she whistled as she loaded her groceries into her Nissan's trunk.

She glanced at her watch. She needed to hurry or Erin would be late for her appointment with the guidance counselor. It had taken much longer than anticipated to find a chain grocery store amid all the organic stores and specialty markets, and her interview with Calum Sloan took a bit more time than she expected as well, but she couldn't complain.

She could scarcely believe she had landed a job so quickly. It was not the sort of position she had imagined herself in, but it paid fairly well. Her benefits would start in a few months, and the position had potential to turn into something more. The thought of having secured a job lifted her spirits immensely, and she sighed, feeling lighter than ever as she pulled the Nissan sedan onto the congested street and turned the car in the direction of their new home. Things were definitely beginning to look up.

The drive didn't take long, despite the heavy traffic, and when she reached the house, Lexie and Jake burst through the front door to greet her.

"You're home!" Lexie ran into her arms as Tarrin stepped from the car.

"Hey," Jake greeted her with a paltry smile.

"Did Aunt Erin tell you my good news?" Tarrin asked with a wide grin.

"Uh-huh," Lexie murmured.

"Yeah, great," Jake replied with little enthusiasm.

Tarrin knew Jake resented the fact she had to work. She had always been a stay-at-home-mom, and going back to work was a major change for her children. She understood Jake and Lexie missed her, and she desperately missed them, but there was no other choice.

Tarrin smiled encouragingly and went on, "Well, it won't be like at the grocery store. I'm working nine-to-five every day, so you won't be at daycare long—only a couple of hours in the evening, after school. I have the weekends off too. There are *so* many places for us to visit here. We'll go on an adventure every weekend. Isn't that great?"

Her daughter nodded and smiled. "Uh-huh."

Jake finally grinned. "Yeah. That's real cool, Mom."

"Where's Aunt Erin?" Tarrin asked, glancing around.

"Inside," Jake replied. "Did you get *Pop Tarts*?" he asked when Tarrin opened the trunk.

"No," she replied slowly. "We're going to have to tighten our budget a bit, and *Pop Tarts* aren't very healthy. So I bought oatmeal, and—"

"Ugh! *Oatmeal*?" Jake cut in.

"Yes, Jake, oatmeal and pancake mix," Tarrin said as she grabbed a few sacks from the trunk. "Here, will you take these?" She handed a bag to each child.

"Hey, I'm ready to head out." Erin suddenly appeared on the porch. Her long, blond hair was pulled back into a pony tail and she wore shorts, which accented her thin, tanned legs. A hot pink tank top hugged her body, and Tarrin regarded her sister quizzically.

"You're going to meet with your University counselor wearing that?"

Erin nodded her head and smirked. "It's not like a real meeting." She bounded down the front steps and walked across the yard toward Tarrin. She gave her a swift hug then added, "Don't act like Mom. And congrats on the job! I'm going to be late if I don't catch the next bus, but I can't wait to hear all about it."

Tarrin rolled her eyes, but grinned. "Good luck with your meeting. What time will you be home?"

Erin shrugged. "Six, maybe? I want to explore the campus a bit and find all my classrooms before the semester starts."

Tarrin nodded thoughtfully. She handed a few more grocery sacks to Jake and one more sack to Lexie. She turned back to face her sister. "Good idea. Have fun, okay? Call me if you need me to come and get you. Are you sure you don't want the car?" she asked.

"Positive. I want to see how the bus schedule works. Love ya." Erin turned down the sidewalk. "Bye, twerps." She waved at Jake and Lexie.

"Bye," Lexie called.

"Let's get these groceries in and fix ourselves a peanut butter sandwich. Are you starving?" Tarrin turned to address her children.

They both nodded unenthusiastically. She knew her children were sick to death of peanut butter sandwiches, but she still needed to be careful. Her new job paid better than she had expected, but with the high price of rent, it still wouldn't be enough to loosen their budget much. Her mood dampened a little at the thought.

Chapter *Three*

$\mathcal{T}$arrin combed her fingers through her hair. She stood and stretched, then laid the *Sloan International Handbook* on the kids' dresser. She would start her new job on Monday, and she had plenty to learn before then. She knelt on Jake's bed and glanced out the wide window. Her eyes dropped to the yard below and she could hear the loud, "Thwump, Thwump," of Jake's soccer ball hitting the side of the house.

After a quick lunch, the children had rushed outside to play while Tarrin went upstairs to finish unpacking and to sort through their toys and clothes. She had stopped for a short break and took a minute to review the handbook. It was nearly five-o'clock. She wondered if Erin would really be home at six. Her sister wasn't known for being punctual, but she hoped they would have time after dinner to search the city for a second-hand store. It would be nice to get some furniture for their new home. She really was getting tired of picnic-style meals.

She sighed and turned from the window just as a shrill scream caught her attention. Tarrin spun around and peered down toward the yard. "Lexie?" she called.

She raised a hand to her chest when Jake suddenly ran across the lawn toward the thick wall of trees. *Lexie? Is she in the woods?*

Her heart picked up pace. "I told them not to go into the woods," Tarrin spoke out loud.

Frantically, she stumbled from the bedroom and rushed down the narrow stairs. She reached the sliding glass door and tugged on the handle.

"Oh, come on!" she yelled when the door stuck.

The sound of grating metal made her cringe as she jerked the door across the runners. The door finally gave enough for her to squeeze outside, and Tarrin raced into the yard. Her eyes scanned the empty expanse.

"Jake?" she called, jogging toward the trees. "Lexie?" She entered the darkened woods. "Jake? Lexie?" Tarrin called again.

Her feet crunched audibly on the forest understory as she pushed through a barrier of ferns. "Ahh-ugh." she moaned when she stumbled through a large spider web stretched between two trees. She brushed at the clinging strands and nearly tripped over a fallen tree hidden in the understory.

"Jake! Lexie!"

"Mom?" Jake's voice sounded from a short distance ahead, and the breath left Tarrin's lungs in relief.

"Where are you? Where's Lexie?" Tarrin called. She turned in the direction of his voice and her shoulders relaxed when she caught a glimpse of Lexie's bright pink shirt through the dense alders and ferns. "Jake, what is it? What's wrong? Lexie? I thought I told you guys to stay out of the woods."

Jake turned to face her as she came through the trees, and Tarrin paused when she read the fear in his expression. Lexie sat on the ground near her brother's feet. She remained still and unmoving. The little girl's eyes were large as she stared ahead. Tears coursed down her young face, but she made no sound.

"Lexie?" Tarrin's heart rate increased and she rushed toward her daughter.

"Mom, there's . . . there's someone hurt," her son spoke and his voice rose anxiously.

"What is it? What's wrong?"

Confused, she glanced through the pines and tall alders surrounding them, her heart pounding in her chest. Jake pointed ahead toward the edge of a spiny blackberry bush. "There's someone on the ground behind that bush," he whispered. "I can see their hand under there."

Tarrin's face paled. A current of fear shot up her spine, and she stepped protectively in front of her children, staring toward the foliage with fearful eyes.

"Jake, what do you mean?" Her own voice trembled, and she turned to look at her son.

"I'm serious, Mom. Look." Jake's eyes were wide; his expression tense.

Tarrin studied her son for only a moment before she turned back toward the wild berry bush. Cautiously, she moved forward. When her foot snapped a twig underfoot, she jumped. Her eyes narrowed, and she could feel her heart beat as she inched her way onward. When the shape of a human hand appeared between the tangled, spiny stems, she gasped.

"Oh!" Tarrin exclaimed.

Her eyes narrowed and she bent closer. The fingers lay unmoving, and small scratches on the skin oozed blood. Tarrin's stomach clenched, and her mouth turned dry.

"Jake," she whispered, her voice hoarse. "Take Lexie back to the house now. Call 911 and stay there," she directed while she stumbled nearer. She raised a trembling hand to the base of her throat. "Hello?" she called. Her voice shook. "Can you hear me? Are you alright?"

Tarrin received no answer and she continued to approach, feeling uncertain. Blood pulsed in her ears, and she took a deep breath. Trembling, she straightened her body to peer over the waist high shrubs. It took only a moment for her mind to process what she was seeing, and a shrill scream tore from her throat. Her hands flew to her mouth.

"No," she breathed when she gazed down into the lifeless face of a young woman.

The woman's eyes were wide, frozen in fear. Her head lay at a strange angle. Blood pooled across her chest and dripped onto the carpet of moss and dead leaves. Tarrin had no doubt the young woman was dead.

"What is it?" Jake's voice suddenly sounded close by, startling Tarrin into action.

"No!" She spun around, shoving Jake back.

"Mom?" he gasped in surprise.

"We need to go back . . . back to the house, now!" Tarrin rushed forward. The hairs on the back of her neck stood on end. "Jake, let's go!" She grasped Lexie and hoisted the girl into her arms. She pushed her son ahead with her free hand and they stumbled their way out of the trees. "Get into the house. Quickly!"

Jake bolted into the house, and he turned to face his mother with wide, frightened eyes. "What happened? What's wrong?" His voice broke.

Tarrin rushed into the kitchen and sat Lexie down on the cracked linoleum floor before she turned to close the glass door. She swore when it stuck, and she tugged at the handle frantically. When the door finally grated closed, she moaned her relief. She flipped the lock securely in place and grabbed her cell phone from off the kitchen counter, then she turned and lifted Lexie, who sat unmoving, into her quaking arms. She carried her into the living room, placing her on the worn, burnt-orange carpet.

"Jake?" Tarrin spun around. "No!" she yelled when she saw him standing in front of the glass doors, watching the woods. "Get away from there. Now! Go into the living room with your sister," she instructed as she dialed 911. Her hands trembled visibly when she placed the phone to her ear. "Hello?" she called.

"Nine-one-one. What's your emergency?" a dispatcher responded calmly.

"I need help. There . . . There's a woman, in the trees behind our house. She's dead!"

Tarrin paused when the dispatcher responded, "You say there is a dead woman in the woods behind your house?" The woman's voice sounded disbelieving.

"Yes," Tarrin replied with a shaking voice. "I . . . I think she's . . ." She glanced toward Jake and Lexie. She stepped away and moved into the kitchen. "I think she was m-murdered," she finished quietly. A shiver ran the length of her spine and her gaze darted toward the woods.

"Did you say *murdered*?"

"I think someone killed her," Tarrin replied weakly. She felt the blood drain from her face.

"Someone *killed* her?"

Tarrin raised a quivering hand to her clammy forehead. She was beginning to feel dizzy. "Yes." She leaned against the wall for support. "I think so. She's dead. I . . . I have two children. My children found her. My daughter . . . I don't know . . ."

Jake appeared in the doorframe between the living room and the kitchen; his expression frightened—his face pale. Tarrin closed her eyes briefly then suddenly felt her skin grow cold. Gooseflesh rose on her arms. The feeling she was being watched assailed her, and she turned to face the glass door with fearful eyes. She took a step forward and lowered the blinds, blocking the yard from sight.

"Ma'am?" the dispatcher questioned.

"I'm here. Yes?"

The woman asked several more questions, and Tarrin tried to calm herself while she numbly answered. After another moment, the dispatcher responded, "I have an officer on the way. You and your children should stay inside. I need you to stay on the line until the police arrive."

"Okay," Tarrin murmured.

"Are you or your children injured?"

Tarrin stepped back toward the living room.

Jake caught her eye. "Mom?"

She shook her head and raised her hand, indicating he should be quiet before she answered.

"We're alright, but I need to help my daughter. Something's wrong with my daughter. I think she might be in shock, but I . . . I don't know." Tarrin moved to kneel in front of Lexie. Her daughter stared ahead, unmoving. "Lex?" She touched Lexie's cheek. The little girl's skin was clammy and cold. "Lexie?" Tarrin encouraged.

Lexie blinked, but she didn't respond.

"Ma'am?"

"My daughter . . . I think she's in shock. She isn't acting like herself. She's cold," Tarrin responded.

"She's been like that the whole time. She wouldn't say anything in the woods either. She just stares," Jake spoke over Tarrin's shoulder.

"Ma'am, you need to get your daughter warm immediately. Lay her down and elevate her legs. I have an ambulance on the way."

Tears burned Tarrin's eyes as she pushed away from Lexie. She stood on trembling legs, then turned to find Jake. "Jake?" she called. She scowled when she caught sight of him in the kitchen once again, peeking through a slat in the blinds. "Get away from there! How many times do I need to tell you?" she yelled. Jake spun around. His pale face twisted in uncertainty. "I'm sorry, Jake. But, listen, I need you to go upstairs and get some blankets and a pillow. And I'm sorry. I didn't mean to yell."

His eyes fell on Lexie when he walked past his mother toward the narrow stairs. He paused and studied his sister with a worried expression.

"Jake," Tarrin spoke as calmly as she could. "Your sister is in shock. I need your help. Do as I've asked, please?"

His eyes shot once again to Tarrin's, and he nodded. "Okay." He turned and rushed upstairs.

"Ma'am? Is your daughter responding?"

"Lexie?" Tarrin sat on the floor.

Lexie raised a thumb to her mouth, but still, she did not look at Tarrin. Tarrin pulled her daughter onto her lap and wrapped her arms about her. Lexie's pants were wet, and she smelled of urine. Her soggy clothing soaked through Tarrin's jeans when she cradled her gently. Tarrin pressed her face against Lexie's hair. "Lexie, are you hurt? What happened? Talk to me."

She turned her daughter's face toward hers, and the little

girl slowly raised her eyes to meet Tarrin's.

"Lexie?" she pressed.

"Here." Jake bounded down the stairs. He tossed the blankets toward them, and Tarrin thanked him.

"I'm going to put the phone down for a second while I wrap my daughter in a blanket. She's responding a little," Tarrin told the dispatcher before she laid her phone on the carpet. She grasped Lexie's favorite blanket, removed her soiled pants, and wrapped her snuggly before she laid her on the floor. Using a pillow, she elevated Lexie's feet. "There. Is that better?" she asked. The little girl blinked as if she was confused, and she nodded weakly. "Are you okay? You aren't hurt?"

Lexie shook her head, wordlessly.

"Is she all right?" Jake asked. His voice sounded uneasy.

Tarrin forced a smile and nodded at her son, hoping to reassure him before she picked up the phone. Just then a loud knock sounded at the front door and Tarrin jumped from the floor.

Jake rushed to the wide living room window and peered out. "It's the cops, Mom."

A small measure of relief washed across Tarrin when she placed the phone back to her ear. "The police are at the house now," she spoke.

She shut the phone and rushed to the door just as the ambulance turned up the narrow street with its sirens sounding and lights flashing. She opened the door and greeted two officers with a grim nod.

"She's . . . The woman is in the backyard. She's in the woods. She's lying in a berry bush about fifty or sixty feet in," Tarrin told them when they entered the house.

"Was there anyone else in the woods?" the taller officer asked tersely.

"No, I didn't see anyone else."

"Are you or your children hurt?"

"I think . . . I think my daughter may be in shock," Tarrin

responded.

"The E.M.T.'s are here. They'll take a good care of her," the second officer exclaimed before he and his partner crossed the small house. "Stay inside," he instructed.

The first officer struggled with the back door for a moment, and he jerked it open with a scowl. They moved cautiously across the grass and disappeared into the trees, guns drawn. Suddenly the medical personnel rushed onto the porch, and Tarrin stepped back, allowing them to enter the home. She pointed toward Lexie.

"She hasn't really responded. She's not acting like herself," Tarrin informed them.

"Mom?" Lexie's confused voice called as the E.M.T. bent over her.

"It's okay, sweetheart. They're just going to check you out. They need to make sure you're not hurt," she tried to calm her daughter.

"We'll need to transport her," one technician responded.

Lexie's face contorted and she began sobbing quietly. Tarrin rushed to her side and watched as the emergency crew lifted her daughter, then secured her to a stretcher. Tarrin glanced out the window when several more sirens sounded in the distance. The street suddenly crowded with cars, and curious onlookers congested the sidewalk.

"Ma'am? We're going to take her to Highline. Don't forget your I.D. and insurance information," one technician instructed.

"Mom?" Jake's worried voice called across the sudden clamor, and Tarrin reached out to grasp his hand.

She squeezed her son's fingers, and with tear-filled eyes, she kissed Lexie's clammy forehead. "I'll be right behind you. Don't be scared. They'll take good care of you. I promise."

"Mama?" Lexie sobbed when the stretcher rolled past.

"I'm going to be right behind you, Lex," Tarrin called to her once again as more officers filled her little house. She watched with an aching heart while her daughter was swallowed from view.

Suddenly a large hand touched her shoulder, and she jumped, turning to face a tall, blond-haired officer who stood nearby. The man observed her closely, his expression concerned, yet business-like.

"Ma'am, are you Tarrin Grace?"

"Yes," she answered before she glanced toward Jake. "Will you go and get my purse, Jake? It's on my bed."

Jake nodded and turned toward the stairs.

"Ma'am, I'm Lieutenant Marzollo, head of Homicide. I realize you need to be with your daughter, but I'd like to ask you a few quick questions if you don't mind?"

Tarrin took a deep, calming breath. "Okay."

"How did you discover the victim?"

"I heard my daughter screaming, and I realized she was in the woods. I was upstairs unpacking, and the kids were playing in the backyard. So, Jake, my son, he ran into the woods to find Lexie. I went in after them, and I found both the kids standing a few feet from her. Lexie was sitting on the ground, and Jake showed me. He saw her—the lady's hand—sticking out from under a berry bush. That's when I found . . . when I found her." She swallowed hard and tried to force the nausea down as the grotesque image resurfaced.

"And what exactly did your children see?" he asked.

"I-I don't know." She felt dazed—overwhelmed.

Jake came down the stairs slowly, carrying Tarrin's purse. He eyed Lieutenant Marzollo with a wary expression. "Here's your purse." He handed Tarrin her worn bag as the officer turned to face him.

He scrutinized her son for several seconds before turning his attention back to Tarrin. "Do you mind if I ask your son a few questions?"

"No," Tarrin shook her head. "Jake?"

Jake shrugged.

"Can you tell me what happened, son? What exactly did you hear and see?"

"I don't know. I didn't know Lexie had snuck into the woods," he answered.

The policeman nodded impatiently. "What happened in the trees? When did you first notice your sister was missing?"

Jake shrugged again, his voice rising. "I didn't know she was gone, but I heard her scream. I found her sitting on the ground. She didn't say anything. That's when I saw the lady in the woods. Mom came right then. That's all," he finished and ducked his head.

"Did you see or hear anyone else?" Lieutenant Marzollo pressed while he jotted a few notes.

"No," he replied.

The detective glanced up. He observed Jake for a moment longer before he smiled and ruffled the boy's hair. The man's teeth gleamed white and his eyes met Tarrin's when he replied, "I'm sure you want to be at the hospital as soon as possible, so I'll let you go now, but I'll send an officer over in an hour or so. I'm afraid we're going to need to question your daughter, and I'll need formal statements filled out by both you and your children. I hope you understand." He winked at Jake.

"I understand," Tarrin replied. Her voice trembled.

"Everything will be just fine. Go and be with your daughter. We'll be right behind you."

"Thank you," Tarrin breathed. Grasping Jake's hand, she turned for the door.

"Take good care of your sister, Jake," Lieutenant Marzollo called. Jake waved unenthusiastically.

With trembling legs, Tarrin stepped out onto the porch. She moved toward her vehicle. The narrow street was crowded with people, including many uniformed police officers. Emergency vehicles lined the road, and another officer directed a stream of traffic through the teeming maze of on-lookers. Tarrin swallowed when she viewed the street. She took a deep breath just as she heard a vaguely familiar voice call her name across the crowd.

"Miss Grace. Tarrin!"

Startled, she turned and watched Calum Sloan, her new boss, separate from the crowd standing on her lawn. He strode toward her, and her mouth fell open. "Mr. Sloan?" she question, baffled by his sudden appearance.

"Are you okay?" he asked.

"My . . . My children discovered a woman dead in the woods. S-she's been . . . murdered. Why are you here?" Her voice rose, uncertain.

"I know about the woman, but are *you* alright?"

Tarrin nodded, attempting to control her emotions. "M-my daughter is in shock. They took her to Highline, I think?"

Tarrin bit her lip hard when she realized she didn't know where the hospital was. How would she get to Lexie? She was beginning to feel the dark haze of panic closing in.

"I live just two houses down—with my nephew, Macin. I wanted to tell you earlier, during the interview, that we lived on the same street, but . . ." He glanced behind him just as a boy about Jake's age joined them.

The dark-haired boy nodded in greeting. "Hey, I'm Macin," he directed toward Jake.

The boys exchanged measuring stares for a short moment before Jake replied, "Jake."

"Oh," Tarrin replied. "You *live* here?"

Calum nodded. "Where did they take your daughter again?"

"Um, High. . . Highline? I-I don't know where that is." Tears suddenly clouded her vision.

"It's Highline Medical Center. I'll be happy to take you, Miss Grace. You probably shouldn't be driving right now," Calum offered.

"*What—is—going—on?*" A shrill, grating voice sounded above the din, and Tarrin groaned when she recognized Edna Cope forcing her way through the tight-knit crowd.

Calum caught Tarrin's eye and frowned. He grasped her upper arm gently. "Let's go. Jake. Macin. Get in," he replied, his voice calm but firm as he took the keys from Tarrin's hand.

Feeling foggy and disoriented, she allowed him to guide her to her car and into the passenger's seat while he jumped behind the steering wheel. Without another word, he started the vehicle and pulled onto the street, just as Edna reached the house. The old woman glared, and Calum waved, flashing a stiff smile in the landlady's direction.

"Well, that was one disaster adverted," he spoke after they'd been on the road for several moments. Tarrin smiled weakly.

Macin laughed. "That woman is scary."

Jake snorted and chuckled a little, but Tarrin could hear the apprehension in her son's voice.

"How are you holding up?" Calum asked.

The man's deep voice seemed to have a calming effect on her nerves. "We're okay. Lexie wasn't really responding. They think she's in shock. Jake seems to be alright, and . . . Oh!" she suddenly exclaimed. "Erin! I forgot all about my sister."

She searched through her purse, frantically looking for her phone, then groaned when she realized she had left it lying on the kitchen counter. Calum's brow rose, and Tarrin closed her eyes, frustrated.

"I left my phone. I forgot all about my sister. She'll be scared to death." She raised a trembling hand to her temple and glared out the window.

Calum reached into his suit coat and pulled his expensive phone from the pocket. He handed it to Tarrin, and her eyes rose to meet his.

"Thank you," she whispered.

She punched in Erin's familiar number then sighed, relieved, when her sister answered after the first two rings. Tarrin struggled to hold back tears while she recounted the events that had just transpired. Stunned, Erin listened mutely.

"Where are you now?" she asked after Tarrin detailed the terrifying situation.

"We're on our way to Highline Medical Center. Mr. Sloan is

driving us there," she explained.

"What?" Erin asked. "Um, isn't that your new boss?"

"Yeah, I-I'll explain later."

"Listen, I'll catch a bus and meet you there." Erin suggested.

Tarrin's shoulders relaxed a fraction. As she ended the call, she glanced toward Jake and forced an encouraging smile.

"Aunt Erin will meet us there," she reported, then asked, "Are you okay, Jake?"

Jake nodded. "Yeah. Sure."

"Dude, what happened?" Macin jumped in.

"Mace, not now, buddy," Calum cut in.

"No, its fine," Jake spoke. "There was a dead lady in the woods," he responded. "My little sister found her."

"Whoa! Really?" Macin asked.

Calum regarded Tarrin curiously. His brows creased in concern, and she added, "I don't know what Lexie saw or whether or not she saw anything at all. She wouldn't respond."

Calum nodded thoughtfully, then after several moments he added, "This isn't exactly a great welcome to the neighborhood. I'm sorry." He pulled the vehicle in front of the hospital. "I'll park the car and leave the keys at the front desk."

Tarrin smiled. "Thank you, Mr. Sloan. Really. Jake, come on—quick."

She grasped her son's hand and slid from the car. With a wave toward Calum, she rushed into the vast building.

CHAPTER *Four*

"Hey, Mom, can I get something from the vending machine?" Jake asked, stepping into Lexie's small, but private, hospital room.

He shoved the rest of a glazed donut into his mouth, then wiped his sticky fingers onto his jeans. Tarrin's lips twisted. "You just had two donuts," she reminded him.

"Yeah, but now I want chips." He talked around the large bite of gooey donut in his mouth. He swallowed. "Besides, I'm still hungry."

"Let's wait until after the doctor comes. When he's done talking to me, we'll go to the cafeteria and get dinner," she suggested.

His face fell. "Where's Aunt Erin?" he asked, licking his fingers.

"Bathroom," Tarrin murmured in response.

Jake came nearer and stood next to Lexie's bed. Tarrin caught his eye, and she reached out to wrap her arms around him.

"*Mom . . .*" he whispered, embarrassed.

She ignored his protest and hugged him tighter. "How are you doing, Jakers? Really?"

"Fine. Honest," he replied. He returned Tarrin's hug, then pushed away. "Hey, can I go watch T.V. in the waiting room?" he asked.

Tarrin glanced toward the clock hanging on the wall. She was surprised it was already eight-thirty. She sighed. "Sure, but don't talk to strangers," she responded as he left the room.

Tarrin let her weary gaze fall toward her sleeping daughter. She touched the little girl's soft cheek and tried, unsuccessfully, to keep back a few tears. She was grateful Lexie was sleeping soundly. After Calum Sloan dropped her and Jake at the main door, she had rushed inside to find her. The doctors treated Lexie for shock, and then they all agreed to keep the little girl overnight, just in case.

Lieutenant Marzollo came by soon after, and she had spent the last few hours speaking with several detectives from his unit. They questioned her children repeatedly about the incident, but Jake could not offer any more information beyond discovering the woman lying lifeless in the forest and finding his sister sitting on the ground in a trance-like state.

The doctors had examined Lexie thoroughly, but found no physical signs of trauma or injury. However, when the detectives questioned her, she could not remember anything about the woods. Lexie's memory lapse left the doctors baffled and the detectives frustrated.

What had her daughter witnessed? Why couldn't Lexie recall anything? Was she scared? Had she seen someone, and was she too afraid to tell? Lexie was so young. It would be hard for her daughter to understand all that was happening right now. Tarrin moaned and leaned her forehead against the cool, metal railings on Lexie's bed.

"Tarrin," Erin's voice sliced into her thoughts.

Tarrin raised her head, and she smiled when Erin entered the room and handed her a cold can of soda.

"You okay, big sis?" Erin asked with a small smile.

Tarrin nodded and reached for her sister's hand. She squeezed Erin's fingers and was once again grateful for her comforting presence. Despite Travis's betrayal, Tarrin suddenly missed him. She felt so alone. Even though the marriage had been over for more than a year, she missed his familiar, strong arms around her during troubling times. He had been there, always, to lend a supportive shoulder, and now . . . She sucked in a deep breath and suppressed a sob. Knowingly, Erin wrapped her arms about Tarrin's shoulders and squeezed gently. Tarrin leaned into her sister and allowed the tears to come.

Tarrin allowed Erin to hold her for several moments before

she pulled away and reached for a tissue from off the bedside table. "I'm sorry," she sniffed.

"Any time," Erin replied. A slow smile spread across her face. "If it helps you feel any better, Mom called."

Tarrin paused and her face fell.

Erin laughed. "I took care of it. I told her you'd call tomorrow sometime."

Tarrin smiled, feeling grateful.

"So, tell me about *Calum Sloan*." Erin wiggled her eyebrows as she sat in a chair and opened her soda with a loud pop.

Tarrin's brow rose and she shrugged. "Apparently he lives just two houses down. Strange, isn't it? That neighborhood isn't exactly where I'd picture a man like Mr. Sloan living. He didn't say anything about it at the interview. Oh, and Edna Cope was on her way over."

"Yikes!"

"Yeah," Tarrin agreed.

"Hmm—so is he good looking?" Erin asked before she took a generous gulp of soda.

"Who?" Tarrin asked.

"Oh, don't be dense," Erin laughed.

"Uh," Tarrin's brow lowered. "He's going to be my new boss, Erin."

"So, *what*? That automatically makes him ugly?"

Tarrin shook her head and smiled. "No. He's very—nice looking, actually. He's a very friendly man."

"Umm-Hmm. So he's *gorgeous*?" her sister pressed.

Tarrin laughed. It felt good to laugh. "Yes," she giggled. "He is very good looking."

Erin grinned. "Aw, well, your good-looking boss called too."

Tarrin's head shot up. "He did?"

"Umm-hmm," Erin went on, noting Tarrin's color.

"Well, what did he say?"

"Oh, this and that." Erin's expression grew ever-more

mischievous and Tarrin suddenly frowned. After a moment Erin giggled and relented. "Oh, fine. He said to let you know he took care of Mrs. Cope. And they locked up the house for us after all the cops left. Oh, and he also fixed the back door. *And* he said he'd like to stop in tomorrow afternoon to check on us."

"What did you tell him?" Tarrin asked.

"I said to come on by, of course."

Tarrin's lips parted in surprise before she replied, "He's just being helpful—neighborly."

"Yeah. Right."

Tarrin rolled her eyes. "You're impossible."

Oß

"Hey, should we get ourselves an ice cream?" Tarrin suggested after spotting a fast-food restaurant on the way home from the hospital.

Jake's eyes widened and his face lit up. "Yeah!" he exclaimed.

Tarrin caught Lexie's gaze in the rearview mirror, and she smiled at her daughter. "How about you, Lex?"

Lexie nodded and stuffed her thumb in her mouth.

"Don't worry. I'll eat the twerp's ice cream for her." Erin glanced toward the little girl.

"Uh-uh," Lexie replied, smiling around her thumb.

Tarrin chuckled when she pulled up to the drive-through window. She placed her order and passed the drippy cones back toward the kids. Erin took hers with a wide smile. "Thanks, sis. I feel like I'm five years old again." She laughed as she licked her cone.

"Hey, you aren't five. I am." Lexie spoke quietly.

Tarrin studied her daughter briefly before she pulled the vehicle back onto the busy road. Lexie hadn't said much since they'd left the hospital. The detectives met with her children once more before they were allowed to leave, but Lexie's memory still had not returned. She could recall sneaking away from Jake to follow a deer into the trees. She remembered the emergency crew loading her into the ambulance and everything after that point, but any memory in between those moments had vanished. It left Tarrin baffled, and she had to admit—scared.

She and Lexie had met with the hospital's child psychologist earlier in the day. The doctor suggested Lexie was experiencing symptoms of post-traumatic stress disorder, and at the proposition of the specialist, Tarrin set up an appointment to meet with a psychologist who specialized in PTSD in children. Tarrin felt apprehensive, despite the appointment being a few days away. She hoped she was making the right choices concerning her daughter.

Tarrin directed her thoughts back to the busy streets of Seattle, and she cringed when she pulled the Nissan into the driveway of their new home. The house that once felt welcoming, now felt sinister. She cut the ignition, and stared jadedly toward the front door.

"Cops are here," Erin spoke, and Tarrin turned in the driver's seat to glance out the side window.

Erin pointed across the street as an officer exited a large, black sedan. He waved and smiled a friendly smile.

"That's Lieutenant Marzollo," Tarrin spoke. She stepped from the car. The children followed, and Tarrin heard Erin's door slam shut. "Hello," Tarrin replied, her tone wary.

"Miss Grace."

He strode toward them and extended his hand in greeting before his gaze fell on Jake and Lexie.

"How are you two?" he asked with a smile.

Jake eyed Marzollo curiously and Lexie watched him with a guarded expression. Her thumb strayed to her mouth again and she inched closer to Tarrin. Tarrin felt the little girl's arms slip around her leg, and she suppressed a smile.

"Lexie," Marzollo squatted to eye-level with the girl, who

was peeking out from behind Tarrin's leg, "did the doctors take good care of you?" he asked.

Tarrin smiled and nudged Lexie. "Can you say 'hi'?"

Her daughter remained silent.

Lieutenant Marzollo grinned as he stood. "It's been a couple of tough days, hasn't it?"

Jake and Lexie nodded mutely.

"Well, I brought you guys a little something. It's waiting in my cruiser. Just a minute, okay?" he replied. He smiled at Tarrin before he walked toward his vehicle.

She waited while he bent inside the sedan. After a moment, he stood straight and shut the door, then ambled back toward them, pulling a bright pink teddy bear from behind his back. "That's from all the guys down at the station for being such a brave girl." He handed the bear to Lexie.

"Thank you," Lexie murmured, reaching for the bear. She hugged it to her chest and gripped Tarrin's leg tighter.

"And this is for you, Jake. Great job, buddy," Marzollo added when he handed Jake a plastic Seattle Police Department badge.

"Cool. Thanks," Jake replied, accepting the gift.

"Thank you. That's very nice, Lieutenant Marzollo," Tarrin turned toward the detective.

"My pleasure. And please, call me Zack," he replied smoothly. His face sobered and he added, "I just wanted to speak with you and let you know what's happening with the case." His eyes strayed toward the children before he asked, "Do you have a minute?"

"Yes. Sure," she replied. She turned to face Erin. "Do you mind taking Jake and Lexie inside?"

Erin shrugged. "Sure. Come on," she called and ushered the children into the shabby house.

She waited for Erin and her children to disappear before she faced Zack.

"Let's sit, Tarrin. Do you mind if I call you Tarrin?" he asked, pointing toward the crumbling staircase.

"No, not all," she replied. She sat wearily on the stairs. He smiled, and Tarrin nodded before she asked, "What have you found?"

Zack sat next to her. He remained silent for a moment while he absently rubbed the back of his neck. "Look," he began. "Really, I'm not at liberty to discuss many details of this case with you, *but* I feel like the information I tell you is in your best interest, and you're going to find out eventually. The woman you found—her name was Katherine Tidwell. She lived in the apartments just north of where her body was discovered. In fact this patch of woods—" He jerked his thumb toward her backyard. "It borders her complex."

Tarrin paled. "Do you think whoever killed her lives that close?"

Zack shrugged. "It's hard to tell. I've got men checking things out. Nobody in the building or the surrounding area happened to see her that day. The last place she was seen alive was in a nightclub in downtown Seattle." He paused and sighed heavily. "She was only twenty-three."

Tarrin shuddered, and her head hung. "Oh, that is terrible. She was so young."

"She was. I can't really tell you much about our investigation, but this homicide seems to be related to three others we've been investigating. All four victims are around the same age, the same build, and they all died about the same time of day—late afternoon. Then to top it off, all four died the same way."

Tarrin gasped. "That's . . . That's awful," she spoke, shocked.

"It is, and if the press catches wind of any of this, my investigation will crumble."

Tarrin's eyes shot to his, and her hands trembled. Would the reporters find them? "Will the press find us? Lexie?"

He held her gaze and smiled. "I don't think they will," he answered. "And don't worry. We've done our best to shield you and your daughter from the media. You might see a reporter or two poking their noses around here, but you shouldn't have a problem. If you do, let me know right away?"

"Yes," Tarrin whispered. "I will. I don't want anyone here badgering us with questions." She shuddered.

"This situation isn't good, but like I said, we'll do our best to keep them away. I can't risk some journalist ruining my investigation because, honestly, I think we have a serial killer on our hands," he finished.

Tarrin felt the blood drain from her face, and she met Zack's blue eyes. "Really?" she breathed.

"I don't want to scare you. That's the last thing I want to do, but these murders haven't been spaced far apart. My department doesn't feel like you or your family is in danger, but I'd like you to know what's happening, and I want you to feel free to contact me, *personally,* night or day with any concerns you might have—questions—whatever you need. Also, if Lexie remembers anything—any details at all—I'd appreciate you letting me know right away."

"Yes. Yes, of course. I'll do whatever I can to help," Tarrin replied.

"I'd like to get this guy behind bars if you know what I mean." He frowned then pulled a card from his pocket and handed it to Tarrin. "I want you to feel safe. This is my private number. Anything you need—just call." He held her gaze for a few seconds.

Tarrin took the card. "Thank you. I appreciate your help."

"I appreciate your cooperation." He stood and Tarrin moved to follow. He turned and shook her hand. "And, uh . . . on a more personal note," he went on, "I don't *usually* do this either—but I was wondering . . . Would you like to go to dinner tomorrow night? I might be in hot water if the chief found out, but it's a risk I'm willing to take." He chuckled.

Startled, Tarrin's expression faltered. "Oh," she stammered, taken aback. "I don't know. I-I guess that would be *okay*?" Her voice rose.

"So, is that a yes?"

A small smile touched her lips and she nodded. "Um . . . Yes, dinner would be nice."

"I'll pick you up at say—seven-o'clock? Too late? Too early?"

"No, seven is fine," she agreed.

"Fantastic. I'll see you at seven." He waved as he turned toward his vehicle.

He slid into his car, and Tarrin's shoulders fell when he pulled onto the narrow street and disappeared down the hill. She blinked toward the empty lane, feeling slightly bemused.

℀

"I still can't believe he asked you out," Erin commented while she filled her plate with noodles.

Shaking her head, Tarrin took a bite of spaghetti. She adjusted her plate on her lap as she sat cross-legged on the kitchen floor.

Erin sat next to her and grinned. "He's cute," she continued. "Are you excited?"

Tarrin's eyes shot toward the living room. Cartoons flipped across the screen while Jake and Lexie sat together on the blankets and pillows spread out across the worn carpet.

"Honestly, I'm really nervous. I haven't been on a real date in a while," she replied.

"It'll be great. Dating a homicide detective—Oh, excuse me—a *Lieutenant.* That's pretty cool," Erin laughed.

Tarrin finished her meal quickly then stood and moved to the stained porcelain sink. She ran the water until it steamed then washed the few dishes left over from dinner. "I miss my dishwasher," she murmured.

"What do you think those two twerps are for? Make them wash dishes." Erin's voice rose to be heard above the television.

"I heard that," Jake called in response.

Tarrin placed another plate on top of the wash pile just as a firm knock sounded on the front door.

Jake rushed from the living room then paused when Tarrin yelled, "No, Jake!" He turned to watch her, his expression growing apprehensive, and she forced a calm smile. "I'll get it."

She wiped her hands on a ragged hand towel and cautiously moved to the door. Peering through the peep-hole, she released a pent-up breath when she realized it was Calum Sloan and his nephew who stood on their front porch. Opening the door, she smiled a greeting.

"Mr. Sloan! Macin! Come in." Her hands fluttered nervously before she hid the dirty towel behind her back.

Calum stepped inside. "Hi," he greeted then held up a plain paper sack. "I brought you a little house warming gift."

Tarrin turned and tossed the towel onto the kitchen counter before she took the bag with a curious smile. "Oh! Thank you," she replied and peered inside. "Donuts! We love donuts."

"Those are the best donuts this side of Seattle. There's a little Hispanic market, about four blocks from here. They make the best donuts and *killer* empanadas," he informed her with a charming grin.

"Yum!" Erin chimed in.

"That will be good to know," Tarrin laughed. "How are you, Macin? Jake and Lexie are watching cartoons. Do you want to join them?"

Macin shrugged. "Sure."

"Those are Lexie's cartoons," Jake muttered and cast his mother a quick glower.

Macin held up a hand in greeting. "That's okay, man. I like SpongeBob." He walked into the living room and joined Jake and Lexie on the carpet.

"Come on in. Have a seat." Erin grinned and pointed toward the floor.

Calum glanced around. His gaze swept across the bare room, and his lips turned down into a frown as Tarrin rushed to explain. "We didn't want to move all the big furniture across states. We plan to buy a table and a couch at a secondhand shop, but—well—we just haven't had a chance to shop yet." Calum nodded his understanding, and Tarrin went on, "Oh, and you haven't met my sister, Erin. Erin, this is Mr. Sloan."

Calum reached out to shake her sister's hand. "It's good to meet you. So, Erin and Tarrin?"

"Yeah. It's good to meet you too, Mr. Sloan," Erin replied. She stepped back with a wide smile then turned to Tarrin. "Hey, listen, I'll be right back. *Um . . . bathroom*," she whispered as an aside.

Tarrin's eyes widened. "Oh! Okay," she replied slowly.

Erin winked before she bounded up the narrow, squeaky stairs, leaving Tarrin alone with Calum. Heat rose in Tarrin's cheeks, and she smiled sheepishly.

Calum chuckled. "I just wanted to stop by and see how everything was. I realize it's late, but I had a few things at the office that kept me. Your daughter is doing well?" he asked.

"Better. She can't really recall what happened. The doctors think she's suffering from some form of PTSD—traumatic disassociation—but she seems fine, other than that. She's acting as if nothing ever happened." She shrugged, then added, "And I appreciate your help yesterday, by the way. I think I was in shock too. I had no idea where to go, and . . . well . . ." Tarrin paused. She realized she was beginning to ramble.

Calum's dark eyes scanned her face and she bit the inside of her cheek when he spoke. "I'm glad I could lend a hand."

"Oh, thank you—for fixing the back door too," Tarrin suddenly remembered. "Honestly, it was driving me crazy."

Calum nodded. "No problem. Ours sticks from time to time. We have to keep it oiled."

"How long have you lived here? I was surprised that . . .

Well, I had no idea that . . ." She paused.

"That I was your neighbor?" he finished for her.

"Yes. I mean . . . It is quite a coincidence."

"It is, isn't it? Like I said, I was going to say something during our interview, but I thought bumping into you would be a bit more fun. I just didn't realize what bad timing I had," he spoke with a grin.

Tarrin chuckled. "You're timing worked out great for me. I don't think I could have handled Miss Cope either. I'm glad you were around."

"Aw, yes. Miss Cope," Calum snorted. "She's a tough woman, but sweet enough once you get past her . . ." He shrugged. "To put it nicely, her less-than-pleasant demeanor. You'll get used to her. Macin's been scared to death of her since they moved in."

"Macin is your nephew?" Tarrin asked.

He nodded. "His mom is deployed with the Navy right now."

"Really?" Tarrin pressed.

"Macin's dad died a few years ago in a car accident. The kid's had a pretty rough time, and my sister hated leaving him. So," Calum went on, "rather than upset his life any more than necessary, I decided to move into their place while she's away. She's been gone nearly eleven months, but she could be back as soon as October. At least, we're hoping she will."

"Wow. I'm so sorry to hear about Macin's dad," Tarrin replied.

"He was a good man," Calum added.

"That's, honestly, really great of you to take care of him."

Calum shrugged. "It's been . . . *interesting*, but I've enjoyed it. I'll actually miss the kid when his mom comes home."

"I can imagine."

"What about you? You moved from Colorado? I never asked what brought you to Seattle."

Tarrin smiled. "Well, I . . . I divorced a little over a year ago, and Erin was accepted to the University of Washington. So, when she suggested I move with her, I did." She paused, thoughtful. "I'm not sure if I made the best choice, but I think the move will be good for us. I felt good about it at the time, but considering all that's happened . . ." She shook her head, but smiled. "We've had kind of a rocky start."

Calum's eyes softened. "You have. I can promise, this isn't the norm."

She laughed humorlessly. "I'm certainly glad to hear that."

Calum chuckled and shoved his hands into his pockets. "I'll let you get back to your dinner. I just wanted to stop in and see how you were—" He paused when Erin's voice suddenly cut across their conversation.

"Tarrin?" Erin called.

Tarrin and Calum glanced toward the stairs just as Erin's pale face appeared near the top. "What is it?" Tarrin asked, growing concerned at the odd note in her sister's usually jovial voice.

Erin's brow furrowed, and she motioned with her hand for Tarrin to come upstairs. "You too," she whispered to Calum.

Tarrin frowned, and Calum glanced at her curiously, but followed up the narrow staircase.

"What's wrong?" Tarrin whispered when she stepped into the hall.

Erin's face was white. Her eyes were large and frightened, and her hands trembled. "I came into the kids' room to get a book, but when I passed the window, I saw a light—out in the woods—moving around through the trees. Someone's out there. They're still there. Come on. I'll show you." She led the way into the darkened bedroom and pointed toward the trees. "Just watch. You can see their flashlight just through there."

Tarrin's heartbeat accelerated and her breathing grew shallow as they peered through the dirty window. They watched the woods below. The dark screen of trees swayed gently with the breeze, and shadows stretched across the tiny yard. Tarrin gasped when a light suddenly appeared within the maze of foliage. The light disappeared and Tarrin, Calum, and Erin waited in silence. Tarrin tore her eyes from the trees to scan the yard below. All was still.

"There! There it is again. You can barely see it, but someone *is* out there," Erin whispered hoarsely. "Do you think it's the guy who killed that girl?"

Tarrin's gaze flew toward the forest, and she caught a glimpse of the light once more before it disappeared again. "I'm sure it's just a reporter or journalist. Or maybe the police?" she offered.

She could hear Calum breathing, deep and even, and she suddenly felt very grateful for his presence, though she hardly knew the man. He was a complete stranger for that matter. Tarrin considered herself a fairly independent woman. She had learned to do many things she had once taken for granted on her own, but still, his presence brought a measure of comfort.

"If I had to guess, I'd say it's a couple of teenagers or kids trying to poke around the crime scene. The news would have spread through the neighborhood pretty fast. It could be anyone. Do you have a flashlight? I can check it out."

Tarrin's eyes widened. "Are you sure?"

He smiled. "It'll be fine. Do you have a flashlight?" he repeated calmly. "Like I said—I'm certain it's just a couple of kids from the neighborhood trying to scare one another."

Tarrin nodded, swallowing hard. Her throat felt dry. She walked down the hall and to her bedroom, where she retrieved a flashlight from the nightstand, then returned to the children's room. She caught Calum's eye through the darkness and he smiled, reassuring.

"I'll be right back."

Calum strode down the stairs, and Tarrin followed close behind. He let himself out the back door, but turned when Tarrin moved to follow. "Wait here. Just in case, huh?" He grinned in an attempt to calm her.

She paused in the open doorway. "Be careful!"

She waited with baited breath as he crossed the dark yard. Eerie shadows stretched across the grass and reached toward the house. She suppressed a violent shudder as a gentle, chilled breeze brushed across her face. She glanced back toward the living room when she heard the children laughing. She was suddenly very grateful they were so enthralled with their cartoons. She turned and watched Calum with an anxious expression when he reached the edge of the trees. She could hear Erin breathing behind her.

"I'm sorry, Tarrin. I just get sick thinking a murderer is still loose out there. You don't think he'd come back, right?" Erin asked.

The flashlight in Calum's hand flared to life just before he disappeared into the woods bordering the yard. Tarrin's heart rate increased and she bit her lip. What if the killer was hiding in the trees? She surveyed the dark mix of conifers and tall alders with ever-increasing anxiety.

"I don't think so. That wouldn't make a lot of sense," Tarrin tried to reassure her sister. But her own doubts played through her mind. Would the killer return? They waited in silence for several moments. The sound of the children's cartoon blended with the noisy city outside, and Tarrin could feel her pulse beating against her throat.

"Where is he?" Erin whispered.

"I don't know," Tarrin whispered in return just as a clamorous rustling sounded at the edge of the trees. Tarrin stifled a gasp, stepping back toward the open door.

"Mr. Sloan?" she called.

"It's only me," Calum spoke, stepping into the yard.

He turned back toward the woods, shining the beam through the bushes and shrubs. Tarrin held her breath while he searched the edge of forest. After a moment, he turned away and crossed the yard. He flipped the light off when he neared Tarrin, and she raised a trembling hand to the base of her throat as their eyes met. He licked his lips and frowned.

"Whoever it was took off when they saw me coming," he informed her.

"You don't think . . . ?"

"That it was the murderer?"

Tarrin remained silent.

"No," Calum said. "I don't. Unfortunately there are a lot of nuts in a city this size. It was probably someone who heard about the murder and was curious. I'm certain everything's fine."

Tarrin stepped back into the house, and he followed. She slid the door shut with little effort and smiled, relieved once again that Calum had taken the time to fix the door.

"Thank you for checking," she whispered.

"Anytime. I'll . . . um . . . look—I'll leave my number. I can be over in less than a minute. All you have to do is call."

She sighed and gave her sister a reassuring smile.

Erin exhaled loudly then looked toward Calum. "Thanks, Mr. Sloan."

"It's no problem. I'm glad I could help. And call me Calum, please? Only my secretary calls me Mr. Sloan and that's because I can't convince her to do otherwise. Speaking of work, Tarrin," he turned to face Tarrin once again, "do you need to start later in the week? I'll hold your position as long as you need."

Tarrin considered the idea for a moment. The next day would be Saturday. She still hadn't found time to register the children for school, but that had nothing to do with what had taken place today. "No, I don't. Thank you, though. I think maybe it'll be best if we just get things back to normal as quickly as possible. Monday will be fine."

"If you're sure."

"Yes, thank you."

"If you change your mind, I'll understand. Also, at the sake of sounding overly helpful, I'd be happy to help you with the couch and table. My sister has a truck, and there are a few second-hand stores close by. I could come and pick up whatever you find. It'll save you the hassle of renting a *U-Haul.*"

"Oh." Tarrin hadn't thought about the bother of renting a truck. She brightened. "That would be very helpful, actually. You wouldn't mind?"

"Not at all."

Erin beamed. "I think that's a great idea. Better yet, why don't you take Tarrin shopping? Go to lunch. Leave the kids with me. I mean the least Tarrin could do is treat you to lunch for all your help."

Stunned, Tarrin's mouth fell open. Heat rushed to her cheeks, and she laughed uncomfortably. "Umm . . ."

Calum nodded, his expression knowing. "I think that sounds like a good idea. What do you think?" he addressed Tarrin. "I know Macin would have fun spending more time with Jake."

Sudden and unwelcome humiliation burned across Tarrin's face. What was she supposed to say? She was going to smother Erin in her sleep—with her own pillow! She glanced toward Erin, and her sister winked once again. Tarrin cringed a little before she met Calum's eyes. "Yeah . . . uh . . . sure. And I-I'd love to treat you to lunch. Really, it's the least I can do."

"You don't owe me anything, but lunch with you *would* be nice, so why don't I plan on picking you up around ten?"

"Yes, ten will be fine."

"Great, and I hope you enjoy the donuts!" Then he nodded toward the door. "If you need me, please don't hesitate to call. I can be right over."

"Thank you, Mr. Sloan . . . Calum," she replied.

"No problem. I'll see you tomorrow."

CHAPTER *Five*

*Y*ou scored two dates in one night. Way to go!" Erin laughed as she flopped into bed and tossed her worn bible onto the nightstand.

"Well, I don't think the second really counted. Calum Sloan was kind of backed into a corner." Tarrin's brows furrowed.

Erin stuck her tongue out, then laughed. "Oh, come on. I saw an opportunity. Besides, you wouldn't have had the guts."

"He's my boss!" Tarrin exclaimed, feeling annoyed.

"So that means *what?*"

Tarrin groaned. "I can't date my boss. It's unethical!"

"Goodness gracious, Tarrin! Just go out tomorrow. Stop being such a wet noodle and have some fun for once. Besides, you deserve it."

"Where am I supposed to take him to lunch?"

Erin shrugged. "Don't know. You'll figure it out." She flipped off the light, immersing the bedroom in darkness. "Stop stressing and go to sleep. Goodnight, sister."

"Goodnight," Tarrin moaned.

After a few minutes of silence, Erin spoke, "I am sorry for putting you on the spot. I just . . . I just want to see you relax and have some fun for once."

Tarrin smiled a little into the darkness and sighed. "I do have fun. I have fun with you and Jake and Lexie."

"You know that's not what I mean."

"I know. And I will. I'm over Travis, but I'm . . . I'm still trying to find *me*, Erin. I don't want to complicate things," Tarrin explained.

Erin laughed a little. "I'm sorry. I am. Next time I'll keep my mouth zipped and let you get your own dates. I promise."

"You do?"

"Well, I should say, I'll try my best," Erin teased.

They laughed before Tarrin added, "You know I love you."

"I love you too. Goodnight, Tarrin. And don't be nervous. It's going to be fine. You'll have a great time tomorrow," Erin finished.

Tarrin stared toward the ceiling as the silence between them stretched. She could hear Erin's breathing relax into sleep, and she focused on taking several deep breaths of her own. She did feel nervous. Spending the afternoon with Calum Sloan, and then going on a dinner date with Lieutenant Marzollo—the thought made her stomach clench. She hadn't been out much since her divorce and the idea of dating again left her feeling susceptible.

She didn't have a whole lot of experience with men. She and Travis had been together since childhood, and they dated exclusively throughout high school and college. Following the divorce, she'd gone out only a handful of times and with only a few different men. There hadn't been many dating opportunities in town, and once the rumors started circulating . . . well, she hadn't bothered dating since.

Fresh start, she reminded herself. She could scarcely believe Erin had managed to get her into such a fix. She rolled her eyes and did her best to relax just as a moan sounded from down the hall. Concerned, Tarrin rolled out of bed and tiptoed toward the kids' bedroom. She peered into the room just as Lexie moaned again, and Tarrin moved to the side of the girl's bed.

"Lex," she whispered, "what's wrong?"

"My tummy hurts, Mommy," Lexie groaned.

Tarrin placed her hand against her daughter's forehead. Her skin was clammy, but not overly heated. "Do you need to use the bathroom?" she asked.

Lexie nodded, and Tarrin helped her from the bed. The little girl padded, barefoot, into the bathroom across the hall and the hinges squeaked gratingly when she shut the door. Tarrin sighed, then noticed the blinds were partially open. She reached across

Jake to grab the cord, but her eyes strayed toward the view. She watched the trees swaying in the gentle breeze for a minute then gasped when a light suddenly appeared between the trees. She froze and studied the woods with baited breath. The light's muted glow appeared ethereal in the darkness.

"I'm done, Mama," Lexie spoke as she reentered the room.

Tarrin stood straight and forced a smile, turning her back to the window. She tried to still her sudden trembling as she tucked Lexie back into bed. "How's the tummy?" she asked. Her voice sounded breathless—frightened.

"It hurts."

Tarrin sighed. "You don't have a fever, but I'll go get you some *Pepto*, okay? I'll be right back."

Lexie's head fell onto her pink pillow, and her curls fanned out from around her face. Tarrin stood and glanced toward the window out of the corner of her eye. The light was gone. Stepping to the window, she scanned the darkened yard below for any signs of movement before she left the bedroom and walked cautiously down the stairs.

Feeling tense, and she had to admit, scared, she peered into the dark kitchen as she came off the last creaky tread. She took a deep breath when she reached for the light, and her eyes swept across the empty room before she moved toward the cupboard where she kept the medicines and first aid supplies. She reached for the *Pepto-Bismol* then glanced at the glowing face of the stove clock.

"Two in the morning," she whispered.

Who is wandering through the woods at two in morning? She caught sight of Calum's number hanging from a magnet on the refrigerator door. *This is crazy. I can't call him at two in the morning. He'll think I'm insane. Worse—he'll probably fire me.*

"Mom, aren't you coming?" she heard Lexie's voice call from above.

Tarrin closed her eyes briefly, then grabbed a spoon before

63

she rushed back up the stairs. She sat on the edge of Lexie's bed to administer the medicine, and she smiled a little when Lexie pulled a face.

"That's gross." Lexie wiped her lips with the back of her hand.

"Mmm-hmm. Lay down now." Tarrin kissed her daughter's forehead then asked, "Would you like me to stay in here with you tonight?"

Lexie shook her head, and Tarrin glanced toward the window. She bit down hard on her lip when she saw the light once again. It moved slowly through the tall alders and dark pines. She wondered if she ought to wake Erin, but she also didn't want Lexie and Jake frightened or upset. Who was in the trees behind her house? Even if Calum were right, and it was only a group of interested kids, why would they have returned after Calum chased them away? The thought made her heart race.

"Mom?" Lexie's voice broke into her thoughts.

She turned to face her daughter. "Maybe I'll stay in here with you? Just for a bit?"

"Okay," Lexie murmured sleepily.

Tarrin crawled across Lexie to sit against the wall, facing the window. She pulled her daughter's head onto her lap and began humming softly. She ran her fingers through Lexie's soft curls and watched the flashlight's languid movement through the dense foliage. Her fingers trembled slightly, and she suppressed a shiver. *I'm sure it's nothing*, she tried to reassure herself.

The glow didn't move closer toward the house. Sometimes, it disappeared for several moments at a time, but it always reappeared in about the same spot, and Tarrin's heart kept up a frantic pace while she kept vigil. *Maybe it's a forensics team, looking for more clues,* she tried to convince herself. *Or some crazy news reporter.* She kept watch on the trees for nearly an hour. Nothing changed. The light continued to appear and disappear. Her eyes grew heavy, and she listened to her children's soft breaths.

This is stupid. There has to be an explanation, she thought, feeling frustrated.

Another hour later, the intruder in the woods finally disappeared. Tarrin waited anxiously for their light to reappear, but everything remained dark. Still, she was reluctant to leave her children alone. With an exhausted sigh, she stretched her length next to Lexie's. Her feet hung from the short bed, and she barely had enough room to squeeze between the little girl and the wall. She lay down and wrapped her arms around her sleeping daughter then closed her eyes and willed her tense, drained mind to relax.

⍧

"*Seven* children?" Calum asked, unable to hide his amazement.

"Yep, seven. I would go down the list of names, but I don't know if you could keep it straight. Most people can't," she replied, laughing.

"Wow! That is . . . amazing. Do you get along? I imagine that makes for some fun family dinners." Calum grinned.

"Yes. Yes, it does. It makes for some very interesting family dinners," Tarrin replied.

"And where do you fall in the line-up?" Calum eyed Tarrin with a smile.

Tarrin liked his smile, and she breathed in before answering. "I'm the oldest. Erin is number five."

Despite how nervous she had been for her date with Calum Sloan, she quickly discovered he was very easy to be with. He was interesting, thoughtful, and she was enjoying their afternoon together quite a bit more than she first anticipated, especially considering her hectic night. By morning, her anxiety over the intruder in the trees had faded, and she felt certain she overreacted. Zack warned her that journalists would probably poke around.

She was doing her best to push the events of the last couple of days behind her, and she could feel herself relaxing with Calum. She smiled then asked, "What about you? Do you have any other brothers or sisters besides Jackie?"

"Just me and Jackie. I'm the oldest. She's two years younger."

"Did you grow up in Seattle?" Tarrin pressed, curious.

Calum shook his head. "No. Downtown Tacoma."

"Do your parents still live there?"

Calum's smile faded slightly. "Well, no. You see—Jackie and I were in and out of foster homes for most of our childhood."

"Oh." Tarrin bit her lip.

His mouth twisted. "My mom was a drug addict. She . . . um . . . struggled. And really, when she wasn't strung out on meth, she was great. I miss her," he finished.

"I'm . . . Wow . . . I'm so sorry."

Watching her expression falter, he laughed a little. "It wasn't easy, but it wasn't that bad," Calum added. "Some days were harder than others. Some homes just weren't a good fit." He shrugged then went on. "Jackie and I eventually ended up with an older couple who adopted us. I was—let's see . . . seventeen. Jackie was fifteen at the time. We weren't exactly the easiest kids to deal with either. We gave them a lot of grief, but they never gave up on us."

"Really? That's wonderful," Tarrin replied.

Calum agreed.

"Are they still around? Your adoptive parents?" she pressed.

"They are, and you've met my mother at the office," he answered, grinning.

Tarrin's eyebrows furrowed. "I have?"

"Um-hmm."

"Mary? Your receptionist?" Tarrin asked.

Calum nodded. "She and her husband, Frank, divorced several years ago. So, I asked her to come in and help me out when my last receptionist quit."

"*Really?*"

"And Frank and his new wife, Kathy, live just up the street from us—over on Seventh Avenue. He and I stayed pretty close despite the divorce, and he and Mary get along for the most part. They left on good terms. Besides, my real dad ran off when I was just a kid. I didn't really know him. So, Frank . . . Well, I couldn't have asked for a better family."

"That's amazing." Tarrin chewed on her lower lip thoughtfully for a moment then asked, "And your birth mom—is she still around? I'm sorry if I'm being nosey. It's a fault of mine." Tarrin laughed.

"I don't mind. Besides, I enjoy talking with you," he added.

Her face brightened, and a soft smile touched her lips as he went on.

"She passed away," he answered. "Several years ago, now."

"Oh, no," Tarrin jumped in. "That's . . . Calum, that's awful."

"She overdosed at a party. They found her face down in the restroom of some back-alley bar in Tacoma, but by that time, Jackie and I had been in foster homes for nearly five years. We hadn't seen or heard from her in a long time. It was . . . difficult. Like I said, when you could look beyond the addiction, she was a beautiful person. She just couldn't get past it."

He took a deep breath and continued quietly, "Jackie and I were lucky. That lifestyle becomes a cycle. My mother's mother was an addict, and I might have ended up on the same path myself. Frank and Mary were there. They helped me see what I could become, not what I thought I would become. Most kids in the system aren't that lucky," he finished.

"Wow," Tarrin breathed. "I can't begin to imagine how hard that would have been. But . . . But Mary seems great—wonderful, in fact. To tell you the truth, she was the first friendly face I'd seen all day. Seriously, I was feeling pretty hopeless. I could have kissed her when she didn't shove my application in a drawer."

Calum chuckled. "She must have liked you too. She was very adamant that I interview you."

Feeling pleasantly surprised, Tarrin hid a smile. "Oh? So, I didn't get the job based solely on my impressive work record?" she teased.

He laughed. "Actually, your year at Sanderson's Shoe Emporium sold me. If you survived a year in the woman's shoe department, you can handle anything, right?"

"I appreciate your confidence in me."

He winked just as he pulled into the crowded lot of a nearby thrift store. "Here we are! There are a few more stores nearby, so we can try those if you can't find what you need here."

Tarrin nodded. "Sounds like a plan."

"Also," he went on, "if all else fails, Frank and Kathy head the community center for our neighborhood. There's a bunch of stuff in storage in the basement, and I'm certain he could find a couch and table somewhere."

"A community center?" Tarrin pressed, interested.

He nodded. "It's great, really. Frank started the center while he worked as a police officer several years ago. He wanted a place for the local kids to hang out—somewhere besides the streets and alleys."

"He's a police officer?" Tarrin asked.

"He retired from the Seattle PD about 8 years ago. Now he works as a spiritual guidance counselor. He spends most of his time working with kids from broken homes or kids who have lived on the streets."

Tarrin's eyes widened and a soft smile curved her lips. "That's amazing."

"Macin spends quite a bit of his time there. Sarah, Frank's step daughter, watches him after school until I get home from work. There's a commons room with a big screen TV, and Macin hooked up a few different gaming systems, so he never argues about hanging around." Calum laughed. "Oh, and if you're interested,

Frank hosts different classes each week for the adults, and a local pastor holds services on Sunday."

"It sounds great," Tarrin replied. "That might be a good place for Jake and Lexie to spend some time, especially if it helps them get to know more kids around here."

Calum agreed then added, "I usually attend the classes. It gives me something to do on Wednesday nights." He grinned. "It isn't easy to have a night life while watching a twelve-year-old boy. And besides, it gives Macin a chance to hang out with some of his friends. Frank coerced me into teaching a class on investing, and if you don't watch out, he'll do his best to corner you into volunteering. He can come up with some interesting topics to teach. We meet once a month for a community pot-luck too."

Tarrin's brow rose. "Pot-luck?"

"You'd be surprised by the culinary talent some of our neighbors possess." He pulled a face. Then added, "Kathy is hosting a luncheon tomorrow after worship service, if you're interested." He faced her expectantly, and Tarrin's eyes broadened for a moment.

Her gaze dropped from his. She hadn't attended any sort of social function or worship service since the rumors about her and Travis began. A few people in her close-knit community were responsible for much of the heart-wrenching gossip, and she had been angry enough to avoid any event in the community, especially church.

She knew the rumors had been a poor excuse to cut ties with her neighbors and friends, but it was all she could do to keep what little pride she had left intact. Her family did the best they could to quell the gossip surrounding her and Travis, but it hadn't helped much. At times it had felt overwhelming. She knew she'd become a recluse. She avoided making friends or forming any sort of relationship, but she was hoping to build a new life in Seattle, wasn't she? It would be nice to get out in the community again and meet new people. It would be nice to attend worship service again. She'd missed that light in her life.

She inhaled deeply before she pulled her mind back to Calum. "I'd like that," she heard herself answer. "Maybe the kids and I will try to come."

He nodded. "Great! I'll let Frank and Kathy know to expect you. Oh, and worship service starts at nine, but don't feel like you need to attend service to join in the lunch. Either way."

She smiled. "Maybe."

The idea was appealing. "Do you attend?" she asked.

"I started attending after Jackie lost Craig, her husband."

"Oh," she breathed. "I'm sure that was very difficult for her and Macin."

"It was. Jackie and Craig were perfect for each other. His passing was hard on all of us." He sighed, and Tarrin remained silent for a moment before her curiosity peaked.

"What about you?" She raised her eyes to his. "Have you ever been married? You . . . You're not married, right?" She hadn't thought about that. It hadn't crossed her mind to ask until now.

A deep blush touched Tarrin's cheeks when Calum laughed out loud. "No, Tarrin. I'm not married," he reassured her, his voice tinged with humor.

"Oh . . . well . . . That's good," she responded. She smiled sheepishly, suddenly feeling very foolish.

He chuckled again then explained, "I went through a divorce about two years ago. Her name was Nicole."

"Oh?"

He shrugged. "We were only married for three years, and honestly, we spent a good portion of that time away from each other. I was busy building my business, and she had her own interests to keep her occupied. We just didn't have a whole lot in common."

"Had you known one another long?" Tarrin asked, curious.

He frowned a little and nodded. "We met in college several years before, and a mutual friend hooked us up again later. We had a good relationship, but—well—" His eyes suddenly danced with humor, and he went on with a smile. "She left me for her vegan yoga instructor. They currently live together in—uh—*Okodorf Sieben Linden*. It's an eco-village in Northern Germany. We're still friends, and it was fun while it lasted, but we were just *very* wrong for one another."

"Do you have any kids?" she asked.

"No." He shook his head. "We both wanted different things. I wanted a family, but Nicole wasn't ready, and it's probably a good thing we didn't have children. Besides, I love meat!" He laughed. "I would have been a terrible example. We have this argument regularly. She feels my life would be better balanced if I embraced my natural instincts—become more of a vegetarian, Paleolithic-type man."

Tarrin smiled. "I can't really see you barefoot and wearing dreadlocks, but maybe."

Calum shared her smile. "Well, you know all about me. What about you? You're divorced?"

"Oh . . . Yes, I am—a little over a year ago." She blanched.

She wasn't ready to discuss the circumstances behind her failed marriage. She'd moved to Seattle to escape the stares, the rumors, and the whispers. She needed a clean start. She wanted to create a future where she and her children would not be ridiculed for her husband's actions. Tarrin knew it wouldn't take a lot of digging for someone to find out the horrible truth. All you needed was an internet connection. Their family's affair had been splashed all over the local news, but Tarrin wasn't ready to openly admit her past to anyone.

This was her new start. She exhaled. "Well," she went on, "it didn't end well. It's difficult to talk about. Not that I still have feelings for my ex-husband." She laughed humorlessly. "I just . . . It was a difficult divorce."

Calum sobered. "I'm sorry. How long were you married?"

"Eleven years," she replied.

He whistled softly. "That's a long time. I can imagine it would have been very difficult. I'm sorry. Really, I am."

"Thank you." She smiled weakly.

He nodded toward the store front. "Should we go in? See what we can find?"

Calum jumped from the Dodge Ram and came around to help Tarrin down. He grasped her hand as he assisted her out of the truck. She felt pleasantly surprised by how tall Calum Sloan was. He towered over her by at least several inches. She blushed when she realized he was watching her, his eyes thoughtful. Laughing self-consciously, she glanced around the crowded parking lot. Jackie's large truck stood out amongst the practical sedans and environmentally-conscious vehicles surrounding them.

Calum eyed her with a knowing grin. "Jackie loves this truck."

CR

He closed his eyes and listened to the soft sound of Tarrin Grace's voice. He enjoyed listening to her talk. Most women's voices just grated on his nerves—set his teeth grinding. But, he liked her voice. He even liked her laughter. It had a soothing effect. He watched her smile as she perused the overwhelming array of used furniture. Once in a while her nose crinkled with distaste. She was cute. He chuckled, quickly looking away so as not to draw her attention.

It was unfortunate her family had stumbled upon him. He'd assumed that house was empty. It had been just that morning. He sighed, knowing he was going to have to keep a very close and calculated eye on the situation. If the girl exposed him, everything he'd worked so hard for would be lost. He wasn't sure yet what course he needed to take, but he knew he would need to act soon. With a sigh, he closed the book he'd been leafing through.

"I like this one," he heard Tarrin exclaim.

Grabbing his jacket he slung it over his broad shoulder and tossed the book back onto the shelf. He moved toward her. Her sweet scent filled his nostrils when he came nearer. She smiled pleasantly. Her smile was soothing. He liked that.

❧

It didn't take long to find a table set and a relatively clean couch. Tarrin settled on a retro-style table, which she loved, and a beige couch. She even discovered a matching recliner for an extra thirty dollars. She paid for her items, and then watched while Calum loaded her new furniture into the back of his sister's truck. He held the door for her before he jumped behind the steering wheel.

"So," he grinned, "are we still up for lunch?"

"Yes. Yes, of course," she replied with a smile.

"I have a favorite café along the piers. They make the best fish and chips in Seattle. Do you mind?"

"No, that sounds great, actually."

"Good, but this will be my treat." He shook his head when Tarrin went to protest. "No arguments. It will be my pleasure to buy you lunch."

CHAPTER *Six*

"This is beautiful," Tarrin murmured when she and Calum were standing on a wooden pier overlooking the grayish-green water of Puget Sound.

The sounds of the café mingled in the distance, and she breathed in the unique scent that seemed to linger along the piers. She hadn't enjoyed a lunch date in such a long time, and the new experience of being in Seattle's Waterfront Neighborhood left her feeling excited.

She held tightly to the little sack of gifts Calum had purchased for her children in Seattle's iconic Ye Olde Curiosity Shop while she studied the water below. It lapped gently against the aged pillars supporting the pier. Long strands of kelp floated lazily along the waves, and colonies of barnacles made their home against the face of the columns and stones. A gull cried as it struggled to scavenge for morsels of food from off the wooden planks. Several tourists milled about, and Tarrin watched in awe when a massive cruise boat docked in the distance.

She turned away from the water and faced the city with its tall skyscrapers and affluent condo towers. "This is so different than what I'm used to," Tarrin murmured, feeling somewhat intimidated by the immensity of the city.

"What area of Colorado are you from?" Calum asked, turning to follow her gaze. They stared toward the tall buildings.

"Delta," she replied.

"Where?" He turned to look at her.

She met his gaze with a smile. "It's a small town, in western Colorado," she answered.

"Oh, I see. So you're a redneck?" he jested.

"Maybe," Tarrin laughed.

"Ya'll fellers come from down on the ol' farm?" he asked in

a terrible version of a western drawl.

Tarrin's eyebrow rose a fraction. "I'm afraid you need to work on that accent, Mr. Sloan."

"What? I thought it was pretty good."

"It was *terrible*," she laughed. "Wait! You aren't going to fire me for saying that are you?"

Calum glared playfully. "I might."

"My grandparents owned a farm." She shrugged. "And Garrin, my brother, worked on a turkey farm in town. He—"

"Wait, wait, wait—" Calum chuckled, cutting her off. "*Garrin*? So Garrin, Erin, and *Tarrin*?" He grinned.

"Oh," Tarrin cringed. "Yeah, I was hoping we wouldn't get to that. You really don't want to know all of our names."

"Yes—I do," he answered, then grinned. "I have to know. Is there a . . . *Karen*?" He raised his left eyebrow.

Tarrin bit her lip. "Yes," she replied.

"You're kidding?" His eyes sparkled.

"No." She smiled sheepishly. "There is also Aaron, Sharon, and Mark."

"Mark?" Calum laughed. His eyes danced.

"Mmm-hmm. Mark. He's my closest brother. We're fourteen months apart. My parents didn't get into their Dr. Seuss mode until after Aaron was born."

"Wow," he replied, his eyes wide. "You're right. I will never keep those names straight. Is there some kind of acronym your parents invented?" He asked, disbelieving.

"No, of course not," she laughed.

"That is amazing. Really! So, you didn't grow up on a farm, but your brother worked on a turkey farm?"

She nodded. "Yes, and I plucked turkeys at the local plant one summer." She shuddered. "I couldn't eat poultry for nearly a year."

A grin spread across Calum's face. "You left that one off your resume, Ms. Grace."

ೂ

Tarrin stood in the small bathroom and eyed her reflection in the cracked mirror. Her mouth turned down into a frown. She pulled her hair up and then let it fall across her shoulders once more, debating whether or not she should wear her hair up or down for her dinner date with Lieutenant Marzollo. Lexie sat on the floor of the carpeted hallway. The little girl held tightly to a matreshka doll Calum had given her with one hand while she watched her mother. Her free thumb hovered near her mouth.

Tarrin gave her a warning look. "Don't suck your thumb!"

Lexie dropped her hand to her side, then stood. She came into the bathroom and wrapped her arm around Tarrin's leg.

Tarrin smiled. "Are you doing okay, sweetheart?" she asked.

Her daughter nodded. Tarrin could hear steps drawing near, and within moments, Erin and Jake appeared in the hallway.

"Hey, Mom. Check it out." Jake showed her his box of jumping beans Calum had purchased for him. "Cool, huh? I named this one Lexie," he teased, glancing at his sister.

"Mom," Lexie whined.

"Just kidding. Geeze, Lex!" Jake disappeared into his room.

Lexie untangled herself from around Tarrin's leg and rushed to join her brother. "Can I build Lego's with you?" she asked.

"No way!" Tarrin heard Jake exclaim.

"Jake!" she warned. Frustrated, she shook her head when she caught sight of Erin's reflection in the mirror. "Are you sure you're up to more babysitting?" she asked, rolling her eyes.

"Sure thing," Erin confirmed with a grin. "Go. Have a great time. And you look beautiful by the way."

Tarrin frowned at her reflection and inhaled nervously, letting her hair fall back across her shoulders again.

"You had a good time with Calum, didn't you?" Erin asked.

A soft smile touched Tarrin's lips. "Yes."

"But did you have a *really* good time*?*" Erin pressed.

"Yes. I did have a really good time," she admitted. "But he's my boss. This isn't going to develop into anything. He's just being a friendly neighbor."

"Yeah, right," Erin challenged.

Tarrin chuckled.

"I still can't believe he lives in this neighborhood. Oh!" Erin's eyebrows rose playfully. "Did I happen to mention that your boss called and offered to stop by tomorrow afternoon so we can follow him to the community center? He said the building was a bit tricky to find."

Tarrin's attention perked. "He called?"

"Yeah. You were in the shower, so I fished your phone out of your purse."

"What did you say?"

"I said yes of course, silly. But when did we agree to attend some luncheon and worship service at a community center?"

"This morning," Tarrin murmured.

"Uh-huh," Erin laughed. "I see. Church, huh?"

Tarrin closed her eyes, then turned to Erin with a sheepish expression. "You don't mind?"

"No, but next time can you please come up with a more exciting second date?" she laughed.

"Church is exciting."

"Um, yeah."

"I'm still new at this, remember?" Tarrin defended.

Erin laughed. "Apparently." Then, changing the subject, she added, "Hey, I picked up the mail. Our address hasn't been forwarded yet, so it's nothing but ads and junk."

"Oh, that's right," Tarrin jumped in. "We need to remember to do that on Monday."

Erin shrugged. "I put the ads on the table. I figured you'd want to look at the grocery fliers. What time is Lieutenant Marzollo coming to pick you up?"

Tarrin left the bathroom, satisfied with her appearance. She followed Erin down the stairs and glanced at the clock above the stove when she reached the kitchen. "He'll be here in half-an-hour or so," she replied.

Her stomach clenched in knots and she wished she hadn't agreed to a dinner date with the homicide detective after all. He seemed like a pleasant man. She'd probably enjoy herself. *So just stop stressing,* she berated herself. She was being a coward. She'd had a pleasant afternoon with Calum, hadn't she?

Tarrin smiled when she recalled her earlier outing. She'd had a very good time with Calum Sloan. He was easy to talk with, and she really had enjoyed getting to know him better. He even took time before he'd brought her home to show her a bit more of the city and had kindly made a point to show her a shortcut to the office. It was a route Tarrin knew she would be grateful for during the heavy morning commute.

Jake and Macin seemed to get along great as well, and Tarrin was happy to see her son making new friends again. Jake had a hard time trusting children his age, due in part to the terrible rumors that were spread across the school by some of his closest friends and cousins, but Tarrin understood. They all had to learn to trust again—to trust and to forgive.

"Hey, do you mind if I eat your leftovers?" Erin asked, stepping to the fridge.

"No, go ahead," Tarrin replied absently while she sorted through the shopping advertisements.

"Yes! French fries!"

Tarrin chuckled quietly then paused when she found a small beige envelope stuck in between the fliers. Her brow creased, curious, and she pulled the envelope from between the advertisements. She turned it over. The wrapper was devoid of any address, but her full name was scrawled across the front.

Feeling somewhat startled, she tore it open and her eyes widened when she pulled out a single photo. She gasped. Her heart stuttered when she recognized her own eyes staring back. She began to shake as she studied the odd photo of herself. In the photo her face appeared in the darkened window of the children's bedroom. Her hair lay across her shoulders in pale waves. She was standing in her pajamas—her eyes large and frightened. With a jolt, Tarrin realized the photo had been taken last night when she stood at the window, watching the light move through the trees. She sunk onto a kitchen chair, trembling.

Erin turned to face her, and her brow furrowed in sudden concern. "Wow, Tarrin, you look terrible. Are you all right? What's wrong?"

Tarrin's eyes shot to her sister's, but she quickly tucked the photo into her lap. She didn't want to scare Erin. She needed time to think. What was going on? What was she going to do?

Tarrin forced a shaky laugh. "I'm fine. I just felt dizzy for a moment," she replied.

Erin laughed. "Goodness gracious, you are nervous! Maybe two dates in one day was too much. Do you need something? French fry?" she offered, holding out the container of microwaved left-overs.

"No, I'm fine. I am nervous though. I'm going to go . . . I think I'll change my shoes."

Erin raised one eyebrow. "Okay, whatever. Those look fine, you know."

"I know, but they're not . . . comfortable," Tarrin muttered, pushing away from the table. She stood on trembling legs and stumbled up the stairs.

"Hey, Mom," Jake called, poking his head out of his bedroom door just as Tarrin reached the hallway.

"Just a minute," she told him, distracted.

She rushed into her bedroom and shut the door. With an inaudible moan, she sat on the edge of her bed and pulled the photo from the folds of her blouse. She examined it carefully. Who had taken the picture? Someone had been watching her. Whoever it was knew her name. Was it the murderer? She didn't understand. What was happening? She propped the photo against the lamp on the nightstand and laid her head into her hands.

She focused on breathing deeply. Had Travis's brother, Brandon, followed her to Washington? Or could it be the serial killer? Maybe the killer learned her name. She grasped the photo again. Brandon still held a terrible grudge against her. Would he go so far as to do something like this?

Tarrin glanced at the bedside clock. Zack would be coming to pick her up soon. Should she mention this to him? If it were the killer, then it would only make sense to let him know, but what if it were Brandon? She closed her eyes. If it were Brandon, had her problems followed her here?

"Mom?" Tarrin jumped when she heard Jake's familiar voice call through the closed door. He knocked quietly, and she stuffed the photo in her purse just as he opened her door.

"Hi, honey." Her voice sounded breathless—trembling. She took another deep breath and forced a weak smile.

Jake moved to her side. He sat on the edge of the bed and stared forlornly toward the floor.

Trying to pull her mind from her frantic thoughts, she faced her son. "What is it?" she encouraged.

He shrugged. "Do you like Mr. Sloan?" he asked.

"Oh! I . . ." she stammered. "I don't know him well yet, but he seems very nice. Why?"

He shrugged again. "I dunno. Do you like this other guy too?"

"Well . . . Yes, I suppose I do. He seems like a nice guy."

Jake nodded then asked, "Are you going to get married again?"

Tarrin regarded her son carefully, trying to pull her thoughts away from the photo in her purse, and feeling unsure how to answer. She knew Jake missed his father, and his life would never be the same. The events that transpired during the divorce were very difficult for her son to handle, and Tarrin's heart ached at the thought of her children's pain and loss.

"That's a difficult question to answer. I would like to one day, yes," she admitted honestly, then added, "I loved your dad, but you know he and I can never be together again, right?"

Jake nodded. "It's okay. I know why. It's just that . . . I don't know . . . . It'll be weird, that's all."

"I understand. It won't ever be the same, but you know—" She paused and inhaled. "There are a lot of blended families out there, and most seem to make it just fine. No matter what happens, we're still a family," Tarrin went on. "Besides, I don't think we need to worry about that quite yet. This is just a first date you know."

He nodded then stood slowly and smiled a little. "I hope you have fun."

Surprised, she answered, "Thank you. I hope so too." Then she asked, "Are you doing okay?"

He nodded again then wiped his forearm across his nose and sniffed. He frowned and said, "I had fun with Macin today. I'm *glad* we moved." His voice held a hint of anger.

Tarrin's face fell. She knew Jake still struggled with many of the changes in their lives. She reached out, wrapped her arms about him, and pulled him into a firm embrace. He resisted for only a moment before he fell against her, and she buried her face in his thick, dusty-brown hair.

"It will be okay, Jakers. Things seem hard now, but one day we'll look back at this time and it won't seem so bad. We'll have made it through this together." Tarrin's heart ached for her son. "I know all of this is so hard to understand right now."

"Nothing makes sense anymore," Jake spoke, his voice angry.

"I know," Tarrin said. She closed her eyes. "It's hard to see past our pain and sadness, but one day it *will* make sense." Jake stifled a quiet sob against Tarrin's shoulder, and she forced back tears of her own. She squeezed his thin shoulders. "Why don't I stay home tonight? We'll have a movie party and play games," she suggested when Jake pulled away.

"Uh-uh." He wiped his nose on his forearm again. "You should go. Aunt Erin's going to make caramel popcorn. She won't make it if you stay." He sniffed again, and Tarrin handed him a tissue.

"So I have to go to dinner just so you can have caramel popcorn?" She laughed.

"Yeah," he replied just as a muffled knock sounded on the front door below. "He's here," Jake murmured.

Tarrin eyed her son carefully. "I can stay home, Jake," she told him.

He shrugged, then grinned. "No way!"

Tarrin smiled a little and she grasped her purse from off the bed. She could hear Erin talking with Zack Marzollo. She kissed Jake's forehead and walked down the hall. She kissed Lexie, who sat building a tall tower with Legos, and the little girl smiled.

"Be good for Aunt Erin, sweetheart," Tarrin reminded her. "Don't fight with Jake."

"Okay," Lexie murmured.

Tarrin walked back into the hall and raised a nervous hand to her churning stomach. Would her family be safe while she went out? Was the person who took the photo still watching their house? Determined to find the answers, she descended the stairs.

She wanted to talk with Lieutenant Marzollo first, and she decided she would as soon as they were alone. She hated to ruin their dinner date, but there was no other choice. He needed to know. She had to protect her family, even if that meant opening up about her painful divorce and facing the demons of her past.

℥

"Wow! You look great." Zack Marzollo greeted Tarrin when she entered the living room.

He pushed up from the sofa and came toward her. His shiny blond hair was styled to perfection. Seeing him out of uniform was odd, and Tarrin noted his casual clothes were neat, clean, and expensive. He grinned. His perfect, white teeth complimented a slight tan, and she had to admit the detective was a handsome man. She had the feeling Zack knew it as well.

He reached out to shake her hand, and a faint smile lit her face. "It's good to see you again, Lieutenant."

"Call me Zack, remember? Besides, I'm not on duty tonight."

He held her hand for a moment longer than necessary, and she pulled her fingers from his grasp with a nod. "It's great to see you, Zack," she repeated before she turned to Erin. "Call me if you need anything. *Anything* at all," she stressed.

"Go. Have a great time. We'll be just fine. Won't we, twerps?" Erin called so the children could hear.

Zack laughed when Jake returned, "You promised us popcorn!"

Erin shrugged. "See?"

Tarrin nodded and turned toward the door just as Zack stepped past to open it. He held the door wide, and she swallowed when she brushed past him and walked down the stone stairs. He placed a hand on the small of her back as he led her toward a sleek, platinum Corvette Coupe and Tarrin's brow rose.

"Wow," she murmured. "Nice car."

He held the door for her, and she slid into the luxurious interior. "It's my baby." He patted the car gently and Tarrin chuckled.

He grinned before he shut the door and slid behind the steering wheel. The powerful engine roared when he pulled the car onto the narrow street. Quiet, classical music played on the customized *Bose* stereo and Zack hummed along with the tune. When they slowed near the bottom of the hill, Tarrin took a deep breath. Determined, she squared her shoulders before she turned to face him. His eyebrows shot up, and he smiled.

"Zack, can you pull over?"

The detective's expression faltered and he shook his head slowly. "Uh, sure. Yeah." He laughed awkwardly and steered the sports car to the curb.

"I need to talk to you. I hate to bring this up. I don't want to ruin our date, but I think you need to see this," Tarrin explained in a rush, her voice trembling.

Zack's smile faded when she reached for her purse and pulled the photo from inside. She swallowed and handed the picture to him. His brows knit, confused, as he took the photo between his fingers.

"This is—*you*?" he asked, confused.

"Yes, I . . ." She swallowed and went on, "I found that in the mail today. It came in an envelope with nothing but my name on it. That's me." She paused and took a deep breath. "I was standing by the kids' bedroom window. That picture was taken last night, by someone—someone in the trees behind the house."

Zack considered her for a moment before he frowned.

"Yesterday," Tarrin went on, "Erin noticed this . . . this light in the woods. Someone was out there wandering around through the trees. So Calum went out to see what was going on, but—"

"Calum?"

"My neighbor," Tarrin explained. "Calum went out to check the woods, but whoever was in the trees took off running. Then, around two this morning, I was checking on Lexie. I saw someone out there again. They were wandering around with a flashlight. I kept my eye on the woods for a while from the window. Whoever was in the trees this morning must have seen me standing at the window. They took *that*. I wanted to talk to you about it first. I'm worried about Erin and the kids. I don't want to scare them, but I don't want to leave them alone tonight either. I needed to talk to you first—alone."

Zack leaned back in the driver's seat. He switched off the ignition and blew out a long, slow breath as he studied the photo silently. His left hand tapped the steering wheel absently, and his brow furrowed in thought.

After a long moment he asked, "And you're sure this was taken last night?"

Tarrin nodded her head. "Yes. Positive. That's why I wanted to talk to you. Is it related, do you think, to the murders?"

His mouth twisted speculatively. "It's hard to say, but I don't know if it could be. We've been investigating other, similar murders, and this is the first time I've heard of something like this happening. Of course you're the first person to have stumbled upon a body so soon after being killed."

Tarrin inhaled sharply and stared out the windshield, frustrated.

"Look, has your daughter remembered anything? Has she come to you with any details?" he asked.

"No." She shook her head, feeling disheartened. "I haven't pushed her either. The doctor said it was best not to put any pressure on her, but I have an appointment on Monday with a child psychologist. They're worried that if she did see anything then she's repressed it. That would explain the memory lapse."

"My concern—" A frown creased Zack's handsome face. "Look, there really is no way to sugar coat this. I'm concerned that Lexie *did* see something. The victim hadn't been dead long—not long at all. This photo worries me. If our killer believes your little girl may have seen him or could identify him, then we have a *real* problem."

Tarrin paled visibly. She rubbed her temple and lamented, "What do we do then?"

"Well to start, I'd like you to take me back into those trees. I need you to show me where you saw whatever you saw. You saw a light? Like a flashlight?"

Tarrin nodded.

"This wasn't taken from the ground. The approach is wrong. Our perpetrator had to be in a tree." Zack studied the photo as he spoke.

Tarrin's heart beat quick. "There is also . . . Well, there could possibly be another scenario. It's hard for me to explain, but the person who took this photo may be my ex-brother-in-law. He's not the murderer or anything, but I've had problems with him before, and this . . . It seems like something he might do to dig at me."

"Your brother-in-law?" Zack's eyebrows rose.

"Maybe. Like I said, I had some trouble with him following my divorce. I had to get a restraining order against him. This seems a bit extreme, even for him, but I wouldn't put it past him either. The envelope had my *full* name written on it—even my middle name. How would the killer know my name?"

Zack pulled his notepad from inside his sports coat. "It would have been simple for our killer to get your full name, but you're right, we should look at all angles. What about your ex-husband? Is it possible he could have done this?"

Tarrin bit her lip. "No," she whispered.

Zack regarded her skeptically. "Are you certain?"

She ducked her head. "He's in prison," she murmured.

Zack's lips parted. "I see. Tarrin, I'm sorry." He paused then spoke, "I hate to ask, but I need to know why and you need to explain about your brother-in-law. It's very important that we know all we can about this." He waved the photo.

Tarrin inhaled. "Travis is in prison for fraud and embezzlement."

Zack's face registered his surprise and Tarrin went on quickly, "He embezzled funds from the corporation he was working for for several years. I . . . I honestly had no idea. I know that sounds ridiculous. I should have known, or at least guessed something was wrong, but . . ." She shook her head then turned to face Zack, unsure what else to say.

"I see," Zack replied. He remained silent for a brief moment before adding, "And your brother-in-law?"

"He blamed me for what Travis did. He said I must have coerced Travis into stealing the money, then he claimed I set Travis up. And when they sent him to prison, Brandon terrorized me. He followed me everywhere. He watched the house. He tried to get me in trouble with my job and with the local police. He and his family spread terrible rumors. They said appalling things. Every chance he could, he found a way to publicly humiliate me. He wanted people to believe that I set Travis up—that I had instigated the investigation to get back at him for having an affair with my son's teacher."

Zack's eyebrow rose and he whistled softly. "Your ex had an affair with your kid's teacher?"

Tarrin dropped her gaze toward her lap and nodded. "Everyone in town knew long before I ever did," she spoke. "Jake . . ." She swallowed. "Jake found out at school one day. He saw them together, and a friend of his confirmed it. It was an awful day for all of us."

"I'm sorry, Tarrin." Zack reached for her hand. He squeezed her fingers gently before she pulled her hand back into her lap.

"Brandon even went so far as to say I embezzled the money and framed Travis. They had to arrest him once. He followed me into the grocery store and shoved me against a wall in front of my kids. He and his wife were angry, even Travis's parents were angry. I understood that. Travis's arrest came as a shock to everyone—especially me. But after the rumors took root, a lot of people *believed* I set Travis up. They said I was angry, and I *was*. Once I found out about the affair, of course I was angry, but I would never tarnish Travis's name like that.

A lot of people thought he had been wrongfully arrested, even after he admitted to the crime. Brandon, his friends, and his family, convinced *so* many people that I was at fault. So did Juliann, the woman he'd had an affair with. Everyone in town liked Juliann, so all of it combined . . . . It caused huge problems for me and my children. Even my parents were targeted because of it."

Zack took notes while Tarrin explained.

"And your brother-in-law's name is Brandon?" he spoke

calmly.

Tarrin could read the empathy in Zack's expression and her shoulders fell. When Erin first suggested she move to Washington while she attended the University, it hadn't taken Tarrin long to make up her mind. Washington was supposed to be her fresh start. The thought left her angry. After all she and the children had been through the past year, now this?

"Brandon Addison," she replied. "He moved away a few months ago. They relocated somewhere in northern Utah. I never cared to find out where. Travis's family still lives in my hometown, and its possible Brandon could have found out about our move."

"Did you give any of your ex-husband's family your new address? You've only been here a few days, but it wouldn't be too hard to trace you," Zack suggested.

Tarrin blanched. She hadn't thought about that. How would Brandon know where to find her? Only her parents knew their new address, and Tarrin knew that neither her parents nor her siblings would give out that information. Would Brandon go through all that trouble just to trace her here? Tarrin closed her eyes. She pinched the bridge of her nose, and Zack touched her shoulder tenderly.

"Hey, don't worry. I'm glad you told me. I'll do everything I can to take care of this. I'll keep you and your kids safe." He waved the photo. "I'm going to keep this. I'll have it checked for prints right away. It isn't likely we'll find any besides yours and mine, but it's worth a shot. I'll check into this Brandon Addison too."

He pulled his phone from the inside of his sports coat and placed it to his ear. He smiled at Tarrin and added, "In the meantime, I'll feel safer if we have a couple officers keeping an eye on your place." He smiled before he spoke into the phone. "Marzollo here. I need a squad car ASAP to keep an eye on the last crime scene. There's been some unauthorized activity and a possible new development. Also, get Chavez over here. I'm going to go over the area again—yeah, now! Get on it!"

He flipped the cover on his phone shut with a loud pop then turned and eyed Tarrin. "I have to say, I'm kind of bummed about our date, but I'm glad you told me. We'll need to go back and meet with my detectives. Can you show me where you saw the light in the trees?"

"Yes." She licked her lips anxiously, but a small smile touched her mouth. She felt a measure of peace. She was glad she had approached Zack with her concerns over the photo.

CHAPTER *Seven*

After returning to the house, Tarrin and Zack quickly explained the situation to Erin.

"You could have told me," Erin said.

"I'm sorry," Tarrin replied, knowing Erin was upset she hadn't told her right away about the photo. She also knew her sister's concern far outweighed her frustration. "I wasn't sure what to do," Tarrin finished.

"Well, then, what do we do?" Erin directed at Zack.

"I need to ask you both a few more questions, and then I'm going to need you, Tarrin, to take me back into the trees to show me where you saw the person wandering around last night." Zack smiled, trying to reassure them both.

"Yeah, alright," Erin returned, and Tarrin nodded her agreement.

They answered more questions about the intruder in the trees and then explained, in detail, Calum Sloan's involvement. Zack's mouth tightened into a firm line when he discovered Tarrin had spent the day with Calum, and he immediately sent another detective to Calum's house for questioning. She felt anxious about Zack's men questioning him, and she hoped Calum wouldn't mind.

Zack asked her to lead him into the woods where she and Erin had first noticed the person in the trees. She felt calm with him beside her, but when they approached the crime scene, flashes of the disturbing image filled her mind and her stomach turned violently when they neared the blood-stained area.

"Tarrin?" Zack asked after catching sight of her insipid complexion.

"I'm fine. Really." Tarrin breathed in deep, trying to calm the nausea that rose to her throat.

Zack glanced at her once more before he crossed through

the thick undergrowth toward a younger detective who accompanied them. The bright flash of a camera illuminated the dim interior of the forest, and Tarrin closed her eyes briefly before she peered through the trees toward her new home. Erin stood, framed in the doorway, her face pressed against the glass while she observed Tarrin and the two officers. Her sister's expression looked worried—frightened. Tarrin felt the same. Her own pale face and large eyes reflected the anxiety she felt.

"Chavez," Tarrin heard Zack address the detective. "What have you got?"

"At first glance, it looks like the perp climbed this tree and took the photo from about mid-height," Detective Chavez reported.

Curious, Tarrin tore her gaze from the house and stumbled toward the officers. A fresh gouge marred the thick bark of a tall hemlock. Zack nodded. "We need to get another team in here tonight. I want this thicket scoured," he directed.

Chavez nodded. "Yes, sir. I'll get right on it."

The detective pocketed the camera and pushed his way out of the thick woods. He strode across the yard, and Erin slid the door open to allow him through the house.

"Why don't you and I go back to the house," Zack suggested, reaching for Tarrin's elbow.

"Yes," Tarrin breathed.

He held her arm gently as he led her back to the edge of the trees, and she felt her body relax a fraction when they moved into the kitchen, where Zack directed her to a chair.

"I'll get my team in here tonight, Tarrin. Don't worry about a thing." He touched her shoulder gently. "How are you holding up?" he asked.

"Fine, really," she murmured. She looked toward her sister, who frowned, but remained silent.

Tarrin glanced at Zack once again. She was grateful he took her concerns into consideration and had been so willing to check things out immediately. The thought brought a small measure of comfort. "Thanks again, Zack."

"Hey, it's no problem." He shrugged then touched her shoulder. "So I was thinking," he spoke as he sat in the chair opposite her. Erin joined them. "It looks like I have a few hours worth of work tonight. Can I convince you to have dinner with me—say—tomorrow?"

Tarrin sighed. "Tomorrow won't really work for me. Maybe next week?" she asked.

"Hmm—no. That won't work for me. Next week is too long to wait." He chuckled. "I have a better idea. Why don't you give me an hour or so to get my men started. I also need to take a moment to question Calum Sloan myself, but once I get things organized, I'll come on back to the house. We can order pizza and just hang out, what do you say?" He momentarily looked toward Erin. "Besides, it'll keep me close in case I'm needed, and it'll give my deputies a break for a couple of hours," he finished.

Erin shrugged. "Sure."

"That would be fine, I guess." Tarrin forced a smile. "We . . . Well, sure. We'd enjoy that."

Q§

Calum stood and stretched his stiff muscles. He groaned as he ambled to the living room window and stared out toward the darkened street. He could see several police vehicles parked in front of Tarrin Grace's home. A couple of officers stood on the curb drinking coffee. His eyes narrowed just as Macin's voice diverted his thoughts.

"Hey, Uncle Cal, I'm headed up to my room for the night," the boy called from the doorway.

Calum turned to face his nephew. He rubbed the back of his neck absently and regarded the boy with a smile. "Did you talk with your mother?"

"Yeah. She IM'd me."

"Oh yeah? How is she?" Calum asked.

Macin shrugged. "A.A.K."

Calum grinned. "In English, kid!"

Macin's mouth quirked. "You mean *old fart* talk?" he teased.

"Watch it, buddy," Calum laughed.

"A.A.K.—alive and kickin'. We talked over instant messenger. We couldn't Skype tonight." Macin shrugged.

"I'm sorry, buddy," Calum responded. "How are you doing?"

"A.A.K." Macin grinned, then added, "Well, I.O.H!"

Calum shook his head, holding his hands up in surrender.

Macin laughed. "Just messing with you. I.O.H—I'm outta here! Good night."

"Good night," Calum replied, chuckling.

Macin left the living room, and Calum listened to his nephew's soft steps as he padded to his room. The door squeaked gratingly then slammed shut. Calum made a mental note to oil the hinges again. His lips twisted ruefully and he stepped back toward the window.

The detective's visit left Calum concerned, and Lieutenant Marzollo's later visit left him irritated. He wondered what was happening at Tarrin's place. The police questioned him about the intruder in the woods, and his involvement, but had not given any other details. What happened last night?

He felt guilty for leaving Tarrin and her family alone, but what more could he have done? He should have called the police immediately, instead of brushing it off as a group of neighborhood kids. And why hadn't she mentioned the incident during their time together earlier that afternoon? He felt terrible. The officers assured him Tarrin and her family were safe, but still, he felt desperate to talk to her, especially in light of Lieutenant Marzollo's visit.

Calum had been forced to recount his statement several times before Lieutenant Marzollo finally took his leave. Calum felt an immediate dislike for the man. Not only did the arrogant detective treat him as a possible suspect, but he had also hinted more than once about his personal relationship with Tarrin. Marzollo made it clear he intended to have dinner with Tarrin and her family tonight, and the man's arrogant manner and accusing tone infuriated Calum.

It shouldn't bother him if Marzollo and Tarrin developed a relationship. That was none of his business. She was his employee and neighbor, nothing more. He pushed away from the window and walked into the kitchen.

He opened the refrigerator and frowned. He knew he should probably take time on Monday to restock their depleted groceries. Macin went through food faster than he could keep it stocked. Living with his twelve-year-old nephew wasn't easy, but he enjoyed it despite the difficulties.

At times, however, Calum missed his condo on the edge of the city. He missed the sound of the lapping water against the shore. He missed the busy hustle and bustle of boats, ferries, and busy cargo ships along the Puget Sound, but he knew once he returned, he would feel terribly lonely. He was used to the kid being around. He shut the refrigerator door and his thoughts immediately returned to Tarrin.

He'd had a great time with her earlier in the day. He felt inexplicably drawn to her, and that thought left him feeling unsettled. He knew a relationship with her was out of the question. She was, after all, his employee, and those types of relationships didn't often work out. The idea was impossible. That sort of relationship was simply asking for trouble.

He groaned as he walked back into the living room. He slumped onto the leather sofa then laid his head back and stared wearily toward the ceiling. He closed his eyes and Tarrin's image surfaced. A relationship with Tarrin Grace would never work. *Then why does it bother me she's seeing Marzollo?* He asked himself, frustrated.

છ

Tarrin laughed at Zack's antics while he played charades with Jake and Erin. She nibbled on a piece of pizza and watched Zack hop up and down. His mouth twisted into a grimace when Jake yelled, "Monkey!"

Zack paused and Tarrin giggled when he scratched his head. His face looked thoughtful for a moment before he pointed toward the ceiling.

"Moon?" Erin guessed.

Zack's expression lit, and he nodded. He turned and began a slow, exaggerated walk across the kitchen and around the table. He winked when he caught Tarrin's eye, and she laughed quietly. He threw his arms wide, and Erin and Jake giggled.

"Walking!" Jake yelled.

Zack paused and nodded, then pointed to the ceiling again.

"Spacewalk!" Jake yelled.

"Phew! Yes!" Zack laughed. "That was rough."

"My turn!" Jake yelled and bounded to the front of the kitchen.

Zack sat next to Tarrin, and he slumped in the chair. "Wow, that was a lot of work," he laughed.

Tarrin grinned and reached for another slice of pizza. "I would have guessed a monkey too." She chuckled.

Zack bumped her with his shoulder. "When is it your turn?" he asked, reaching for a slice pizza.

"Oh, no! You can't get me up there. We would be here all night. I'm terrible at charades," she replied.

"How's the pizza?"

"Fantastic. Some of the best I've ever had."

He shoved a large bite into his mouth. "This sure beats the restaurant I picked out, but I still say I need a rain check, Tarrin."

"Alright, I'll give you one," she returned with a smile.

"Good. I'm looking forward to it."

She remained thoughtful for a moment then replied, "Thanks for dinner. Jake is having a great time, and I . . . I appreciate all the work you're doing to keep us safe. It means a lot."

"That's my job, and I'm *good* at it! It won't be any time at all and I'll have this nut bag behind bars. You don't worry about a thing." He touched her fingers gently, and Tarrin caught her breath. She withdrew her hand and smiled.

She really was having a fantastic time with Zack, despite the undercurrent of fear that still hovered on the edge of her mind. He did an amazing job calming her family's nerves. Jake and Erin laughed and teased with him throughout the night. Lexie remained aloof, but that didn't come as a shock to Tarrin. Since her father's arrest, Lexie was wary of police, and the little girl had remained firmly seated on Tarrin's lap most of the night. Eventually she had fallen asleep, and Zack graciously offered to carry the little girl to her bed.

Tarrin liked Zack, and he made it no secret he was attracted to her as well. But thoughts of Calum continued to intrude, and she felt reluctant to accept many of Zack's advances throughout the night. She didn't want to hurt the man's feelings, but she was beginning to feel rather overwhelmed and confused.

She hoped Zack would take the subtle hint and slow things down. Tarrin liked him, a lot, but she wasn't sure she was ready for any kind of relationship with him or—she bit her lip gently—Calum Sloan. The divorce and Travis's infidelity left her vulnerable, and she wondered if she would ever be able to trust enough to allow a romantic relationship in her life again. She hoped she could, but the thought of romance suddenly left her feeling terrified.

She could feel Zack's eyes on her while she watched Jake's attempt at charades, and she laughed at her son's actions.

"You look like a goat," she shouted.

"No!" Jake replied in a disgusted tone. "I'm not a goat. Geeze!"

Zack caught her eye. "Giraffe!" he yelled.

Jake's shoulders fell and he frowned. "Aw, how'd you guess so quick?" he asked as he slumped to the table.

Zack ruffled the boy's hair. "It's my job to be good at these things, son. I'm a *detective.*" He wiggled his eyebrows.

Jake shrugged and turned toward his mother. "It's your turn."

"Hey, you know what?" Zack cut in. "I better get going. As much as I hate to call it a night, I probably need to get back to the station and get some paperwork done."

Tarrin stood. "Thanks, Zack. This was fun."

"This was *great,* Tarrin."

"I'll walk you out?" she offered.

"I won't say no. Goodnight." Zack nodded toward Erin and Jake as he grasped Tarrin's elbow. They walked onto the front porch, and Tarrin inhaled when she gazed up toward the hazy sky. The thick covering of clouds reflected the city lights. She missed the stars.

"Tell me what you're thinking," Zack suddenly murmured near her ear.

She jumped a little, but laughed. "Not much. I was just thinking I miss the stars at night. The sky was full of stars back home. Things are so different now," she admitted.

He glanced up and inhaled. "I've lived in a city my whole life," he sighed. "It's a real treat when I get the chance to see a sky full of stars. Once in a while, I'll take my schooner out past the Sound—on out to the Pacific during the halibut season, and I stay a few nights. The sky can be amazing."

Tarrin smiled. She liked the picture he painted. "Sounds wonderful," she murmured. "Did you grow up in Seattle?"

"No, Atlanta."

"Really? I wouldn't have guessed that," she responded.

"I lost the accent a while ago. I've been in Seattle for nearly twenty-years now. I moved here when I was just starting out. I managed to get on with the Seattle PD as a deputy and worked my way up."

"Have you always wanted to be an officer?" Tarrin asked.

His brow creased. "I learned early in life I have a knack for this sort of work. I've bagged a lot of bad guys." He shrugged. "And I have an amazing team. We always catch our man."

"I'm glad," Tarrin returned. "This has been so hard. I've never experienced anything like this," she admitted. "Some days, I feel like this is just a bad dream."

"I understand." Zack faced her. "But we'll keep you safe, Tarrin." He reached out and gently tugged on a lock of her hair that had fallen across her shoulder before he added, "Listen, I did want to give you just a bit of advice before I left. I don't know who took that photo—yet. We'll find out. In the meantime—you're new here. If our killer did take that photo—just keep in mind—he'll use that to his advantage. Don't talk to a lot of people. Don't trust anyone with any information. There's a lot at stake here and I just want you to stay as safe as possible."

He reached for her cheek, cupping her face against his palm, and Tarrin took a deep breath. She could feel her hands grow moist, but she smiled and took a step back. "Thank you. I really do appreciate the time you spent with us tonight."

Zack's expression looked slightly pained when she pulled from his embrace, but he recovered quickly. "Me too. You take care now, and I'll see you soon."

⅋

He slumped low in the driver's seat of his nondescript vehicle and watched with lowered lids as Tarrin Grace and her children returned home from Sunday services. He enjoyed the way Tarrin's long, black skirt flowed about her slender, shapely ankles. She was indeed a beautiful woman. Her sister wasn't half bad either. Tarrin paused at the front door, and he chuckled in amusement when she struggled with the lock. Her daughter wrapped her arms about her leg, hindering Tarrin's effort, and he groaned.

It was unfortunate the girl had wandered into the woods that day. She was an attractive child. Her silky blond curls framed a delicate, cherub face. She looked like her mother. He inhaled slowly. He couldn't take the risk of Lexie's memory returning. The little girl's memory lapse had been a lucky break, especially considering he wasn't able to get close enough to take care of the child yet.

He considered smothering her at the hospital, but the nurses and doctors never left the girl's side. Everything that he'd worked so hard for would be lost if she had the chance to expose him. The thought was never far from his mind. He needed to work fast, but he also wanted to play his cards right. He had to admit, he was having fun with Tarrin Grace. He hadn't intended on killing her in the beginning, but he knew now, he would have to kill her in the end to reach the girl. The thought hadn't been very pleasant, at first. Now, however, he was beginning to change his mind.

He enjoyed watching Tarrin. He took pleasure in seeing her vibrant eyes fill with fear, but yet there was also a glint of determination within her gaze that appealed to him. The mixture of fear and courageousness was a heady combination—one that was difficult to resist. Most of his victims were fairly tedious. Tarrin Grace intrigued him, and he was thankful to have a bit more time to explore the many facets of her personality.

Unfortunately, her daughter did pose a problem, but perhaps a few more days wouldn't make a difference. He would keep a very close eye on the situation. He was, after all, in control. He could end the game anytime he chose. Killing a kid would be unfortunate, but it had to be done. Killing Tarrin Grace . . .

He enjoyed this new challenge, and he smiled as he started his vehicle. "See you soon, babe," he murmured when he drove past the familiar, little green house.

His latest gambit suddenly paled in comparison to stalking

Tarrin. Perhaps it was time to change his 'modus operandi' after all.

CB

  Tarrin moaned when her alarm sounded near her ear. With little enthusiasm, she rolled over and pressed the clock's snooze button. She laid there for another minute or two then forced her body out of bed and glanced at the glowing clock face in the dim light of the small bedroom. The time showed only six-thirty. She still had a few hours before she needed to leave for work. *Work,* the word popped into her head like a hammer. *No.* Tarrin moaned again and laid her head against her palms. Her first day of work had been a disaster. She was grateful Calum was a patient man; otherwise, she would probably be looking for a new job. She hoped her second day would go a bit smoother. Tarrin had gone into work on Monday expecting customer service to be a breeze, but her first two calls left her a nervous wreck. Her mind seemed to draw a blank every time a customer became irate, and she had a difficult time remembering all the complicated terminology and jargon.

  Calum had been understanding and patient. Her immediate supervisor, Walter, had not. She had overheard Walter's scathing remarks regarding her performance, and to her mortification, Calum caught her after work. His eyes held a glint of humor as he attempted to encourage her, but he had reminded her to review the handbook and to ask for help. She felt regressed from a confident, thirty-two-year-old to a high school student barely entering the job market.

  The hours following work hadn't gone so well either. Lexie refused to speak with Emalee Edwards, the hospital's child psychologist, and she had clung desperately to Tarrin, burying her face against her neck. Doctor Edwards was very patient, but after hearing the details of Tarrin's divorce, she immediately recommended family therapy as well.

Tarrin felt emotionally exhausted. She rarely spoke the details of her divorce. Over the course of the past year, she hadn't confided in anyone besides her closest family members. Now suddenly, she found herself having to confide in strangers. Her old grief was resurfacing, and she was trying desperately to quell those feelings. Washington was supposed to be her new beginning. Would she and her children ever be free from their past?

She rubbed the back of her neck and tried to focus her thoughts elsewhere. She reflected on her weekend. Saturday had been a very eventful, stressful day, but Sunday had gone well. Tarrin enjoyed her Sunday lunch at the community center. She hadn't taken pleasure in a social gathering for such a long time. It felt nice to sit among a new group of neighbors who didn't watch her with contempt or pity; no whispers could be heard as she and her children passed by.

Tarrin knew only a few select women, including Juliann and her tight-knit group of friends, had been the cause of her grief, but it was enough to make attending any event in town a nightmare. Even her closest friends had fallen away from her after Travis's arrest. They continued to smile and offer condolences, but Tarrin hadn't escaped their pitying glances, and more than once she had walked in, mid-conversation, on the gossip surrounding her and her family. Hearing the gossip was painful, and eventually she had cut most ties.

She was grateful for the opportunity to make new friends, and she loved watching Jake and Lexie take part in the fun and games with the other children who lived in the area. The community center seemed like a great place for them to spend some of their time, and Calum's father, Frank, was a very kind man. Calum had met her, Erin, and the kids on Sunday afternoon, and he was happy to introduce her to Frank and his family. However, after introducing her, he'd gone his separate way.

He'd sat across the room next to his family. Tarrin caught his eye a few times throughout the lunch, and he always smiled politely, but his sudden reserve left her feeling quite depressed, and she moaned, frustrated.

Why does it matter? She asked herself, feeling annoyed. *Calum Sloan is my boss for Pete's sake,* she reminded herself with a scowl. It didn't matter that he was handsome, friendly, and easy to talk to. The possibility of a relationship was non-existent, and she knew he probably just thought of her as a fool, especially considering her first, botched day on the job.

"Ooooh! What time is it?" Erin whined from across the room, pulling Tarrin from her thoughts.

Tarrin glanced at the bedside clock. "Six-forty," she murmured. Standing, she stretched her stiff muscle then walked to her closet.

"What are you doing up so early?" Her sister yawned.

"I was thinking I might go for a run," Tarrin replied. "Will you be okay?" she asked and moved to the window.

She opened a slat in the blinds and peered down toward the street. The squad car remained parked across the lane. Tarrin could see the two officers inside, drinking cups of coffee. Zack had been adamant about keeping a couple officers posted nearby to keep an eye on Tarrin and her family for a few days. He had called on Sunday to let her know they were still checking into Brandon Addison, but they hadn't been able to pull any prints from either the photo or the envelope. Zack assured Tarrin he and his unit would do all they could to find out who had taken the photo of her.

Zack Marzollo seemed like a genuinely nice guy, and she enjoyed spending time with him on Saturday evening. He seemed fond of both Jake and Lexie, and Jake had really appreciated the game and pizza night, but a part of Tarrin found his advances toward her unsettling. She just wasn't ready for that sort of relationship, was she? She thought of Calum, and a blush tinged her cheeks. Was she ready? She shook her head, feeling ever more frustrated.

Erin had badgered her since Saturday about both Calum and Zack, and she smiled at her sister's unfounded, romantic notions. She did find Calum Sloan very attractive, but she was positive a relationship between them was not likely. Calum was friendly and gracious, nothing more. Zack, on the other hand, made it no secret he was interested in her.

Tarrin wasn't quite certain how she felt about that. She wasn't sure how she felt about anything for that matter. She felt tense—keyed up—and suddenly she needed to escape. A good run would help clear her mind, and she turned from the window with a firm resolution to remain in control of her ragged emotions.

"I'm going out for a bit. I won't be gone long," she told Erin as she opened her closet.

"Yeah? Do you think it's safe?" Erin murmured, burying farther into her blankets.

"I won't go far," Tarrin reassured her.

Erin moaned then shut her eyes. "Be careful."

Tarrin dressed in her running shorts and shirt then found her shoes before she tiptoed down the stairs. The stairs groaned loudly and she paused, listening for any sign that she had disturbed Jake or Lexie. Satisfied she had not awakened either child, she moved to sit at her vintage, retro-style table.

She sat on a red, vinyl chair and placed her arms on the gray Formica table top. Her eyebrows rose in amusement. The table and chairs definitely fit in with the era of the outdated kitchen. She donned her shoes then took a moment to stretch before she left the house. The officers glanced her way, bored, when she stepped onto the sidewalk. Tarrin's eyes narrowed against the brightness of the early morning sun peeking through the haze and she began a slow jog down the hill.

Tarrin ran only a mile before she found a marked recreation trail. She was pleasantly surprised to discover the wooded lane in the middle of the city. A few joggers waved when they passed, and she turned onto the track. The sunlight filtered through the trees and left molted patterns on the black pavement. Birds called from within the woods, and Tarrin smiled. She could smell the spicy scent of the forest and earth, and the song of her feet on the pavement calmed her jagged nerves.

Maybe I can get through a few calls without botching things today, she mused while she ran along the twisting trail. Another jogger passed from the opposite direction and she smiled and waved. She glanced at her watch. She didn't have a lot of time left before she needed to turn around, and she didn't want to leave Erin and the kids alone for too long. But she wondered how far the trail stretched. She could see a few tall buildings through the trees and it left her feeling intrigued.

She knew she didn't have time to explore the area today, but it would be a good place for her daily run. She decided to go just a little farther before she turned around. Picking up her pace, she ran around a sharp bend in the track. Shadows stretched across the black top, and she studied the dappled light as it danced along the pavement. She breathed in the crisp, fresh air. Closing her eyes momentarily, she relished the feel of moving her body, letting the motion soothe her stress away. Opening her eyes, she inhaled deeply then slowed when she noticed a pile of white feathers lying in the middle of the trail. Her face contorted in disgust when she neared a dead mourning dove. The animal lay stiff and lifeless. She stopped and eyed the dead bird with a frown.

Poor little thing, she thought, glancing around in alarm. What happened to it? Had it been hit by a bike? She turned away, repulsed, and had taken only a few more steps before she noticed the trail ahead was littered with pure, white feathers and several squares of paper. *Photos.* Her breath caught in her throat. An abrupt sense of apprehension assailed her, and she paused before moving cautiously forward.

She raised a hand to her throat, and her stomach turned just as the hairs on the back of her neck stood on end. She felt suddenly nauseated and she glanced around at the woods surrounding her. *It's nothing*, she told herself. *This is nothing*. One of the square photos lay on the black pavement scant feet away, near the edge of the trees. With a hammering heart, she stumbled toward the closest print on trembling legs. She let her gaze fall toward the ground.

A breeze kicked up, swirling the feathers around her legs as she stared at the photo. Her face drained of color, and she stifled a scream when she recognized herself, Jake, and Lexie sitting on the front porch of their new home, dressed in Sunday clothes. Her eyes shot to the other photos. The same print lay scattered across the blacktop, their smiling faces frozen in time. Spinning around, Tarrin faced the dead bird, and her knees grew weak.

Her heartbeat sounded loudly in her ears and her chest tightened with fear. A couple of joggers suddenly appeared around the bend, and she stumbled back, her eyes expanding in terror. She screamed. The joggers slowed, and the two men stared at Tarrin, their expressions shocked. She watched the men, fearful, and her body tensed, ready to defend herself.

"Whoa, lady! What's going on here?" the taller of the two men demanded while the second man reached for his cell phone. Tarrin stared at the men in fear. Who had done this? "I . . ." She shook her head. "I *d-don't know*. I need help," she returned, unable to hide the tremor in her voice. "I need to call the police. I need Lieutenant Z-Zack Marzollo." Her voice cracked, and a wave of weakness threatened to make her lose consciousness. *Pull yourself together*. She focused on taking deep breaths.

"Right," the man spoke.

His eyes raked across the dead bird and feathers lying in the middle of the trail, and he studied the photo near Tarrin's foot. His gaze shot to Tarrin, then back to the photo. He bent to retrieve a feather then glanced at his partner. He nodded.

"Call," he said.

Tarrin tore her eyes from the men and she looked toward the forest. Her skin crawled and goose bumps rose on her arms.

Feathers floated on the breeze and swirled into the woods. Somewhere within the trees, she knew someone was watching her.

CHAPTER *Eight*

"Here, drink this," Zack commanded gently as he sat next to Tarrin on the pavement. He opened a can of orange juice. The tab popped, and he handed her the chilled drink.

"Thanks," she whispered before she took a small sip.

"I have a team of officers standing in with your sister and the kids," he informed her.

"Who's doing this? I don't understand. H-how could this be here? I hadn't planned on coming this way. He must have followed me. The whole time—he's been following me. I don't understand. I-I don't know."

"You've never been on this trail before?" Zack asked. His voice rose in alarm.

Tarrin shook her head. "Never. I've never been here before. I didn't even know this trail existed until this morning. I wanted to run before I left for work. I just . . ." she groaned. "Oh, *shoot!*"

Zack sat back abruptly. "What is it?"

"I forgot about work!" she lamented. "What am I going to do? I can't lose my job on top of everything else."

Zack smiled and rubbed her back. "Hey, relax. You can give your boss a call in a minute. If you'd like, I'll explain the situation."

"No. No, I can explain. I work for Calum Sloan. I—"

"Sloan?" Zack asked. His eyes tightened. "I hadn't realized you worked for Calum Sloan."

She nodded and rested her head against her forearms then looked up at Zack with tortured eyes. "What am I going to do? Who's doing this to us?" she questioned, frustrated. "I can't let some psychopath terrorize me and my kids."

She glared into the trees. She could see several officers searching the surrounding woods. Camera flashes popped around her, and several on-lookers watched the crime scene with avid interest.

"We do know one thing. Whoever it is, it isn't your ex's brother. I made some calls. A Utah officer checked Brandon out. He lives in Logan and hasn't left the state in months. Tarrin, by any chance, would your ex-husband send someone after you?" Zack enquired.

Tarrin felt shocked. "No! Travis wouldn't do that. Not to me or to the kids."

Despite her and Travis's problems, she knew he held no grudge against her. Travis knew from the moment of his arrest what would become of his life, and as far as she was concerned, he had not held her or the children responsible in any way. Only his family and a few close friends held any animosity toward her. Tarrin knew the shock of Travis's conviction was very hard for them to accept. She understood it was difficult for everyone who knew Travis to accept what he had done, but she could not believe Travis was responsible for this.

Even Brandon wouldn't go this far. She'd known that the moment she saw the photos scattered across the ground. This was not someone she knew, but whoever it was *knew* her and the thought scared her senseless.

"You're certain?" Zack's voice tore through her jumbled thoughts.

"Yes," Tarrin whispered.

Zack sighed heavily. "Okay," he breathed. He swore quietly under his breath.

She closed her eyes. It wasn't Brandon. That only left one other viable possibility. Whoever murdered the woman in the woods was still at large, and he was now terrorizing Tarrin and her family. What had Lexie seen? Had her daughter witnessed the killer in the act? Was that why the murderer was targeting her?

"Look, Tarrin, I want you to know that I will do everything—*everything*—I can to keep you and your kids safe. I hate to tell you this now, but it looks like we *are* looking for a serial killer. Earlier this morning another body was found. A young woman."

"What?" Tarrin asked feeling weak. *Another body?*

Zack nodded. "The victim was found a few miles from your place. We believe she was murdered Sunday afternoon, but we're still waiting on autopsy results. At the scene of the crime, we found a piece of paper. The killer placed a note in the woman's hand. Tarrin—"

Tarrin grasped her stomach before she raised her face toward his. Their eyes met, and she could read the profound disquiet in his expression. She gritted her teeth and closed her eyes, already fearing the unknown words written on the note.

Zack tensed. "Your daughter's name was written on the note," he finished.

Tarrin bit her lip hard enough to draw blood. "No," she whispered.

She felt dizzy, and she struggled against the overwhelming desire to faint. Zack's hand steadied her, and he held her upright. His arm wrapped about her shoulder.

"Just breathe," he murmured.

She struggled to hear past the sharp ringing in her ears. "No," she sobbed.

"Tarrin, lean over and put your head between your knees," Zack instructed. "We need a medic over here!" he called.

His voice sounded very far away although she could see his face was mere inches from her own. She could feel his hot breath brush across her clammy forehead.

"No. No, I'm fine," she murmured, dazed.

Not Lexie. Not Lexie. Not my baby, Tarrin's mind screamed. Why? Why was this happening to her and her children? Hadn't they been through enough? *Why? Why is this happening to us?*

"Miss Grace?" a female emergency technician touched her shoulder.

"Tarrin?" Zack grasped her hand.

Her eyes finally focused and the ringing in her ears began

to subside. Her hands trembled and she shivered. The attending technician wrapped a prickly wool blanket around her thin shoulders.

"Miss Grace, I'd like you to lie down."

"No!" Tarrin shook her head. "No, I'm fine. It's passing." She breathed hard. "He knows her name? He is targeting us then, because she saw something? She must have," she murmured.

Zack's brows creased. "We believe she may have."

"What's being done to find him? What leads do you have?" She turned to face him. She clenched her fists together and raised determined eyes to his.

He frowned and gazed at the ground as he spoke, "As of right now, not a whole lot. There were no viable prints, but we've sent the note in to the handwriting analysis team. We're still waiting to hear back from forensics. We've found a few bits of evidence, but nothing real solid."

"I'm not going to sit here and let this maniac terrorize me and my children!" Tarrin glared at Zack. "He won't touch Lexie! I'll die first!" She gritted her teeth.

"Believe me, we won't let him. Tarrin," he reached for her shoulder and his mouth twisted into a grimace. "I will keep you safe," he finished.

Tarrin felt her body relax a fraction. She nodded slowly then asked, "Do you think we should leave? Go back to Colorado or somewhere else? I'll go anywhere!"

"No!" he jumped in. "That's the last thing you should do right now, as strange as that seems. He'll follow. You'll only make things easier for him if you leave. It might even endanger the rest of your extended family. There's no saying what could happen. Stay here where I can keep an eye on you and your kids."

"Well, what can I do then? I'll do anything. Just tell me what to do. Maybe I can get him to come after me. Maybe I—"

Zack's expression mirrored his sudden confusion. "Whoa, Tarrin, what are you trying to say? We aren't going to use you as bait. Is that what you're trying to say?"

"If it will help catch this guy sooner, then I'll do anything!"

"Yeah? Well, that isn't going to fly. Now listen to me. I made Lieutenant for a reason. I've bagged more homicide cases quicker than any other man, and I've put several serial killers behind bars. There is nothing you can do!" His gaze met hers. "And you *certainly* better not do anything that puts you at risk. Setting yourself up as bait doesn't do us any good. It'll just get you killed. You let us handle this. I've told you before, I always get my man!" His expression hardened.

"So then what? What now? What happens next?" she asked feeling more disturbed than ever.

How could she possibly sit around and wait for this slaughterer to find her daughter? She would protect Lexie at all costs.

"I'll keep you safe. You have to trust me." He touched her shoulder. "The best thing you can do is go on with your life. We'll keep an officer with you and your kids, but you need to keep on living. It could be days, weeks, even months, before he tries anything again."

Tarrin closed her eyes for a brief moment and nodded. "Okay." She paused then added, "I'm . . . Zack, I'm so scared," she admitted on a whisper.

He rubbed her back gently.

Tears burned the back of her eyes, and Zack reached out to touch her cheek. She leaned into his gentle caress for an instant, taking comfort in a friend.

"Let me take you home. From here on out we won't let you or the children out of our sight. If I'm not with you, then one of my men will be. I don't want you, your sister, or the children leaving the house without someone around. I know this will be a huge intrusion, but until this nut is behind bars—and make no mistake, I'll get him—I want you and your children to be as safe as possible."

Tarrin rubbed her temple. "How much does Erin know? I

don't want Jake and Lexie to know more than what is absolutely necessary."

"My detectives informed her there's been a situation, but that's all. I have a few men scouring the streets and neighborhoods. There has to be more evidence we've over-looked. It's obvious he's been following you—closely. He's been watching the house too, so I don't think he's going to give up, but he is going to slip up sooner or later, and when he does, I'm going to be there."

Tarrin nodded, and Zack squeezed her fingers. "Do you want me to take you home now?"

"I guess . . . Yes. I need to get ready for work. I don't want the kids to get scared. They'll wonder if I stay home. They've been through enough already. They don't need this," she whispered. "You will watch them? You won't let my kids or my sister out of your sight? I'll tell Erin what she needs to know, but you won't let this guy near Jake or Lexie?"

"No, I won't. My men are amazing. We can tell the kiddos and your sister this is just a precautionary measure. They don't need to know any of the details. Now, let me take you home, and then we'll get you to work. I'll explain the situation to Sloan, and we'll have an officer stand guard at the office."

"I hate to have you go through so much trouble," Tarrin replied, her voice weak and strained.

"Hey, it's our job, and we're good at it."

☙

"Tarrin!" Mary exclaimed when Tarrin and Zack entered the spacious office. Mary's concerned eyes met hers, and the older woman stood, rushing around the large maple desk. "Are you all right, dear? What's happened?" Mary asked, placing her plump arms around Tarrin in a motherly hug.

Giving in to a moment of weakness, Tarrin leaned into the woman's tight embrace. Mary's arms felt warm and comforting.

Tears burned the back of Tarrin's eyes, but she forced them back, determined. At the moment she wanted nothing more than to fall into the kind woman's arms and sob frantically, but she knew she had to keep it together. She needed to be strong.

"What's going on?" Mary directed at Zack. "Tarrin, dear, you're trembling."

"I'm fine," Tarrin sniffed, pulling out of the older woman's embrace.

"I need to speak with Sloan privately, please," Zack's tone was businesslike, and Tarrin gave him a wary look.

Mary glanced, confused, back and forth between Tarrin and Zack.

"It will be fine if Mary knows," Tarrin replied.

Zack turned and eyed her for a moment before he nodded curtly. "Is there a place where we can all speak in private, then?"

"Certainly, we can talk in Mr. Sloan's office. Follow me." Mary fidgeted as she led the way toward Calum's office.

Tarrin's heart picked up pace when Mary knocked on his closed office door. She could see Calum sitting behind his desk, his ear pressed to his phone. He swiveled around and caught her eye then smiled before his gaze fell on Zack Marzollo. His smile faded, and he called, "Come in." He placed the phone back on the desk.

Mary opened the door. "Son," she spoke, "they need to speak with you."

"Come in and have a seat." Calum stood as he watched Zack step into his office. "Tarrin. Officer Marzollo," Calum greeted.

"*Lieutenant* Marzollo," Zack corrected.

Tarrin cast Zack a quick glance before her eyes fell back toward Calum.

Calum regarded Zack for what seemed like several moments before he spoke calmly, "Excuse me." He paused. "*Lieutenant* Marzollo," he finished then turned to face Tarrin. His expression softened considerably. "What's happened, Tarrin?" he asked.

115

Before she could speak, Zack held up his hand to stop her. "Let me explain." He turned to face Calum.

It didn't take long for Zack to describe the events that transpired earlier in the day, and Calum listened with a scowl to the horrifying details. Mary looked pale, and she held on to Tarrin's hand tightly when Zack finished.

"Oh, dear," Mary murmured with a shaky voice. "You poor, sweet, thing! Oh, Tarrin, how awful!"

"What's being done to keep her and the children safe?" Calum questioned.

Zack's brow rose. "You don't need to worry about that, Cal. We'll handle it. You can, however, expect an officer on scene to keep an eye on—*things.*"

"Hmm," Calum's forehead furrowed. Annoyance flicked across his handsome features. "The name's *Calum,* Lieutenant, and I'd like to do what I can to help. It's important to me that I keep *all* my employees safe, especially Tarrin and her family."

Calum eyed Zack carefully, and Tarrin was surprised to see a quick spark of anger in Zack's eyes. "It's being taken care of, Sloan. You need to understand that until we have apprehended the perpetrator we need all involved in this case using discretion. It's a need-to-know basis. We don't want our investigation or Tarrin's safety compromised in any way."

"I understand," Calum replied.

"Also, I need to ask you a few questions".

"Sure." Calum's eyes narrowed skeptically.

"Where were you this morning at say," he shrugged, "seven-o'clock?"

Tarrin gasped and her eyes shot to Zack. "Zack, I don't think . . . This isn't necessary!" she replied, stunned. Embarrassment stained her cheeks.

"I don't mind, Tarrin," Calum answered. He turned back to face Zack. "I was home. I cooked breakfast for myself and my nephew, Macin. We ate at seven-thirty. I puttered around the house, and at eight-o'clock I left and drove straight to the office. I've been here all morning."

"Isn't it true you usually run in the mornings?" Zack asked calmly, but Tarrin could easily detect the accusatory tone. She felt Mary stiffen and the older woman glared at Zack.

Calum smiled tersely. "I do. I usually run along that trail. In fact, I *did* run on that trail earlier in the morning. I left at five and returned at six-thirty."

Zack jotted a few notes onto his notepad and Tarrin's heart beat a frantic rhythm. What was Zack doing? Why was he treating Calum like a suspect? Calum's face remained stoic, but his body tensed.

"Just one more question, Sloan?" Zack spoke, and Tarrin groaned, annoyed.

"Zack, this isn't necessary, is it?"

"Just doing my job. We need to look at every angle, don't we?"

Calum's eyes hardened. "What else would you like to know, *Lieutenant?*"

"What brand of running shoes do you wear?"

"I own a pair of Brooks."

Zack jotted a few more notes then smirked. "Got it! I appreciate your cooperation, Sloan."

"No problem," Calum returned dryly.

Zack turned to Tarrin and laid a hand on her trembling shoulder. "I'll leave Chavez posted outside. If you need anything at all, let him know right away."

She nodded uncomfortably. She could feel Calum's eyes on her. "Thanks," she whispered, irritated.

"Tarrin," Zack whispered. "I'm going to do everything I can, to keep you safe, remember?"

She exhaled and nodded. "Erin, Jake, and Lexie?" She raised her face toward his.

"I'll keep my men posted close by to keep an eye on things.

No one will get near them. I have this under control. Don't worry about a thing."

Relaxing a little, she nodded.

"Let me know if you need anything," he reminded her with a lopsided grin then he turned to Calum. "I'll be seeing you," he leered.

Calum nodded abruptly and his brows knit together in consternation when Zack left the office. Tarrin waited silently while Zack disappeared before she turned to face Calum.

"I'm so sorry about all of this," she offered meekly.

Calum's severe expression softened. "You have nothing to apologize for."

"No, dear, you don't. Calum . . . What . . . ?" Mary shook her head.

He glanced toward Mary briefly before he turned his attention back to Tarrin. "How are the kids?"

She shrugged. "Confused and scared. They don't know the details. They think this is just a precaution. I think Erin suspects a lot more. I won't be able to keep this from her for long, but Jake and Lexie . . . They can't find out."

"No, of course not. Look, this might not be the best moment to bring this up, but have you thought about contacting Frank? It might be a good idea to let him know what's going on. He worked for the Seattle PD for years. I think he could help."

Tarrin bit her lower lip in vexation. "I . . . No. I don't want to involve anyone else."

"I understand, but he may be able to provide a bit more . . . I guess you could say guidance and insight. It might help to let him know."

"Oh, yes. Frank would know what to do," Mary cut in.

Tarrin's face twisted in uncertainty. "I'll think about it."

He frowned. "How are *you?* Do you need some time off?"

"No." She shook her head. "I need to just keep going. I'm not going to let this maniac control me or scare my family into hiding."

Mary hugged Tarrin tightly before she left the office, and Calum nodded.

"Okay," he said.

CHAPTER *Nine*

A malicious smirk spread across his face when he thought about Tarrin Grace—her smile, her face, and especially her eyes. He could clearly picture how those wide eyes filled with fear and uncertainty, and he chuckled. Did she really believe those incompetent detectives could keep her safe? Her naivety made him laugh out loud.

This was quickly becoming a very interesting game. He hadn't enjoyed himself to such a degree in years. He grinned as he eyed the tall building where Tarrin worked. The experience was new and exhilarating. His previous victims hadn't evoked any sort of emotions. He felt nothing but contempt for his latest prey. They were too easy, but Tarrin—this took work—cunningness—and he realized he was good at it. *Of course, I'm good at everything I do*, he laughed silently.

He loved watching Tarrin's reactions. He would hate to see it end, but her death was inevitable. He needed to kill Tarrin Grace and her daughter. Still, the idea of killing a kid caused him grief. Only crazies killed kids, but he really had no choice. If her memory returned . . . He needed to do what needed to be done. *I have no choice,* he reminded himself, *but Tarrin . . .*

He smiled slowly and hummed a little tune. He let his head fall back against the rough bark of a tree growing alongside the curb. Stretching his legs out in front of him, he closed his eyes. He would need to return to his office soon, but he wanted a moment with his thoughts.

℆

Just having returned from a quick walk along the pier, Calum tossed his coat onto a nearby chair. He turned toward the wide window and stared out across the bustling city of Seattle. He tried to relax while he observed the boats on the water, but it was no use. It was obvious he was being considered a possible suspect. He wondered if he ought to contact his lawyer. He cringed a little before his thoughts turned to Tarrin.

She had looked pale and weary. What kind of emotional toll was this taking on her? After Marzollo left, she hadn't lingered in his office long, but joined the other employees across the hall. He wondered how she was faring. She'd had a difficult time with customer service the first day, and he could only imagine she was having an even harder time today, especially considering the circumstances. Calum turned away from the window. He could see Officer Chavez sitting on a chair outside the door. He looked like he was asleep. Calum rubbed a hand across his jaw and glanced at the clock on the wall.

He wondered at Tarrin's reaction if he were to ask her to lunch. He'd considered approaching her during an earlier break, but changed his mind. He was anxious to talk with her. Did she believe he had anything to do with the murder? He exhaled noisily then walked into the main office just as everyone began to break for the lunch hour. Mary greeted him with an anxious smile. Calum's adoptive mother looked worried—her expression, tense.

"I'm going out for lunch, Mom. Can I get you anything?" he asked her with a reassuring smile.

"No, thank you," she replied quietly.

He nodded just before he caught sight of Tarrin exiting the call center. He smiled one last time at Mary before he stepped through the double-glass doors.

"Tarrin," he called.

Tarrin paused. She and Detective Chavez glanced his way curiously and Calum held a hand up in greeting while he walked toward them.

"Do you want to join me for lunch?" he asked, then nodded toward the officer. "You would be included of course."

Detective Chavez glanced at Tarrin and she shrugged. "I . . . um . . . sure. I'd love to. Will that work for you?" she turned to address Chavez.

"Yeah. Whatever," he replied.

When she turned back to face him, Calum noticed she looked weary, but he could also read no fear toward him in her wide-eyed expression.

"Can you give me a minute to call Erin and the kids?" she asked.

"Sure. Of course. You're welcome to use my office if you'd like," he offered, then added, "You know? If you'd like, we could head home for lunch. I make a mean pastrami sandwich, and Erin and the kids can join us at my place. Besides, it would give me a chance to check in on Macin and Sarah." He shrugged and shook his head. "The kid wasted no time telling everyone about the body in the woods. Sarah's been nervous ever since."

"Oh," Tarrin breathed. Then asked, "Sarah?"

Calum smiled and explained, "Frank's step-daughter. She watches Macin when I'm at work." He relaxed a fraction when she smiled and her expression turned thoughtful.

"Oh, that's right," Tarrin exclaimed with a quiet chuckle. "I knew that. I'm sorry. I think I'm completely frazzled." Then, "I think . . . I think I *love* that idea. I'd really like to see Jake and Lexie, too. I hate leaving them alone, especially after what happened this morning. I mean . . . I know Zack has officers watching the house, but still. . ."

Calum nodded, understanding. "But still. It would ease my mind to check-up on things too," he added.

☙

Tarrin leaned jadedly against Calum's kitchen counter, and watched his large hands while he made several sandwiches. She could hear the children laughing in the living room while they played a video game with Officer Chavez, and she sighed wearily.

"How are the calls at work going today?" Calum asked quietly. "Walter seems to be in a better mood."

Tarrin cringed, but smiled. "They're going better, I think," she answered.

"And how are you doing? After this morning?"

She shook her head a little. "I'm okay, I guess. I'm not sure how to feel. Scared? Angry? Both?" She laughed humorlessly. Then asked, "Can I help?" when she caught Calum's concerned gaze on her.

"Sure." He shrugged. "Can you get the mayo out of the fridge?"

"Of course." She moved to the refrigerator. Opening the door wide, she reached in for the salad dressing, and placed it on the counter next to him.

"Butter knives are in there. Do you mind?" he asked, nodding toward the drawer next to his hip.

"No, not at all," she replied, reaching around.

She took a deep breath as she stepped nearer, and she suppressed a pleasant shiver when she brushed past him to reach the drawer. She pulled on the handle and reached in for a knife. She could smell Calum's expensive aftershave, and he smiled when she caught his eye.

"Here." She could feel a slow blush creep up her face. She placed the knife next to the salad dressing, and took a step back. "Anything else?"

"No, that's everything. Thanks." He reached for the jar.

The silence stretched between them and Tarrin sighed when she heard her sister's familiar voice draw near.

"Those look scrumptious," Erin announced when she entered the kitchen. She was followed closely by Sarah, Calum's step-sister.

Tarrin gave a little wave and Sarah returned it with a smile. Erin and Sarah had become quick friends, and Tarrin was pleased

124

to discover she would soon begin classes at the University of Washington as well. The girls had made plans to ride to school together in the mornings, and the thought comforted Tarrin. She didn't like the idea of her sister traveling on the bus alone, especially now.

Erin took a moment to peek over Calum's broad shoulder at the stack of food he was making before she sauntered over to stand next to Tarrin. "I'm starving." She laughed, then asked quietly, "You okay?" She nudged Tarrin gently with her elbow.

Tarrin gave her sister a quick hug and nodded before she turned her attention toward Sarah. "How are you?"

"I'm doing fine," the girl answered. She sat on a chair in Calum's kitchen, then went on, "Erin was saying you've been looking for daycare for Jake and Lexie."

"I have," Tarrin responded. "Although, I haven't had much time to look yet—"

"Sarah can watch them," Erin cut into the conversation.

"Really?" Tarrin's brow rose.

"Yeah, I'd love to," Sarah added. "I watch Macin while Calum's at work, so I can watch them here at the house with him. And when school starts, my classes only go until the afternoon. I'll be here when they get off the bus. What do you think, Calum? Would that be alright with you? I'm sure Jackie wouldn't mind."

"I think that's a fantastic idea. Tarrin?" Calum asked.

"Well, yes, of course. If you really don't mind, I think that would . . . Well, it'd be great," Tarrin responded. "You don't mind?"

"Not at all." Sarah smiled. "I'd love to. Lexie is just a little doll," she added.

"Thank you. Really. I know that will make Jake happy too. He loves hanging out with Macin."

Tarrin smiled, feeling slightly relieved. Finding suitable daycare would be one less thing she'd need to worry about in the coming weeks and she felt immensely grateful. Not only would her children stay close to home, they would be with a friend. *And a police officer.* The thought suddenly filled her head and she cringed. What would the coming weeks bring?

"Then it's all settled." Sarah's voice broke into Tarrin's thoughts as she stood, and hugged Tarrin quickly.

Surprised, Tarrin returned the embrace. Calum regarded them silently when he moved to the table holding a plate piled high with sandwiches. Sarah turned to face him and reached for a sandwich from the top of the stack. "Hey, Calum?" she addressed him. "I'm going to run up and check in with Mom and Dad real quick. Do you mind?"

Calum shook his head. "No, not at all. Grab a bag of chips and a can of Coke before you leave. Oh, and would you mind letting Dad know Macin and I'll be coming by for dinner this Sunday?"

Sarah nodded. "Sure," she replied. "I'll be back in a few."

She left the house, and Tarrin waved before she shut the door. Erin stood still for a moment, a smile plastered on her face. Then suddenly, she spun around to face Tarrin with a scowl.

"So when are you going to tell me what's going on?" Erin whispered, her voice harsh. "I'm *not stupid,* and I'm not a *child,* Tarrin. What happened this morning?"

"Erin, it's nothing really," she lied.

Calum took a step closer. "You know, this is probably none of my business, but I think she needs to know, Tarrin," he offered. He glanced toward the living room for a moment, making certain the children weren't listening before he went on, "Knowledge of a situation this dangerous can protect her better than ignorance. I don't agree with Marzollo, I think she needs to know."

Tarrin's eyes widened in surprise and her lips parted while she contemplated Calum's words. Annoyance flitted across her face for a brief moment, but she knew he was right. It would be better for Erin to know the truth. She didn't want to scare her sister, but the truth was, they were in a very frightening situation. There was no getting around the fact. If Erin knew, would she be better able to protect Lexie and Jake? She would be more cautious, and caution right now was of the utmost importance.

"Maybe . . . You're right, I guess. I just . . ." She sighed.

She glanced toward the living room. Jake, Lexie, and Macin were engrossed in their video game, and Officer Chavez laughed loudly from the sofa as he joined in the virtual battle. She smiled a little. She liked Officer Chavez. He seemed like an easy going young man, and he didn't hover. She turned back to face Erin. Calum set the plate of sandwiches on the table while Tarrin explained the situation that had taken place earlier in the day. Erin listened, pale faced, and a mélange of expressions played across her face.

"*Oh, my gosh,*" she spoke. "He's coming after Lexie? What are we going to do?"

"I thought about leaving. Maybe going back to Colorado, but Zack said this wacko would just follow and it could be worse. But I have to protect Lexie, somehow."

"That note doesn't necessarily mean the killer is coming after Lexie. I personally think it's just a scare tactic, but Marzollo does have a point," Calum interjected with a frown.

"So this isn't Brandon? I was so positive this was Brandon. I wasn't even all that worried. I just thought . . ." Erin's voice cracked.

Tarrin cast a quick, uncomfortable glance toward Calum. "No, this *isn't* Brandon, and for the first time in my life, I wish it was," she admitted.

Erin groaned. "Well, what now?"

Tarrin shrugged. "Well, whatever we do, this man isn't going to get near Lexie," she replied.

Calum's eyes shot to hers. He fixed his gaze on her for a long moment. Tarrin was amazed at how strikingly brown his eyes were. She could read his concern for her in their lively depths and she was touched that he cared. His sudden friendship was comforting.

"What are we going to do?" Erin repeated.

Tarrin tore her eyes from Calum's. She faced her sister. "We just . . . wait."

∞

Tarrin was quiet on the drive back to work. She tried to force her tense body to relax as she rode next to Calum in his Honda sports coupe. He glanced her way several times, and she had the feeling he had something on his mind. She caught his eye again and his mouth twisted.

"What is it?" she encouraged.

"Well," he began, "during lunch, Erin mentioned someone named Brandon. I realize it isn't my business, so please don't feel like you owe me any kind of explanation. I don't mind if you tell me to butt-out, but I was wondering if Brandon is your ex-husband."

"No," Tarrin hesitated. "No, Brandon is my ex-husband's brother."

Calum's eyes broaden curiously. He remained silent and she wondered how much to divulge. If Calum knew the truth, what would he think of her? As crazy as it seemed, Tarrin felt she could trust him. He was becoming a good friend, very quickly, and she enjoyed being in his company. He remained silent as he pulled his Honda into the building's dim parking garage.

Detective Chavez pulled up alongside them and she waved at the man before she turned to face Calum. She could read the troubled curiosity in Calum's expression.

"Brandon . . . he's caused a lot of problems since my divorce. It's a long story," she murmured as old memories rushed to the surface.

"I understand if you don't want to talk about it, but if I can help, I'd like to," he replied. When she didn't answer he asked, "Do you want to tell me about it?"

Tarrin licked her dry, trembling lips before she heard herself whisper, "Yes, I do." Shocked at her forthright confession, Tarrin felt her cheeks warm. "But I'm so . . . I feel so much shame over the whole incident still," she admitted.

"Shame? Why should you feel ashamed?" Calum probed.

She sucked in a deep breath, and let it out slow. "Everything with my divorce . . . It's all just so complicated." She closed her eyes. "We came here for a fresh start, but now . . . Everything's changed, and I'm so . . ." She groaned. "Scared," she finished.

Her voice trembled. Tears shimmered along the length of her thick lashes, and she felt Calum's strong hand close about hers. She seemed to draw strength in his nearness. What was it about him that compelled her to be so open? She'd never been the sort of person to form relationships on a whim, but Calum Sloan . . . Why did he appeal to her? What was it about him that seemed to draw her in?

"I'm not here to judge you. We all have our skeletons in the closet. Whatever it is, I'm here to listen and help in any way I can. I want to help you. I really . . ." He paused for a moment. "Tarrin, I care about you. I know we've only known one another for a few days, so I feel a little strange admitting it out loud, but I really do."

Their eyes met. "That means a lot," Tarrin whispered.

He brushed a tear from her cheek. "What happened?"

Inhaling deeply, her tears spilled free as she recounted the details of her divorce and the dark months following Travis's arrest. "I had no idea. We were sitting down to dinner. Lexie answered the door. I didn't understand what was going on at first. Then, the police took Travis outside and arrested him. And Jake and Lexie . . . They watched from the window," she sobbed. "They watched as the police arrested their father. How could they possibly understand? I didn't understand, and the kids were so young."

"Then, when the rumors started . . . Brandon helped that along. He and his family—his wife—his kids—they told such awful stories. Jake knows most of what happened. He found Travis and Juliann together. He trusted his father. He trusted his teacher. This has been so hard for him. Lexie, she understands more than I hoped, but one day, she'll know everything."

"Is that why you left?" Calum asked, his eyes narrowing.

"Partly," Tarrin admitted. "I needed a change. The kids needed a change, and once the rumors started, it was hard to stay. As if I didn't have a hard enough time facing our old friends. They all knew about Juliann and Travis long before I did. Then to add unfounded lies—that I somehow framed him—" She placed her fingers against her temple.

"Some days it felt like more than I could bear. I could hardly stand the knowing looks and pitying glances. I just wanted to escape," she whispered.

Calum sat back against his seat and stared out the window. He remained silent for a minute, then replied, "I'm sorry, Tarrin. Honestly, this world is a real messed up place sometimes. It hardly seems fair." He shook his head, then went on. "But, you understand, don't you, that your past and your *husband's* mistakes don't define who you are, right?"

Tarrin exhaled quietly as he went on.

"I personally think you are an amazing woman, especially to have overcome what you have. And this . . ." He groaned. "This thing will pass. That man—whoever he is . . . Let me help you. Talk with Frank. I know how hard it is to trust after feeling the pain of betrayal. I know that pain. Every time my mother promised to come clean—to give up her addiction—I'd believe her. And for years I felt like nothing ever came of my faith. I stopped believing in everyone. I loved my mom, and it hurt when she couldn't give up her physical needs for me or Jackie, so I understand that pain, but Tarrin, try to trust Frank. Like I said, he can help you. He has other connections. Connections Marzollo doesn't have. Marzollo has . . ." He let his words fade and groaned again while he ran a hand across the bottom of his jaw. "Besides," he went on, "Frank is an amazing counselor. He's worked as a spiritual advisor for years. I realize faith is a very personal thing, but he's worked with women from all manner of broken relationships. You're not alone here."

Tarrin brushed at the tears dangling along her jaw line. "I don't know how to trust anymore," she whispered.

"It isn't easy, is it? You can't just flip it on and off like a switch, but I promise you, you're not alone. Frank's a good man, and he can help protect you and your family." He paused. "Personally, I don't know Marzollo. But," he sighed. "I don't trust him, Tarrin."

Tarrin chewed the inside of her cheek and cast a quick glance toward Detective Chavez. The officer stood outside his patrol car and eyed them lazily. She looked back toward Calum. He regarded her carefully, his expression, troubled. She understood why he had a difficult time trusting Zack. She'd felt stunned when Zack questioned Calum so boldly. Actually, he hadn't questioned Calum, he interrogated him. He'd treated Calum like a suspect.

Tarrin liked Zack. He seemed to care about keeping her and her kids safe. The knowledge that he was keeping an officer with her and her family brought a small measure of comfort, but she had to admit, having a policeman within her line of vision at all times was a bit unsettling. She knew it was worth it if it meant keeping her kids and Erin safe, but the points Calum made also made sense.

She knew she needed to trust someone. She trusted Zack, but could he keep her and her children safe? Did Frank have enough connections to provide more protection? She sighed and leaned her forehead against her palms. She felt emotionally drained. How could she possibly bear this? How much more was she capable of handling? It would be nice to talk to someone about her feelings—her fears. It would feel good to release a bit of the emotions churning inside.

"Will you come with me?" she whispered. "To speak with Frank?" She hadn't really thought it through completely, but as she voiced her request, Tarrin realized speaking with Frank felt right. She couldn't explain it, but she knew he could help.

Calum nodded and she frowned when she caught his eye. "Besides," she laughed a little. "I'm worried Frank will think I'm insane when I tell him a serial killer might be stalking me. It would help to have a witness." She smiled wryly.

Calum chuckled. "Yes, I will go and bear witness to your sanity whenever you're ready." He smiled. His white teeth gleamed in the dim interior.

"Tonight?"

"Yes, of course. I'll call him as soon as we get into the office. I'll let him know to expect us."

"Thank you," Tarrin told him with a smile.

"No problem." He reached out to gently touch her cheek. "It's nice to see a smile on your face." He dropped his hand and his fingers trailed slowly down her arm. Tarrin's eyes widened when he grasped her hand then brought it to his lips and kissed her fingers tenderly.

His warm breath sent pleasurable waves up her spine and a slight blush touched her cheeks when her eyes dropped to his lips. His mouth curved into a small smile and she jumped, startled, when he suddenly nodded toward Detective Chavez. "Maybe we ought to go up. I think he's starting to get edgy."

Tearing her gaze from his mouth, she spun to face the window. A deep blush crept up her neck, and she laughed breathlessly. She had momentarily forgotten about the detective, and she stared out the window, embarrassed. *What is wrong with me?* Detective Chavez paced back and forth in front of his car, and Tarrin forced a quiet laugh, pulling her thoughts from Calum. "You're right, he's starting to look perturbed."

Calum's calm laughter joined hers as he exited the car and came around to hold her door. Keeping her eyes toward the ground, she slid from the car just as he grasped her hand in his.

"Remind me to thank the security guard for sending you up to the office." He squeezed her fingers. "And remind me to give him a big, fat raise. I owe him."

CHAPTER *Ten*

arrin," Calum caught her after work. "Can I see you in my office for a minute?" he asked.

A few of Tarrin's fellow employees glanced her way, and she smiled awkwardly. "Um . . . sure," she replied. "If this is about that last call . . . I know Walter was really annoyed, but I just couldn't remember what I was supposed to say," Tarrin spoke quietly while she entered his office.

Officer Chavez followed, but paused just outside, and Calum shut the door. "*What?*" He turned to face Tarrin.

"Is this about that call?" Tarrin asked sheepishly.

"Did you mess up another call?" Calum suddenly grinned.

"I . . . Well, yes," Tarrin admitted.

Calum laughed out loud. "No, Tarrin. This isn't about a call." He stepped nearer. "I talked with Frank. I wanted to let you know he agreed to meet with us. He's waiting at the center."

"Oh." A frown touched Tarrin's lips, but Calum continued to smile. "Okay," she went on. "That's . . . um . . . good. Really?" she hesitated.

"It'll be fine. I promise," he added. "I was thinking we could just drive together, if that's okay. Chavez can come too, or follow, either way."

Tarrin's lips twisted in uncertainty. Was she ready to talk with Frank? She sighed then said, "Okay."

"You're sure? I don't want to pressure you, but I really do think this is a good idea." Calum touched her hand.

She smiled just a little. "No, you're right. And I'm ready."

Calum squeezed her fingers then grinned again. "Maybe later we should talk about that call."

Tarrin cringed. "Yeah," she breathed.

She was quiet on the drive through the city, and Calum

caught her eye several times to give her an encouraging smile. Her stomach twisted into knots, and she could feel her hands tremble as they lay in her lap. Questions played through her mind. What would she say? Zack had asked her to keep the investigation to herself. Was she doing wrong going to Frank? Frank would undoubtedly ask about her past as well. How could she open herself up once again, and face the demons that always seemed to follow her? She wondered if she were making the correct decision trusting Frank with her past or her future.

When they met previously, Tarrin had immediately liked the older man, though she wasn't given much of an opportunity to get to know him. Frank reminded her in many ways of her own father, and suddenly a longing for family and home assailed her. She wondered again, had she made the right choice moving her children to Seattle? Back home, the only thing on the line was her family's reputation. Now, she worried about their lives. Gossip and rumors seemed to pale in comparison. Would the killer really try to get to Lexie?

She closed her eyes briefly, and silently prayed for strength. Calum reached for her hand, and their eyes met briefly before he turned his attention back toward the busy city streets. His presence always seemed to comfort her. She studied his profile as they pulled up to the newly constructed community center.

"Everything's going to be fine, Tarrin," Calum spoke, facing her.

Turning from his penetrating gaze, she looked at the building. Double glass doors surrounded by potted rhododendrons lent the building a welcoming feel. Tall hemlock and spruce surrounded the grounds and she moaned quietly when Frank stepped outside. The kind man waved, and Tarrin moved to exit the car. Calum came around to hold her door, touching her elbow gently.

"You're late," Frank chuckled, moving toward them. Tarrin smiled faintly when the older man grasped her hands between his in a comforting embrace. "I'm glad you're here. Come on in." He waved to Officer Chavez, who had just pulled in beside them.

Tarrin followed the two men as they entered the building, and she swallowed hard when Frank stopped in front of his office door.

"Calum, son," he addressed Calum. "Why don't you wait outside for a moment, while I get to know Tarrin a little better?"

Calum looked to Tarrin. "Okay?"

She nodded. "Yes."

"I'll wait right outside," he returned.

Frank laughed good-naturedly. "Don't look so nervous. I'm not as mean as he lets on." He cast a wink at Calum.

Frank ushered her inside his cramped, yet comfortable office, and she couldn't help but smile when he offered her a huge chocolate muffin. "No, but thank you," Tarrin laughed a little nervously.

"Are you sure? My wife, Kathy, is one amazing cook, as you can see." He chortled and patted his ample waistline. "Now," he said as he sat next to her. "Let's talk. I've heard a little bit about why you're here, but first, I want to get to know you better."

Tarrin clasped her hands tightly in her lap, but she could feel her nervousness dissipate slightly as the older man studied her with caring eyes. It took several moments for her to know how to start, but while Frank listened, Tarrin found herself speaking openly as she described the circumstances of her previous marriage. Under his compassionate presence she spoke of her past struggles, her current feelings of insecurity, frustration, and grief, and Frank was empathetic and honest in his counsel. It left her feeling more hopeful than before, but when the conversation turned to the murder and Zack's investigation, Frank was shocked at the information she related concerning the serial killer, Lexie, and the events earlier in the day.

"I'm going to be honest with you," he said, standing. "This isn't a good situation. Not at all. But . . ." He paused. Turning, he opened the door. "Calum, come on in here, son," he called before spinning back to face her. "But," he continued. "We're going to do something about it."

Tarrin waited in silence as Calum entered the office. His broad shoulders filled the doorway, and she smiled when Frank slapped him on the back. Calum sat next to Tarrin, then, noting her tear-stained face, he pulled her trembling hands into his.

"Are you alright?" he whispered, leaning close.

"Yes," she returned.

His warm hand closed about her fingers, and Tarrin drew comfort in his touch. Her hand felt right in his. The thought took her by surprise, but she quickly forced her mind back to Frank and listened carefully while he devised a plan to keep her and her family safe.

"This is something we have to cautiously, as well as prayerfully, consider," Frank spoke. "We need all the help we can get. The police seem to be doing a swell job, but I think we can do more. I'll contact Officer Gomez. He's an old friend of mine still working down at the station, and we can get the neighborhood watch captains to patrol the streets," he proposed.

He tapped the desk with his forefinger for a moment as he considered his plan. Then he went on, "Tarrin, I'd feel much better if your sister and the children would agree to spend their time during the day at my house with my wife and I, just until this man is caught. I don't think any of us should risk being alone.

"Talk with Lieutenant Marzollo, and let him know the change of plans so he can get a patrol car out to my place as soon as possible. Also, I think you and Calum would be wise to carpool to and from work until this man is apprehended. I'll get right on a neighborhood watch. Everyone on your street and within the vicinity needs to be notified. I understand the detectives' need for confidentiality concerning their investigation, but the more people who are aware of the situation, the safer we'll all be. I don't agree with Marzollo keeping this quiet. I never liked the way that man worked. I only worked with the kid for a few years before I retired, but I never liked the guy. Calum, you'll organize the watch captains into teams?"

"Of course," Calum agreed. "I'll get right on it."

"Well, we have work to do," Frank stood. "Kind of feels like old times," He laughed a little. "I miss my days on the force." He looked to Tarrin. "And don't you worry about a thing. You and you're kids—you're going to be just fine."

♋

He stared at the bedroom window. The muted light glowed from behind the shutter drawn down across the glass. He knew Tarrin was getting ready for bed. Her lazy sister was probably already asleep. He could see the patrol car parked next to the curb. Two officers sat in the seats, gorging themselves on coffee and scones. He knew two more officers were keeping an eye on the patch of woods behind the house, hoping for his return.

The thought made him chuckle. In a few hours the two overweight goons in the patrol car would be asleep, and he knew the officers patrolling the woods would soon grow indolent and give up. He smiled. He knew his way into the old house. He knew how to get inside without making a sound, and he could hardly wait to see her.

He yearned to see her hair fanned across her pillow, with her pale skin glowing in the ethereal moonlight. Her chest would rise and fall as she breathed in her last breath. He could do it easily, and silently, without waking another soul in the house—even Tarrin's annoying sister. His skin tingled in anticipation, then he thought of the girl. His euphoric mood dissipated and he scowled. He had to do what had to be done. He forced his emotions down. Serenity washed across his body and he smiled, leaning back in the driver's seat of his vehicle. Only a matter of hours before it would be finished.

ॐ

Tarrin tip-toed into the darkened hall when she exited the bathroom. The toilet groaned as it flushed, and she cringed. She glanced in toward Jake and Lexie. Both children remained deep asleep. She was grateful for that. *Leaky faucet, broken window lock, and now something is wrong with the toilet,* she smirked as she quietly made her way back to her bedroom.

She wondered if she would dare broach the subject of repairs with Edna Cope. The thought sent a shiver down her spine and she nearly laughed aloud. After all she had endured the last few days, Tarrin was amazed that her landlord still evoked anxiety. She smiled. She knew she could ask Calum for help, but he had done so much for her already.

The thought of Calum made her faint smile grow, and her stomach knotted pleasantly. After accompanying her to visit Frank, he had joined them for dinner. She prepared spaghetti and breadsticks, and he and Macin thoroughly enjoyed the home cooked meal. Both Jake and Lexie liked being with Calum. And, Lexie, usually withdrawn and quiet, warmed to him almost immediately.

After dinner, the little girl had climbed into his lap. She'd wrapped her skinny arms tightly around his neck and asked him to read her a story. Calum had obliged with a grin, and he spent nearly an hour reading aloud. Lexie had laughed at Calum's attempt to create different voices for the characters. Tarrin found she was enjoying the time they shared. Just being near Calum sent Tarrin's pulse rate soaring in a pleasant way, and she felt rather breathless whenever he happened to touch her or glance her direction. She hadn't felt these new stirrings of awareness in years, and it left her feeling confused, but happy.

She closed her eyes and her body grew weary as she reflected on the day's events. The horror of the morning seemed distant and surreal, but she knew the danger she was facing was very real. With renewed purpose, she vowed to keep her kids and sister safe. She felt very grateful for the new, caring friends in her life, and with a small smile, she flipped off her bedside lamp, drowning the room in darkness.

◌ଃ

His body tensed when he slowly slid from his car and inhaled the crisp, brine-scented air of Seattle. He closed his eyes and focused on taking several deep, relaxing breaths. He could feel power and determination fill his body—flood his veins with strength—and his eyes opened. A smile spread across his hard face, and he knew it was time. The moment had come at last.

He glanced around the darkened street. He had parked several blocks away to avoid detection when he left the scene. Not that he would get caught. No one ever saw him. Well, despite Lexie, but that would quickly be remedied. Besides, how could he have possibly foreseen a child wandering into the woods that day?

He finished his quick, meticulous search of the dim alley. Vapor street lamps cast eerie shadows across the narrow road. He glanced up calmly and watched as a western pipistrelle bat darted in and out of a cloud of insects. Mesmerized, he observed the bat for several moments before he turned down the sidewalk. He pulled his jacket tighter about him then reached into the pocket of his jeans.

Slowly, he removed two surgical gloves. He had already taken precautions earlier in the night to alter his fingerprints with superglue, but he pulled the gloves on, just in case. He knew how to be invisible. He had done this many times. He grinned when he turned the corner to the next street, and he glanced around carefully as he avoided areas of bright light. Only another block and he would be there. He sighed in anticipation. He had planned this perfectly.

ભ

Tarrin suddenly bolted awake. Her eyes opened wide, and she sat up, listening. She heard Lexie moan, and she shot out of bed then padded down the hall, barefoot, toward the kids' room. She cursed softly when her foot came down on one of Jake's *Lego's,* and she stumbled into the room. Grasping Lexie's footboard for support, she steadied herself. She stood straight and winced, rubbing the arch of her foot just as Lexie moaned again and tossed in her sleep.

The little girl's princess blanket twisted about her skinny legs, and Tarrin moved to untangle the soft cover. She pulled the folds of Lexie's blanket from around her feet and spread it across her daughter's body. She touched her head tenderly and leaned down to press a kiss against her brow. Tarrin stood straight. She sighed, then suddenly, she froze when a quiet thud sounded from below. Was someone in the kitchen? Her heart rate kicked up, and she held her breath.

She raised her head and listened for several moments. Had she imagined the sound?

Her body relaxed when no more unfamiliar sounds met her straining ears, and her erratic heartbeat began to slow as she stepped into the darkened hallway. She passed the stairs, and the hairs on the back of her neck suddenly stood on end. Gooseflesh prickled along her arms, and the air seemed frozen in her lungs. She turned to face the dark stairwell. Something wasn't right, but Tarrin saw nothing. Her heart raced once again. She strained to hear past the rush of blood pulsating in her ears, but she heard nothing. Frozen, she eyed the stairs with wide, nervous eyes, and she leaned forward, trying to see into the dark kitchen.

"Erin?" she whispered.

She knew Erin was deep asleep. *My imagination is running wild,* she thought as she squinted through the darkness.

"Mom?" Lexie broke the eerie silence.

Tarrin's pent-up breath whooshed from her lungs, and she took a deep gulp of air, trying to calm her ragged nerves. She tore her gaze from the stairway and stumbled back toward Lexie's room. She peered around the doorframe. Her daughter sat up in bed, her soft hair was sticking out from around her face. The little girl groaned and wrapped her arms across her stomach. Tarrin moved into the room, concerned. "Are you alright, sweetheart?" she inquired.

"My tummy hurts," Lexie cried.

Tarrin sat on the edge of the bed. She reached for Lexie's forehead and laid her hand across the girl's face. She didn't have a fever. Tarrin caught her bottom lip between her teeth, frustrated. "Your tummy hurts again?"

"Mmm-hmm," Lexie murmured.

"Do you need to use the bathroom?"

"No." Lexie shook her head and groaned in pain.

Tarrin nodded. "I'll go and get the *Pepto*. Just stay here. I'll be right back."

Tarrin stood and walked to the staircase. She swallowed her fear and advanced cautiously down the creaky stairs. Her heart thundered in her ears, and when her foot touched the landing, she swallowed and peered toward the living room. When a cool draft brushed across her face, she gasped. She spun around to face the glass, sliding door, and her eyes grew wide when she realized the door was slightly ajar.

Her lungs seized and she took a tentative step toward the kitchen. Her heart hammered painfully against her ribs. Then, without warning, a loud bang echoed through the house. A scream froze on her lips as she heard a shout, and she turned to face the front door with fear-filled eyes. *What is going on?*

"Tarrin!" A deep voice called through the closed door. "Tarrin! Open the door!"

Her mouth fell open when she recognized Calum's frantic

voice. She glanced behind her toward the open glass entrance before she turned and rushed to the front door. She paused. "Calum?" she asked.

"Yes! It's me! Open the door!"

Tarrin unlocked the dead bolt with trembling fingers, and then flung the door wide. Calum stepped past her, knocking into her as he rushed into the kitchen. His expression faltered when he noticed the glass door ajar. He bolted through the small kitchen and peered outside, his expression severe.

"Calum? What are you doing? What is it?" Her voice rose with ever-increasing alarm.

He turned and his eyes shot toward the stairs. "He's in the house."

Tarrin felt the blood leave her face. "*What?*" she whispered. She turned to face the open back door.

Calum didn't wait for permission as he raced up the stairs. Tarrin followed quickly, and she waited, terrified, as he searched the bathroom and closets. She ran to check on her children. Her heart pounding wildly as she flew into their room. Lexie sat up, wide-eyed, and she studied Tarrin quizzically before Tarrin darted down the hall toward Erin's room. She rushed into the room and could hear her sister's even, quiet breaths. She quickly checked the closet then spoke, "Erin, get up! Get dressed" Her voice sounded breathless. Erin stirred slightly. "Get up!" Tarrin yelled before she rushed from the room and back toward Calum.

"Did you check the kids' room," he whispered, and Tarrin nodded.

He brushed past her and stepped into the children's room. "Calum!" Lexie called when the little girl caught sight of their neighbor.

Her sleepy eyes lit excitedly, and Calum smiled tersely at the little girl. "Hey, princess," he spoke before he turned back toward the stairs.

Bewildered and frightened, Tarrin turned toward her

daughter. "Lex, wake up Jake. Go into my room with Aunt Erin. Don't come out until I get you, okay?"

Lexie's expression mirrored her confusion, but she did as Tarrin asked.

"What do you want? Leave me alone," Jake muttered when Lexie shook her brother awake.

"Jake, wake up!" Tarrin spoke loudly, stepping into the hall just as Erin appeared, looking bewildered and confused.

"Tarrin, what's going on?" her sister asked, disgruntled.

"Stay with the kids," Tarrin instructed. "Someone was in the house." She didn't wait for Erin's response before she raced down the stairs to find Calum.

"Calum? *Calum*?" she called when she reached the landing.

She noticed he was standing outside with a flashlight and she moved to follow, but paused when she caught sight of a newspaper article printed on a new sheet of paper. The article was sitting in the middle of the table. Certain it had not been there the night before, Tarrin turned and scanned the paper carefully. A gasp burst from her trembling lips when she realized it was the story of Travis's arrest. Her face paled, the blood draining in a rush, as she examined the document. In bold marks, different words were circled within the story. Her mouth fell open as she read each circled word in consecutive order. *You—never—know—when—I'm coming—for—you—nice—dreams.*

"Tarrin, I saw him! He came into the house, and . . ." Calum suddenly stood behind her, and his words faded when he saw what held Tarrin's attention. He swore quietly then placed a hand on her shoulder. "I'm going to go wake up the two imbeciles who are supposed to be guarding this house. I'll be right back. Will you be okay for a minute?" he asked and Tarrin nodded mutely.

She turned to face him with agonized eyes. "He was here," she murmured.

"I know. I'll be right back. I won't be gone more than a second."

What was she going to do? The killer had been in her house. She closed her eyes briefly and her heart hammered against her ribs. She felt near collapse.

"I'll be right back," Calum whispered, then paused. He took a step toward the kitchen drawers. "Where are the knives?"

She pointed to the second drawer weakly.

"Here." He jerked the drawer open. He pulled out a large butcher knife and placed it in her hand. "I'll be back." Placing a feather light kiss against her brow, he turned and stormed toward the door.

Tarrin stared in silence as Calum disappeared out the front door before she turned and watched the backyard. The tall trees cast eerie shadows across the thick lawn and she could hear the soft breeze whispering through the ancient pines. The trees creaked. She moved closer toward the open doorway and caught her breath. She could feel unseen eyes on her. She knew he was watching her and with renewed determination, she stood straighter, keeping her eyes locked on the trees. She glared, her fingers grasping the knife tightly.

"You will not win. I won't let you!" she spoke aloud.

The hair on her arms stood on end and she shivered. *You will not win,* she repeated silently. She watched the swaying trees and the rustling ferns for another moment before she backed up toward the stairs. Placing her hand on the rail, she kept her gaze focused on the dark woods beyond the house. *He's watching me now, taking pleasure in my pain and fear,* she thought with a pounding heart.

"Tarrin!"

Tarrin jumped when Erin's trembling voice broke through her tumultuous thoughts. She tore her eyes from the woods and turned to peer up at her sister's bewildered, frightened expression.

"Tarrin, I mean it! What is going on?" Erin asked, her voice quaking.

"Erin, someone was in the house," she answered,

attempting to keep the panic from her voice. "Will you stay up there with the kids, please? Let me find out exactly what happened. Just keep the kids safe."

Erin's face blanched. She frowned then nodded. "T-Tarrin," she replied breathlessly. "I'm scared, Tarrin. What's happening? What are we going to do?"

"I don't know," Tarrin answered. "Calum went to get the officers. He'll be right back. I'll come up as soon as I can," she replied.

Her sister nodded and then disappeared just as Calum returned with the two, weary-eyed policemen. Macin followed close behind. The boy's short cropped hair stood in untidy tufts, and his expression looked weary, yet anxious. Calum glanced toward Tarrin.

"Can he go up with Jake and Lexie?" he asked.

She nodded and gave Macin a small, forced smile as the boy walked up the stairs. Calum's face clearly showed his frustration as they waited for Macin to disappear. They heard the bedroom door shut, and Calum spun around to face the two officers. Irritation showed plainly on his face.

"While you two were sleeping, someone came into this house! I was awake, and I happened to look out my window. A man crossed this street, right in front of you! So I came outside to check on things. I saw him come through this door! Right in front of you!" he finished.

Tarrin's eyes broadened, and she lifted her face toward the front door. How was that possible? The door had been locked. The dead bolt had been set, but yet someone had been in the house. The back door was open, and the newspaper article . . . She felt her knees grow weak, and she shook her head, frustrated. Calum rushed to her side. His hand grasped her elbow, and he encouraged her to sit on the bottom stair. She sat, and then eyed the two bemused officers with worried eyes.

"I'm not sure I'm following you. You say you *saw* him? Did

you hear anyone?" the officer turned to address Tarrin.

"I didn't know . . . I-I didn't *see* anyone, but earlier I did hear a noise. It startled me. I thought maybe . . ." She shrugged. "Something didn't feel right, but I thought . . . Well, I thought maybe someone was down here, b-but I can't really say why. Then Lexie woke up with a stomach ache. I came down into the kitchen to get some medicine.

"That's when I discovered the back door was slid open. Someone *was* in here," she whispered as the reality of the situation began sinking in ever deeper. "Calum knocked just then, and I answered the door, but I don't understand. The door . . . *That* door was locked. The dead bolt was set. I don't understand. If he came in that way, he would have needed a key, wouldn't he?"

Calum turned questioning eyes toward the policemen and they waited as one officer stepped to the door and examined it carefully. "There's no forced entry," he replied. He turned toward Calum.

"He came in that door. I saw him. He opened *that* door." Calum pointed toward the front door. "And he came into this house. He must have gone out the back when he heard Tarrin coming down, but he left *that!*" He turned and pointed toward the table with a scowl.

One officer moved to the table. He eyed the newspaper article with a frown before he stepped toward the open glass door. The second officer studied Calum. "Now tell me again. How did you see this guy? You just happened to be awake?" he inquired, his voice accusing.

"I forgot to plug in my cell phone. The battery was dying. It sounds an alarm whenever it gets too low. So I woke up and went downstairs to find my charger to plug it in. I keep a charging station in the living room, on the entertainment center by the window. I happened to glance up right as a man crossed the street.

"It concerned me when I noticed he was heading toward Tarrin's place. I came out onto my porch just as he entered the house through the front door. I realized you two were asleep, so I came running. I yelled, hoping to wake you, but that didn't do any good," Calum finished, his tone biting.

"Hey, check this out," the officer standing near the table called. He pointed toward the newspaper article. "Is this article talking about you? Your name's in it."

Tarrin blanched visibly, and she leaned her head into her hands. Calum's fingers squeezed her thin shoulder, and she focused on taking deep breaths. *Why?* She asked again. *Why is this happening to us?* The killer had been so close. He had been in her home. He could have killed Lexie, and she had gone downstairs without any sort of protection. If Calum hadn't intervened when he did, would the murderer have come back? Had he heard Calum shouting? Was that why he'd left?

"Calum," Tarrin whispered his name.

She felt grateful for his presence. He knelt in front of her just as a sob broke through her tightly pressed lips. He opened his arms, and she fell against him. His strong arms wrapped around her trembling body, and she could feel his warm breath on her neck as he buried his face against her hair. Hard, aching sobs wracked her body, and she tried desperately to quell the sudden hysteria.

"What's happening here?" Zack Marzollo's deep voice suddenly echoed through the small house.

Calum's arms dropped from around Tarrin and he stood straight, turning to face the detective.

Tarrin took several deep, gulping breaths as Zack brushed past Calum. "Tarrin," he spoke her name tenderly.

"Oh . . ." She inhaled when Zack's arm came around her shoulder.

Tarrin stiffened momentarily then leaned her head against his broad shoulders for a moment. She could smell the spicy scent of freshly applied aftershave. He held her for a second longer before she pulled away. He frowned as he stood and faced his men.

"I want answers now! I radioed in, and when I didn't get a response, I figured I'd better get down here. I guess it's a good thing I did," he finished, giving Calum a scathing look.

Calum's mouth twisted in distaste as he eyed Zack. The two officers scrambled to explain, and Zack listened with a scowl. He stepped to the table, and eyed the article closely. He nodded toward the note. "Clifton, take care of this. I want it sent to forensics immediately." He pointed toward Calum. "Take him down to the station."

Calum swore. "If I have to go down to the station, then I can take myself."

Zack's face contorted angrily and he regarded Calum for several long second. "Cuff him," Zack directed his officer.

"You're *arresting* him?" Tarrin's eyes shot to Calum's, and then back to Zack. "You can't arrest him! He saved my life!"

"Sloan isn't under arrest, but I am detaining him. I don't have probable cause for an arrest *yet!*"

Tarrin glanced at Zack, shocked. "What exactly do you mean? Calum hasn't done anything. You can't do this!"

Tears burned the back of Tarrin's eyes and she watched in horror as Zack's men cuffed Calum. Calum scowled, but remained silent.

"You can't do this!" Tarrin repeated. "Calum?" She shook her head, frustrated. "Let him go!"

"Tarrin, it's fine," Calum spoke calmly, but she could hear the frustration behind his words. He glared at Zack. "If I'm not under arrest, then I can take myself downtown, Marzollo. There's no need for this. And I'm not talking until my lawyer is present," Calum told him. "You know you have no probable cause to detain me."

"Whatever you say, Sloan," Zack returned. "You two!" he directed toward his officers. "Get on this! I want a unit out here now, before our crime scene is compromised more. Clifton, escort Sloan down to precinct."

148

"No," Tarrin breathed and Calum forced a small smile for her sake. She stood and moved to his side. "Calum, I'm sorry." A sob broke through, and she dropped her eyes. "I'm so sorry. You—"

"You have nothing to be sorry for. I won't be long, Tarrin." He paused, then said, "Can you call Frank and Kathy? Will you send Macin up to their place?" he asked.

"Yes, of course," she whispered.

Calum leaned in close. His breath brushed across her ear. "Don't stay here tonight. Go to Frank's house. Please, just trust me on this. Don't stay here. Get out of here as soon as you can."

The officer pulled him back, and Tarrin met Calum's eyes. She could read his concern in their pleading depths. She swallowed hard and nodded. "I'll think about it."

His frown deepened. He went to reply, but shook his head instead as he exhaled loudly. He leaned in and placed a feather-light kiss against her brow. His lips lingered for only a moment before he was pulled away once again and shoved out the front door.

Tarrin spun around quickly when she felt Zack's hand on her shoulder. "You didn't need to do that! He isn't a suspect, Zack! He saved our lives," she spoke.

Zack's face contorted into lines of anger for a brief moment, then he pinched the bridge of his nose and sighed. "Look, relax. It's all under control."

"What do you mean, 'It's all under control'?" she spat. "*This* is *not* under control! Someone was in my house! Those doors were locked, so whoever it was has somehow managed to find a key! Then ... then you arrest the man who saved our lives?" she asked, her tone incredulous.

Zack regarded her silently for a long moment before he spoke, his voice calm. "I know you're upset, but I wouldn't have detained Sloan if I didn't have good cause. Look, I hate to tell you this, but Calum Sloan is a probable suspect."

Tarrin paled, and her eyes grew disbelieving. "What do you

mean? That's impossible."

"Is it, Tarrin?" he asked. "Think about it. Look at the facts. He's been around from the get-go. He never has a solid alibi, and we've found a few bits of evidence that may just tie him to this case."

Tarrin felt her knees grow weak and she stumbled. Zack's hand snaked out to steady her. He led her to the kitchen table and she sat on a chair weakly. "No," she whispered." That's . . . It's not possible. I don't believe it."

"The night you saw the light in the woods—"

"Calum was *here* in the house with us. It can't be him," she cut him off.

Zack sighed. "We discovered a metal wire hanging in a tree. The wire was in the immediate area where you saw the light."

Tarrin's lips parted in bewilderment. "That isn't possible. I don't understand."

"He hung a light on the wire, Tarrin. When the breeze came, it would have looked as if someone were moving. The thick brush would have caused it to disappear and reappear."

"He wouldn't do that," she murmured.

"He was jogging on the same trail yesterday morning," he went on. "We found tread marks that look to be about the same size as Sloan's, and the only one who can verify his whereabouts is his twelve-year-old nephew."

Tarrin ducked her head and focused on taking deep breaths. "It can't be him," she replied.

"And tonight, he just *happens* to be awake in time to see a man enter your house through a locked door?"

"But *someone* was in my house!" Tarrin defended.

Zack sighed. "Obviously someone has been in your house, Tarrin, but it may have been Sloan."

She shook her head. "I don't believe that. It can't . . . couldn't be him."

"Look," Zack's voice raised a fraction. He stood and walked

to the table. He glanced down at the newspaper article lying in a plastic evidence bag. "Has Calum Sloan been in this house recently? Before tonight?"

"Yes, but—"

"Did you tell anyone other than me about your ex-husband?" Zack faced her, and her mouth fell open.

No, I don't believe it. It can't be. Her wide, horror-filled eyes fell on the article.

"Did you tell Calum Sloan about your ex-husband?" Zack pressed.

"Yes, but he wouldn't—"

"You'd be amazed at who would." He moved closer and touched her forearm. "I've known husbands, mothers, nurses, doctors, even religious leaders. Everyone said they couldn't do it— '*Not them*'. Tarrin, this is what makes serial killers so dangerous. They aren't the typical freaks or maniacs you'd expect. They're often the nice, every day, Mr. Rogers-type."

Tarrin's body trembled. It wasn't Calum. It couldn't be him. But hadn't she thought the same thing when the police arrested Travis? She hadn't believed Travis was guilty even after he admitted to the crimes. It had taken months for reality to sink in. Could it be happening again? She didn't *really* know Calum, but it wasn't possible, was it?

"It just can't . . . it can't be," she whispered, feeling weak.

"Yes, it can. I've done a bit of homework on Sloan. Look, I know you don't want to believe this—no one ever does—but Sloan has a criminal history with three previous arrests on his record, including a felony."

Tarrin felt weak. "What?" she asked. How was that possible? She ducked her head as the blood rushed from her face, and she closed her eyes when Zack went on.

"He had a tough childhood. He had a drug addicted mother and a dead-beat dad. He was tossed from one foster home to the next. Now, I'm not saying that automatically qualifies him as a serial killer, but the women being targeted have all been drug addicts of one kind or another."

"He has a criminal history?" she asked.

"Yes, and I'm afraid to say it, but Calum Sloan is a very probable suspect. I wish I had told you sooner. I hadn't realized that you two were so . . . close. But that makes him even more dangerous. Most serial killers like to get as close to their victims as possible. He fits the profile."

CHAPTER *Eleven*

arrin's breaths were shallow, and she struggled to remain calm. A tear rolled down her cheek, and she jerked slightly when Zack tried to wipe the moisture from off her face. He pulled his hand back and frowned.

"I'm sorry. Look, I know you're upset, and I can stay here tonight. Just in case. I can crash on the couch, and—"

"Tarrin, is Uncle Calum down there?" Macin suddenly called from upstairs.

Zack paused mid-conversation and his eyes shot to hers. Flustered, she jumped out of the chair. Zack caught the chair before it fell to the floor while Tarrin swung to face the stairs. *What am I going to tell him?* She thought frantically.

"Who is that?" Zack questioned.

"Macin, Calum's nephew. What am I going to tell him? I forgot to call Frank."

"*Who?*" he asked.

"I'll explain in a minute," she whispered just as Macin came down the steep staircase.

She brushed at the tears that still lingered on her cheek, and she tried her best to mask her emotions when the young boy entered the kitchen.

"Uncle Cal?" he called warily.

"Macin, he isn't here. The police asked him to go down to the station and answer some more questions. He asked me to call Frank. He wants you stay at their place until he comes home. I just need to call him real quick."

She reached for her purse and fished out the post-it note with Frank and Kathy's number scrawled across it. She found her cell phone and tried to steady her trembling fingers as she dialed. She could feel Macin's confused eyes on her, and she forced a smile. She caught sight of Zack out of the corner of her eye and an annoyed expression flitted across his face. After a few rings Frank answered, his voice sleepy, and Tarrin rushed to explain, being careful to avoid the subject of Calum being considered a possible serial killer.

Tarrin sighed her relief when the older man agreed to come right over and pick Macin up. She ended the call and smiled at the boy. "He'll be right here to get you."

"I'll go back up and get my shoes," he murmured. His shoulders slumped as he turned and ascended the stairs.

"Who is this coming over?" Zack asked.

"Frank Sloan, Calum's father," Tarrin explained.

He nodded, his lips curving into a frown. "How are Jake and Lexie?"

Tarrin shrugged. "I don't know," she replied. "I need to go check on them. I really should let Erin know what's going on. Do you mind?"

"Not at all. My team will be here any minute," he replied when she turned away. "Tarrin?" he called.

She spun to face him. "Yes?"

"Do you want me stay? I don't like the idea of you and your kids being alone."

Tarrin shook her head. "No, really, Zack." She bit her lower lip anxiously. "But, will some of your men be here?"

"Of course. I'll keep a couple men posted in the front and the back, and I have men circling the neighborhood now. But I can stay if you need me."

Tarrin exhaled and closed her eyes momentarily. "No," she answered. "We'll be fine, I think, with your men here."

Zack frowned. Rubbing a hand across his jaw, he glanced down toward his feet and said, "Alright." He shrugged. "I've got to get back to the station and make sure we get this wrapped up. My men will be here for a few hours. And like I said, I'll keep some posted nearby through the night."

"Thank you, Zack," she murmured.

He took a step toward her and reached for her hand. His hands felt cold when he squeezed her fingers. "Tarrin, you need to stay alert," he warned. "You and the kids—if you feel like you need me, just call. Come down to the station if you need to. We can fix up a place for you to stay." His eyes bore into hers. "Just be safe."

He tugged her closer, and Tarrin could feel his hot breath on her wet cheeks. With a trembling sigh, she allowed him to pull her into an embrace. He placed a kiss against her brow before she took a step away, removing her hand from his.

"I will—call—I mean—if I need anything," she assured him.

He nodded. "Okay, I need to go. I'm going to have a little chat with Sloan."

Tarrin winced. Then, with a heavy and troubled heart, she climbed the stairs. When she reached the bedroom, she knocked. The door flew open. Jake and Lexie bolted into Tarrin's arms while Erin and Macin sat on the floor, the remnants of a card game scattered near their feet. Erin placed her cards on the floor and glanced at Tarrin with worried eyes.

"Everything's going to be fine," she tried to reassure them.

"I don't want to live here anymore, Mama," Lexie replied.

The little girl wrapped her arms around Tarrin's leg, and Tarrin patted her daughter's head gently. She hugged Jake against her side, taking comfort in their familiar presence. How close had she come to losing her precious children tonight? She agreed with Lexie, she didn't want to live here either.

Jake leaned back. "Where's Calum?" he asked.

"He went with the police down to the station. They need him to answer more questions. He'll be back soon." She cringed inwardly.

Would he be back? She felt as if she were in a dream. Calum couldn't be the killer, could he? Her eyes strayed toward Macin. He moved closer to Jake, and despite his attempts to be brave, Tarrin could read the fear and worry in the young boy's expression.

"Did they arrest him? I was awake when I heard him yell at me to wake up. He came over then. He didn't do anything wrong, honest," the boy came to Calum's defense.

"I know. They don't believe he did," she lied. "They just want to find out what he saw. But, can you tell me what happened?" she asked.

Macin shrugged. "Yeah. I woke up 'cuz I heard his phone beeping. Guess he forgot to plug it in again. He went downstairs. After a minute, I heard the front door open. I looked out my window, and I saw Uncle Calum on the steps. He was looking toward your house. He came inside then, and he hollered at me to wake up, so I came downstairs. He was getting dressed. He told me to stay put, then he bolted. I stayed in the living room until he came to get me."

Tarrin nodded soberly. "That's good, Macin."

"Who was in our house, Mom? Was it the guy who killed that lady in the woods?" Jake asked.

Tarrin shook her head. "They don't know. That's what they're here to find out."

"But, Mom?"

"Just a minute, Jake. Macin?"

Macin's gaze rose to meet hers.

"Before you leave, will you speak with the detectives and tell them what you told me? Tell them what you saw and heard."

She briefly wondered if it were legal or ethical to ask him to do so, but if anything could help Calum's case, she was willing to ask. Everything in her told her Zack was wrong. *But you thought that about Travis too,* another voice reasoned. Tarrin sighed when Macin nodded.

"I want to go stay with Macin's grandpa too," Lexie murmured. "He's nice."

"Yeah, Mom. He's an ex-cop and a preacher, so we'd be safe there," Jake interjected.

"I'm with the kids on this one," Erin added quickly.

"I don't know," Tarrin's brows furrowed. "And he isn't a preacher. He's a spiritual guidance counselor," she murmured.

"So. He still has an 'in' with God," Jake returned.

What if associating with Frank and his family posed a risk to them? What if the killer followed her and the children there? Would he hurt the older man or his family?

"Hello?" a voice called from the stairs, and Tarrin turned from her thoughts.

She spun around to see Frank's head appear. He stepped into the hall and walked toward the open bedroom. His face was a mask of concern, and Tarrin greeted him with a grimace. Macin brushed past Tarrin and ran into the man's arms. The boy threw his arms about Frank's ample waist and buried his face against him.

"There, there," Frank patted Macin's back affectionately before his eyes met Tarrin's over the top of the boy's head. "Looks like there's a lot we need to discuss. Tarrin, I'd feel much better if you and your family came to my place for the rest of the night too."

"I understand, but I just . . ." Tarrin shrugged as Frank went on.

"I have the means to protect you. There's safety in numbers," he spoke. "Erin can share a room with Sarah, and we have plenty of room for you and your children. You shouldn't be alone. Besides," Frank winked toward Jake, "Kathy has eggs and sausage cookin', and I bet she's even made some flapjacks. I'm going to need some help eating all that food. What do you guys say to an early, *early* morning breakfast?"

Calum had asked her to go and stay with his father, and she had no desire to stay in the house. The police would probably stay for a while to conduct their investigation, but she briefly wondered how Zack would react.

"Please, Mama?" Lexie's voice trembled, and the sound tore at Tarrin's heart.

Her daughter was in danger. They were all in danger.

Would staying be safer? Or would there be safety in numbers as Frank had suggested? Tarrin closed her eyes, and after a moment's hesitation she nodded her agreement.

"Good. Get your stuff together. I'll speak with the detectives downstairs before we leave, and then we'll get you youngsters fed and back into a nice, soft bed," he replied with a comforting smile. "We'll talk some more at the house."

⍚

He stood still as he watched the house. He knew she was in there. She probably felt safe. He laughed. If she only knew. Angrily, he balled his hands into tight fists. Did she really think that anyone could keep her and her brats safe? If the little girl hadn't woken up, he would've had her. He'd brought the newspaper article just in case, but the knowledge that he'd missed his big opportunity sent hot anger rushing through his veins. He thought of the way Tarrin's skin felt beneath his fingers, and his nostrils flared in rage. He would make the little girl pay for interrupting his plans, and Tarrin—Tarrin would suffer for her betrayal. Did she think she was safe? He laughed bitterly, then turned, and stalked off into the darkness.

⍚

Tarrin jumped when Frank's phone rang, interrupting the quiet of the house. He stood and moved to answer it, and Tarrin waited nervously for him to return. When he returned to the kitchen, he smiled calmly.

"That was Calum. He called to say he's been let go. He thinks its best, given the circumstances, if he just comes by in the morning to get Macin. He's gone to stay at his condo tonight," he answered Tarrin's unspoken question.

Tarrin's brow furrowed, and she nodded mutely.

"He asked about you. He sounded concerned, and he said

to tell you he was thinking about you all," Frank finished.

He sat across from her, and Tarrin glanced down toward her plate of untouched food. Kathy had fed the children an hour ago and put them all to bed. At Sarah's suggestion, they all congregated in the downstairs family room with sleeping bags and pillows, and even Kathy and Frank had moved their belongings to a downstairs bedroom to remain close-by.

Sarah had made up the hide-a-bed for Tarrin and turned on a movie to help the children relax. Once the children had fallen asleep, Tarrin, Frank, and Kathy returned to the kitchen to talk. Tarrin quietly told them about the suspicions placed on Calum, and they had listened with sullen expressions.

"I don't believe it," Kathy replied.

"What do you think, Tarrin?" Frank asked calmly, but firmly.

"I don't know," she answered. "I don't believe it. Everything tells me it isn't him, but I've been wrong before. I didn't believe Travis was guilty either." She placed her head in her hands.

Kathy patted her arm, trying to offer comfort, and Frank frowned thoughtfully, then replied, "I can appreciate that. You haven't known Calum long at all, but what does your heart tell you, Tarrin? Let go of the past for a moment. I'm not speaking as his father, but as a counselor and a police officer. Sometimes you have to let go of '*facts*'. Search your heart."

Tears pooled along the brim of Tarrin's eyes, and she wiped at them, aggravated by her weakness. "I don't know," she lamented. "I don't know. I don't want to believe he's guilty." She paused then went on more calmly. "I don't think he's guilty. It doesn't feel right, but when Travis was arrested . . ."

"Tarrin, honey, I'm not trying to turn your thoughts one way or another, but think back to that moment, the very moment, when your ex-husband was arrested. You told me yourself that you'd thought things weren't quite right with your husband for some time. You said there had been warning signs, but you hadn't realized it until after the fact."

Tarrin's lips twisted, and she considered his words. Frank was right. Deep down, she had felt that something wasn't right with Travis. When he'd been arrested, if she admitted her real feelings, she had known Travis was guilty even though her mind rejected the possibility. Calum . . . She hardly knew Calum. Could she trust her heart to lead her?

Tarrin's heart, not her head, rejected the idea he was guilty of such atrocious crimes. However, she'd known Calum for mere days, whereas, she had known Travis nearly her whole life. She reflected on Zack's words. It was true serial killers came in all sorts of nicely wrapped packages. Wasn't that why they were so dangerous and able to kill so many before being caught? Everybody would reject the idea that a close friend or a loved one was capable of killing.

"I haven't really known him long," Tarrin murmured.

Frank nodded understandingly. "I realize that."

She lowered her aching head toward the table. "I don't want to believe it's him."

The older man grimaced. He ducked his head and replied slowly, "I've known Calum since he was a boy. I know his sister Jackie, and it's true, they had a rough start in life, but I know, beyond any doubt, Calum isn't guilty. But you need to follow your heart. Only you can decide what you believe. The best advice I can offer you tonight is keep a prayer in your heart and trust in the Lord to guide you," the man offered. He patted her hand, then stood. "I think it's best if we get some rest now."

Tarrin smiled wearily and nodded her head in agreement. As she fell into bed, she fervently searched her heart for the answers, and more than anything she hoped that her heart would be open enough to receive them.

෴

Calum ran a hand across his haggard face as he slid out of

his vehicle parked in front of Frank and Kathy's house. He stood on the sidewalk and glanced at his watch. It was already nine-o'clock. He'd called the office earlier to let Mary know he wouldn't be in. His adoptive mother had detected the note of strain in his voice, but he quickly made an excuse. He'd told her he wasn't feeling well. He felt guilty for the little, white lie, but in essence it was true. His head pounded, and his muscles ached with the strain of excess stress.

He had spent hours at the police station. His lawyer agreed to come right away, and Calum had been interrogated thoroughly. He knew the Seattle police department considered him a suspect, and he scowled openly. The thought made him angry, and he groaned when he thought of Marzollo and his smug face. It was obvious Marzollo had taken an immediate dislike to him, and he in turn felt the same of Marzollo. However, the man's open antagonism left Calum worried. His shoulders fell as he strode across the lawn toward his father's newer, modest home.

He was relieved Tarrin and her family had agreed to stay with them. It helped ease much of his worry the night before. He ascended the stone stairs and rang the doorbell. He heard footsteps draw near, and the door opened wide. Calum took a step back in surprise when Macin shot out of the house and fell into his arms.

Calum knew this ordeal was taking a real toll on the boy. It was bad enough his mother was clear across the globe, but now his uncle was being considered a serial killer. His frown deepened and he patted Macin's back just as Lexie and Jake appeared. Jake smiled and waved while Lexie ran to Calum's side. Tarrin appeared in the entryway, and she watched with wide eyes as Lexie wrapped her arms firmly about Calum's leg. Tarrin's mouth opened in surprise. Macin pulled away and Lexie stretched her arms up toward Calum. With a quiet chuckle he lifted the girl into his arms, then met Tarrin's eye warily. What did she think of him? Did she think he was guilty too? They regarded one another for a long moment. Varying emotions flitted across her expressive face. She walked forward slowly, and he felt pleasantly surprised when she fell against his side.

"I'm glad you're back," she whispered.

Calum set Lexie on her feet, and with a sigh, he pulled Tarrin in against him, holding her trembling body. He caught Frank's eye over the top of her head, and the old man grinned knowingly. Calum returned the smile then kissed the top of Tarrin's head. He could smell the sweet scent of her shampoo, and he breathed in while he held her close. He was quickly falling in love with Tarrin Grace. The thought took him by surprise.

She pulled back after a moment and he cupped her cheek in his large hand. "Tarrin, you know, don't you, that I couldn't . . . I would never harm you or do *anything* like this."

Lexie wrapped her arms around Calum's leg once again, and he glanced down at the little girl, then back toward Tarrin. She studied him for a moment. Her eyes searched his before she nodded slowly.

"I know," she whispered.

He licked his lips, and then slowly, he leaned in and kissed her. His own spontaneity took him by surprise as his kiss deepened. His heart thundered in his chest while he tried to gauge her reaction. When he pulled back, she smiled shyly, and he released a tightly held breath.

"Come on in, son. Kathy has some more breakfast waiting," Frank called when Calum and Tarrin drew apart.

Calum smiled a little, relieved. He stooped to pull Lexie off his leg and into his arms. The girl grinned. She touched his cheek with her soft, little hand and he gazed into her innocent face. "What do you say, princess? Are you hungry?"

Lexie smiled and nodded. Calum turned to face Tarrin, and he grasped her hand in his as they followed Frank into the kitchen.

☙

Tarrin stared thoughtfully toward the Sloan's backyard. Jake, Macin, and Lexie were giggling as they bounced on the large trampoline. It felt good to see her children smiling and care-free after such a difficult night. She laughed when Jake attempted a lopsided flip, just as she felt Calum come up behind her. She held her breath when he placed a hand against her waist, and she smiled when he caught her gaze in the glass door's reflection.

Her heart fluttered when he turned her around to face him. "How are you feeling?" he asked.

She studied his haggard expression for a minute. She did not believe he was a serial killer. Zack was wrong. He had to be. "I'm okay."

Calum's eyebrows rose. "Good." He nodded, then whispered, "Now how about the truth?"

Her shoulders relaxed a fraction. "Honestly," she answered, "I'm tired. I'm tired of being scared."

Calum pulled her into an embrace and she rested her head against his hard chest. She could hear the heavy pulsation of his heart, and she listened to his lungs as he breathed in and out, deep and even. She felt peace in his arms. She felt safety in his presence. Being near him felt right, and for the first time, in a long time, she felt the volatile, novel stirrings of new love. *Zack is wrong,* she thought.

"What are we going to do, Calum?" she spoke against his chest.

He drew in a deep breath then exhaled. "I think—"

"Well, I personally think there's no sense dwelling on what you can't change," Frank interrupted. "We don't have a lot of options concerning this current situation," he spoke from across the room.

Calum released Tarrin, and they turned to face the older man.

"I say, you both have the day off, so why don't you two go

163

on out and enjoy it? Don't let this maniac keep you holed up," Frank suggested, giving Calum a pointed look. "Besides, I have a bit of bad news."

Tarrin tensed immediately.

"A friend of mine in the department just called," Frank went on. "The press caught wind of this. They'll be here in a matter of minutes, I'm sure."

Tarrin inhaled sharply. "No," she breathed.

Calum reached for her hand as Frank continued, "Calum, I think you and Tarrin need to leave the city. At least for the day. You'll be safer."

Tarrin's brow creased, and Calum frowned while he considered Frank's words.

"It's a beautiful day, Calum. Why don't you take Tarrin and the children to the coast? Westport or Port Angeles, maybe," Kathy suggested.

"I can't handle the press," Tarrin replied. She couldn't stand the thought of her family being splashed all over the news once again. The thought terrified her. "I'll need to talk it over with Zack first, but—" She jumped a little when she heard Calum swear loudly.

"Why?" He suddenly turned to face her.

Tarrin's eyes widened a fraction as she faced his frustrated expression. "What?"

"Why do you need to talk it over with Marzollo?" he questioned with a scowl.

Startled, Tarrin raised her eyes to his. "Well, I thought—"

"Those goons of his aren't doing you a bit of good, Tarrin, and I don't trust Marzollo!" he replied.

"Calum, I understand why you feel that way, but . . ." She paused, and her eyes closed briefly.

"I can take care of you and the kids today. Leave Marzollo out of it. Please?" he asked. "You can trust me, can't you?"

He rubbed his temple wearily. Tarrin realized he was drained. Dark, half-moon circles shadowed his eyes, and she bit her lip. "Yes, Calum, I do trust you," she replied. "And it would be nice to get away for a while, without a police escort, but I'm just not sure." How would Zack react if he found out she had snuck away from town with their prime suspect?

Calum shook his head and raked his fingers through his thick hair. His expression looked haunted when he spoke. "Tarrin, they're trying to pin this on me. Marzollo hasn't liked me from the beginning." He groaned. "He's determined to make me a suspect only because they have no other leads. I'm sorry. I understand if you feel safer speaking with him first. I don't mind. Really."

Tarrin glanced at Frank and the old man smiled encouragingly. Was she making the right choice? Would it be better to leave the detectives out of their plans? Tarrin knew Zack wouldn't agree. In fact, he would be incredibly against her going with Calum. Calum was right, after all, he was their main suspect.

"If you aren't comfortable going alone with me, I understand." Calum sighed. "I mean, I am their 'probable' suspect, right?" he finished, and Tarrin could read the despair in his eyes.

Her mouth turned down into a frown and she considered her options carefully. She didn't want to let the killer corner her by keeping her and the children shut in and hidden, and she certainly couldn't handle facing the press, but would she risk her and the children's lives if they ventured out to the beach? A day away from the city could help clear her mind, and she knew the children needed a break from the situation as much as she did.

"Like I said," Frank spoke. "You'll be safer if you leave the city for a bit. I'm not trying to tell you what to do, but you need to get out from under Marzollo's men, just for a while. I have some phone calls to make. I have connections Marzollo doesn't have. And the beach will be crowded. This guy isn't likely to try anything in a crowd that size," he added. "You risk more by staying cooped up in the house. There's strength in numbers. In the meantime, I'm going to get a few old friends searching the streets—looking into leads Marzollo might have missed. "

Tarrin nodded slowly before she turned to face Calum. "Okay," she answered. "Honestly, I would really like to leave. I can't face the press, and Frank's right. Maybe he can get more information than Zack has." Her eyes briefly met the older man's and he smiled, nodding his agreement.

CHAPTER *Twelve*

arrin knew she had made the right decision to spend the day with Calum on the beach. They had avoided the journalists as far as they knew. Her body relaxed visibly when they left the bustling city behind them and drove toward the west coast. She could hear the children snickering in the back seat, and she cast a quick glance their way. Jake and Macin's heads were bent over Macin's portable video game system. Lexie held tightly to her sand bucket as she stared out the window with an excited expression.

Erin had decided to stay behind for the day and explore the University's campus with Sarah, while she and Calum took the children out for the day—away from the city and away from the press. She worried about leaving her sister behind, but Frank assured her Erin and Sarah would be safe. He'd arranged for an old friend to stay with them during their trip to campus, and knowing Erin had a police escort helped to ease her mind. Kathy had packed a generous picnic lunch, and Jake and Lexie eagerly loaded their swim gear and buckets into the trunk of Calum's vehicle. Tarrin had to admit, despite the horrific events the night before, the day held an air of excitement, and she smiled before she turned back to face the front.

Calum cast her a sideways glance and he grinned before he asked, "What are you thinking?"

Tarrin sighed. "I was just thinking how much we needed this," she replied.

"We did, didn't we?"

Her lips twisted thoughtfully. "It's nice to see open spaces again. I'm not used to cities," she admitted.

"I understand that. I used to live in Port Angeles, and I loved it. It was quiet—peaceful. I bought the condo for convenience after my divorce, but one day, I'd like to sell it and settle out here again," he admitted. Then after a moment of silence, he said, "We're coming up on Aberdeen. There are some fun, little antique stores in town. Do you want to stop?"

"Yes, I'd love to."

It didn't take long to reach the port-city of Aberdeen. She smiled when they entered the quaint logging town situated at the very tip of Grays Harbor County. Tidal lands met river, and a sea of trees surrounded the picturesque town. Calum drove through the narrow side streets, and Tarrin delighted in turn of the century homes, weather-beaten fishing boats, and harbor-side businesses. He pulled into the parking lot of a charming antique store, and he and Tarrin stepped out onto the graveled drive. The small pebbles crunched under her feet and she waited for the children to join them.

"Can we just wait out here?" Jake asked, eyeing the store with distaste.

"Yeah, we'll just crash on the grass," Macin added.

Calum shook his head. "Considering the circumstances— not a chance. Come in and sit by the door."

The boys frowned, and Calum led the way to the front of the store. He held the door open and ushered them inside. A little bell above the entrance jangled softly to announce their presence.

"Have you ever been in here?" Tarrin questioned.

"No." Calum shook his head.

"This is neat," Lexie murmured. "Look at the pretty dolls, Mama."

Tarrin walked toward a display of antique dolls and studied their aged faces. "They are pretty."

Calum moved behind them, then kneeling next to Lexie, he whispered, "Pick one."

"Oh," Tarrin spoke. "No, Calum. They're too much."

"Tarrin," he smiled. "Let her pick one."

"Really?" Lexie asked, studying the dolls. "I can really have one?"

"Sure." Calum pointed toward a pretty blond doll. "What about that one?" he asked.

"She's perfect," Lexie whispered. "She looks like a princess."

"Just like you." Calum patted the top of Lexie's head then stood to face Tarrin.

Tarrin shook her head. "Calum, you don't need to do that."

"I know I don't. I want to." He grasped her hand in his and led her toward a shelf filled with antique fishing gear. He studied the display and picked out a few items.

After studying the interesting array of antiques, Tarrin turned to face him. "I didn't realize you collect old fishing gear."

He shrugged. "I found a couple of old floats when I was a kid, and I've collected ever since."

"Where did you find those?" Tarrin asked, intrigued.

"You can find them once in a great while along the beach. I hitchhiked out to the coast once, when I was living with another foster family in Tacoma. I stayed out there for days, picking through the garbage cans and fighting with the seagulls for scraps of food.

"I found this little cove with cave-like holes in the cliffs and a fresh water stream." He picked through the items on the shelf nonchalantly while he talked. "I felt just like Robinson Crusoe on my own little deserted island," he laughed. "I collected a float, just like this, when it washed ashore." He held up a blue-colored glass ball. "I found a couple of antique wooden floats too. I still have them." He smiled. "They're some of the only things I have left from my childhood. I don't have a huge collection, but I have some neat pieces. You'll . . . uh . . . have to come by the condo sometime and see." He looked at her.

"I'd like that," she answered, then laughed. "I can't believe you ran away. How did you get back?"

Calum grinned. "They found me. Some local fishermen noticed me coming and going, so they called the cops. By that time, I wasn't too put out either. I was hungry. I wanted to go back, and at the time, I didn't realize how dangerous it was either."

"Wow." Tarrin laughed a little.

Her brow furrowed as she thought about what Zack had revealed concerning Calum the night before, but she quickly shook the thought away when he asked, "What about you? Did you ever get into any sort of scrape as a kid? What were you like?" He grinned as they continued to explore the narrow aisles.

"I was . . . well, I wasn't shy," she laughed. "I was a feisty little tom-boy actually."

"You were?" Calum's eyes broadened.

Tarrin nodded. "I did get myself into a few scrapes. Not like yours, but I caused my parents a lot of problems sometimes."

"Like what?" Calum encouraged.

"Well, one time, when I was eight, I went camping with my family. The river was swollen and running pretty high, so Mom and Dad warned us not to get too close. I promised I wouldn't, but I did." She smiled, remembering. "I snuck away from the campsite one afternoon, and while I was playing on the bank I slipped and fell in. The current was *so* strong. I wasn't a very good swimmer and the current kept pulling me under. I called for help, but nobody could hear. No one knew where I had gone. I thought for sure I was going to die. Then my shirt snagged on a tree branch hanging in the river.

"It caught me, and I used the branch to pull myself back onto the bank." She laughed. "I tried to sneak back into camp, but I was shivering and soaking wet. Karen found me and told my parents. They had a fit, but I didn't care. I was alive," she finished.

She hadn't thought about that event in her life for many years, and suddenly Tarrin could see the parallel with the recent events. Her life felt like the rushing river. She felt as if she were being carried away on a swift current she couldn't control. How was this new turmoil in her life going to end? When would it end?

Calum held her gaze, and she smiled just a little. He squeezed her fingers, but remained silent while they continued shopping. They paid for their items, and Tarrin grimaced when the kindly cashier rang up the antique doll Lexie clutched to her chest. Calum reassured her again and Lexie grinned.

"I love her!" the little girl announced when they exited the store. "I'm going to name her Poppy."

"Poppy? That's perfect!" Calum said, helping her with her seat belt.

Tarrin's heart warmed to see Lexie so happy, and she thanked Calum once again. "You don't know how happy you made her."

ᐂ

The ride to Ocean Shores was breathtaking. Once to the beach, the children and Tarrin were amazed at the huge beachside resorts and expansive panorama of coastline. Thousands of people lined the seaside.

"Wow, look at all the pretty kites, Mama," Lexie spoke as they stared at the conglomeration of beach goers, all engaged in various activities.

"Do you like kites?" Calum asked when he came around the side of the car.

Lexie smiled and nodded, running to him with a wide grin. Calum swung the little girl high into his arms and then placed her atop his broad shoulders. Lexie laughed happily, and she smiled down at Tarrin. Tarrin returned her smile, shocked her daughter had grown attached to Calum so quickly. She felt pleased she had. Seeing her daughter's eyes full of life again made her heart soar. She loved Lexie's familiar, beautiful smile.

"Hey, man! Come on!" Tossing his game system into the Honda's trunk, Macin grabbed a football.

Jake ran after him, and Calum called, "Macin, stay close kid."

"Yeah, no problem," he returned.

Tarrin watched the boy's race toward the water's edge. The

view of the Pacific was spectacular, and sunlight shimmered against the cresting waves in the distance. She caught sight of a few surfers attempting to ride the swelling waves and she pointed toward the water.

"Look, Lex, surfers," she said.

"Wow!" Lexie exclaimed while she sat high on Calum's shoulders.

"Should we find a spot to spread the blanket?" he questioned.

"Sure," Tarrin answered.

"*And* I brought a kite just for you, Lexie. Do you think we can get it to fly?" he asked, pulling a multi-colored kite from the trunk.

Lexie squealed in anticipation when she saw the rolled up, colorful fabric. "Is it a big kite?"

"Probably bigger than you, pipsqueak!"

Lexie giggled her reply, and Tarrin laughed. It felt good to laugh. She could feel the tension leaving her body as she pulled Kathy's old-style picnic basket from the trunk. Calum led the way toward an open spot along the sandy beach. She spread out the giant patchwork quilt Kathy had packed and watched with a grin as Lexie scrambled from Calum's shoulders to join Jake and Macin at the water's edge.

Calum and Tarrin sat in comfortable silence while they kept an eye on the three children splashing in the foaming surf. Jake laughed when a wave soaked him to the knees, and Macin tossed the football into an oncoming swell. The boys dove into the water after the ball. Lexie squealed in delight when the water rushed around her skinny ankles. The little girl glanced toward Tarrin. Her face lit up, and she giggled and waved before she turned back toward the ocean.

Tarrin relaxed against the blanket. A faint brine-scented breeze brushed past, stirring the strands of hair that had escaped the confines of her elastic. She brushed them from off her forehead and smiled. The sun felt warm—comforting—and the evils of the past few days seemed almost distant. It was wonderful to see her children smiling and carefree. Lexie raced toward the spot where Calum and Tarrin sat. Grasping her bucket and doll, she rushed back toward her brother and Macin. Macin sloshed out from the water and sat next to Lexie. Tarrin watched, a smile hovering on her lips, while he helped the little girl build a sandcastle.

"He's a great kid. I'm happy he and Jake get along so well," Tarrin commented.

Calum nodded. "He is, isn't he? I'm going to miss him when Jackie comes home."

"I bet," she murmured. "Jake has a great time with him."

"He likes Jake. Your kids are wonderful. Lexie's a little angel. She looks just like you." Tarrin smiled softly, and Calum reached for her hand. "Despite everything that's happened, I'm glad you're here," he added.

"So am I. I couldn't handle this alone. Calum, if you weren't here . . ." She shrugged.

"I'm not much help. I wish I could do more." He leaned back on his elbows and stared out toward the water.

"Just having you near is enough," she murmured. He smiled a little. "Is this the beach where you came when you ran away?" she asked after another moment passed.

Calum's smile broadened. "No, I ended up on some secluded beach in Ilwaco, near Astoria. I was a long way from home," he admitted. "It's a beautiful area though. I've gone back a few times. I'd love to show you one day."

"I'd like that," Tarrin replied. "One day." *One day*, she repeated silently. Would they have a 'one day'? Would she ever be free of the maniac who was determined to ruin her life? She'd love to spend more time with Calum, but she wanted to spend time with him free of fear and uncertainty.

He turned to glance her way, and his mouth curved into a frown. He sat up and asked, "Tarrin, does Lexie remember anything from that day?"

Her eyes swung to meet his, and she regarded him closely.

"The reason I'm asking," he went on. "They have me pinned as a suspect." He sighed. "I have a good lawyer, but Marzollo is determined to make a case against me. It would help if Lexie could recall something. Any detail at all," he finished.

"I'm sorry, Calum. She doesn't. We met with a psychologist on Monday, but nothing really came of it. We have another appointment in a few days, but I only wanted the doctor to conduct sessions with Lexie once a week. I didn't want to push her, but considering everything, maybe I should try again."

He nodded, returning his eyes toward the vast ocean. Tarrin followed his gaze to the horizon. A small plane flew low over the water. The hum of the engine pulsed through the air. She loved the sound of airplanes. The sound was soothing to her jagged nerves, and she listened as the vibrations of the engine faded into the distance while she thought about all the indiscretions Zack accused Calum of. There were so many questions playing through her mind. She chewed her bottom lip, then spoke, "Calum?"

He caught her eye, and his brow rose. "What is it?"

"Can I ask you a personal question?"

"Anything." He sat up straighter.

"Zack told me . . . He told me that . . ." She paused.

Calum's broad shoulders fell and a frown darkened his face. "What did Marzollo tell you?"

"He said you had a criminal record. He said you had a couple of arrests, including a felony," Tarrin rushed to explain.

Calum licked his lips. His brow furrowed. "So that's it? That's Marzollo's angle?" He raked a hand through his hair. "He's right. I *had* a criminal record," he admitted.

"Can you tell me about it?" she questioned.

"Yes," he responded. "I told you about my childhood?"

Tarrin nodded and waited for him to go on.

Calum frowned in thought. "I also told you I had a few

rough years, as a teen. I was arrested three times. Once when I was fifteen, again at sixteen, and the last time was right before I turned eighteen. I stole a car and was charged as an adult, but my charge was later reduced from a felony to a misdemeanor, and since then, I've had all these charges expunged."

"What happened?" Tarrin pressed when he paused.

"When I was fifteen the state let Jackie and I go home with our mom, but things weren't better. I really struggled. I didn't know which direction I wanted my life to go, and really, I'd known no other life. The foster parents who Jackie and I had been living with were great, and I'd had a small taste of a very different life—a life that was alien to me. I wanted *that* life, and it made me angry that I couldn't be born into that sort of situation instead. It made me angry that my own mother couldn't give up her need for drugs to give me that kind of life.

"I was having an identity crisis, like I said. So we'd been living with our mom again for about a month when things turned from bad to worse. Her boyfriend moved in, and she started using again. Things were tough to deal with. Eventually, I joined a gang. It wasn't like belonging to the major drug gangs or anything, but we made mischief. I was caught lifting a watch and a box of donuts from a K-Mart. They arrested me, and I served some community service, of course. After that, the state stepped in again." He paused and his mouth twisted.

Tarrin could read the pain in his eyes as he recounted his past, and her heart ached for the child who Calum had been. She remained silent while he continued.

"Jackie and I found ourselves in yet another foster home. This time it just wasn't a good fit. I struggled to keep the right sort of friends. I struggled to do the right things to keep people happy. Trust me, I understand all too well what it's like to be shunned for a past that is out of your control." He frowned and shook his head. "When I was sixteen, I was on my fourth or fifth home. I fell in with another bad lot and got caught during a graffiti sting. A few of the

175

guys I was with were caught with drugs. I never touched the stuff, but I took the fall with them. Another kid in our group was packing a nine-millimeter he'd lifted off his brother. That kind of sealed my fate.

"I served a month in juvenile detention for that. Then, after my month in juvy, they shipped me off to a new family. They sent me and Jackie to separate homes. That was the hardest part—being separated for so long. Right before my eighteenth birthday, I decided I'd had enough. I was sick of being shuffled from one family to the next. Jackie and I'd both had enough, so one day, I stole my foster parent's car and I picked up Jackie. We hatched up this crazy plan that we'd head out East. I'd get a job, and we could find a cheap place to live. She'd stolen a big wad of cash from her foster family, and we really thought we had a fool-proof plan." He laughed humorlessly.

"What happened?" Tarrin encouraged. She reached over to grasp his hand in hers.

He squeezed her fingers. "We didn't make it far before we were caught." He paused, then a smile touched his lips. "Frank was the arresting officer. That was when he and Mary stepped in. They changed our lives. So Marzollo's right about *one* thing. I do have a criminal record. Jackie and I have both struggled with the ghosts leftover from our childhood, but my past does *not* define who I am now. I've never believed in profiling. I might have a rough background, but it doesn't mean I've turned into a killer—a cold, heartless murderer," he finished, his voice rough with emotion.

Tarrin's heart wrenched when he finished the story of his difficult past. She knew it was not easy for him to recount. Her heart ached for the young Calum and again, she was grateful for people like Mary and Frank, who were so willing to lay aside their reserves and judgments and open their hearts and homes for children like Calum and Jackie.

She wondered if she would have the strength to do what Mary and Frank had done in adopting two troubled teens. Her own childhood had been quite easy considering Calum's difficult past. At times it had been a burden to be the oldest of seven children. Her parents were unnaturally strict, but they had provided a good home where she and her brothers and sisters always felt safe and loved.

Tarrin suddenly realized that her immature grief over missing extracurricular activities so she could help care for her younger siblings paled in comparison to other children's difficult lives. Her divorce had been a nightmare, but she had her family to lean on. They were always there to offer their comfort and advice.

She raised her troubled eyes to meet Calum's. "Thank you for telling me. I believe you, Calum. I wouldn't be here if I believed you were a killer," she replied.

His brow knit. "That means a lot. I may have a troubled past, but I'm no psychopath. Marzollo is barking up the wrong tree, and he better get his act together so they can put the real killer behind bars."

Tarrin's gaze fell toward the children, who were still laboring over their sand castle. Jake sat in a huge hole with only his head and the tops of his shoulders visible. Macin and Lexie worked to build a sand wall. She inhaled deeply before she turned back to face Calum.

"Calum," she whispered. "I'm so worried. So scared. How could that man get inside my house? The dead bolt was still set. The only way through that door was with a key. How did he get a key? I keep mine with me all the time, and I know Erin does the same."

Calum leaned back on his elbows. "I don't know." He shook his head. "I wish I had some answers. I've worried over the same thing. It was too dark to see well. I should have gone out the minute I saw him cross the street. I should have done *something*. This could all be over with if I had just acted more quickly."

"Or you could be dead, and I'd still be in just as much danger—or worse. He was so close," she whispered and her face grew pale when she thought about how near she'd come to losing all that was so precious to her.

Calum shook his head, and they both wrestled with their troubled thoughts in silence. The deep, guttural roar of breaking surf mixed with the sound of gentle waves helped calm her troubled mind. Gulls cried loudly as they fought for scraps of food. People all around them laughed and talked. Parents chased their young children, and teenagers played Frisbee and volleyball in the sand. A few motorized scooters zipped past along the hard packed sand, and she watched while they darted up the beach and disappeared into the mist.

"Hey, didn't we come here to have a good time and forget our troubles, if only for a little while?" Calum suddenly spoke. The frown disappeared and a good-natured grin spread across his handsome face.

Tarrin's shoulders relaxed. "We did," she replied.

He nodded toward the kids' haphazard sand castle. "What do you say we go show those three how it's done, huh?"

CHAPTER *Thirteen*

He kept a close eye on Tarrin. A slow smile touched his handsome features. Did she believe a day at the beach was safe? Sometimes her callowness shocked him. Did she think she even had the remotest chance of escaping him? She was right where he wanted her. No one escaped him. *No one*! He never failed, and he would not fail with her. He chuckled as he watched her eyes light with pleasure.

She played alongside the children, and she laughed when she tried to escape an oncoming swell. The frigid water rushed up around her ankles and the kids' laughter joined hers.

"Oh, no!" Her sweet voice sounded in his ears as the receding tide washed away the remains of their sand castle.

He loved to hear her laugh. He loved to see the light in her eyes—and the fear. He chuckled. Nothing brought him as much pleasure as seeing her vibrant eyes fill with terror, and soon the laughter would fade. Fear would fill the depth of her soul.

That smile spread across her face would disappear, and her full, soft lips would tremble with dread. Did she think she could escape *him*? It would be easy to get her away from the throngs of people occupying the beach. Just a few carefully chosen words were all it would take, and then she would be his. His eyes closed as he envisioned her last moments. He could clearly picture her face in his mind—how she would look, and the words she would say.

Tarrin would be determined to live. He could imagine how her eyes would spark with anger, and her face would light with purpose. She would fight him, he knew that. He looked forward to the struggle, but she would not escape. He had planned it just right, and the beach would work wonderfully for what he had in mind. He grinned at his turn of luck. Yes, his plan was perfect. He would wait. He knew he would find the opportune moment to enact his plan.

Her death was inevitable. *Funny,* he thought, *that a moment of error has led to such an enticing game.* He hadn't known when he began his quest to silence the little girl that he would fall in love with her mother. A frown suddenly touched his lips. His feelings for Tarrin were something he had never before experienced, and certainly he had never planned to fall in love with her. He wondered if it would be a real letdown after it all ended. The thought suddenly sobered him.

03

Tarrin laughed out loud as another swell rushed across the sand. She breathed in as the icy water of the Pacific swirled about her ankles and rose above her knees. Lexie squealed with delight and she raced up the sandy beach, trying to escape the water. Calum caught the little girl as she ran into his arms, giggling with delight. He lifted her high into the air when the gentle surf approached.

"Over here," Macin called as he and Jake ran deeper into the water.

The boys splashed wildly while they tossed the football back and forth. Tarrin grinned when Jake fumbled the ball and fell back, disappearing beneath a wave for a brief moment. He stood and shook the salt water from his face, blinking.

"Hey, Uncle Cal?" Macin reached for the ball, then tucked it under his arm.

"What d'ya want, kid?" Calum replied with a chuckle.

"Let's go do that horseback ride thing. Mom took me last time we came. It was awesome," Macin replied.

"Horseback ride, huh?"

"Oh, yes! Pleeeeease?" Lexie grinned and grasped Calum's face between her palms. She looked him in the eye as she begged,

"Can we, Calum. Can we?"

Calum smiled into Lexie's face, and he squeezed her tightly before he glanced at Tarrin.

"What do you think?" he asked. "I mean, how do I say *no* to this?" he smiled at Lexie.

"Cool," Jake interjected. "That would be awesome. Can we, Mom?"

Tarrin shrugged. "I don't know. I've never been on a horse before."

"You were born and raised in Colorado, and you've never ridden a horse?" Calum asked.

She shrugged and smiled self-consciously. "No, never."

"Can we please, Mama?" Lexie asked again.

"Well, I don't know. I guess we could give it a try," Tarrin responded after a moment deliberation, and Jake whooped excitedly.

He and Macin raced out of the water, splashing Tarrin when they passed. Tarrin and Calum followed, and Lexie wrapped her arms around Calum's neck. He smiled at Tarrin then reached out to grasp her waist as they followed behind the boys. The walk to the stables was pleasant. They took well-worn paths that cut across the dunes. She was amazed at the abundant vegetation that thrived in the soft sand.

"The plants protect the beach. The grass holds down the sand with its root system." Calum explained when she asked about the abundant flora.

"This is amazing. It's absolutely beautiful," she replied in awe, taking in the panorama of grey-blue waters and cresting waves.

Calum stopped for a moment and followed her gaze toward the horizon. "It is, isn't it? This is by far one of my favorite— this one, Ilwaco, and Ruby beach."

"Ruby beach?" Tarrin questioned.

"It's a beach on the Olympic Peninsula. It's honestly," he

shrugged, "amazing. You'd love it. There are sea stacks, tide pools, and the sunsets are . . . well, amazing." He laughed.

"I'll have to keep that in mind."

"I'll take you before summer's end, if you'd like," he suggested.

Her stomach twisted pleasantly at the thought of spending more time with him and a smile touched her lips. "I can't think of anything else I'd rather do," she replied.

Calum studied her face for a brief moment, then he spoke, "Neither can I."

She felt heat rush to her cheeks and her smile broadened. She hugged her stomach then jumped when Lexie suddenly squealed, "There they are! There are the horses. Oh, I want the white one! Can I, Calum?" she asked, her voice rising in pitch.

Tarrin laughed at her daughter's eager expression. Calum chuckled as he swung the girl down from off his broad shoulders. While Lexie bounded ahead, Tarrin reached over to brush the sand from his shirt left by Lexie's bare feet. Calum caught Tarrin's hand in his and held her fingers against his hard chest. She could feel his heart beating beneath his shirt, and she held her breath when he bent closer. He kissed her upturned lips slowly. Tarrin could taste the ocean on his skin, and she closed her eyes and sighed when his lips left hers to explore her face. He trailed gentle kisses along her cheekbones and after breathless moments, he pulled back and grinned into her wide-eyed expression.

"There. I've wanted to do that all day," he chuckled.

"You have?" she whispered.

He nodded. "I have. And, honestly," he inhaled, "I feel like a teenager again. I get nervous, tongue-tied, and sweaty-palmed every time I get near you. I haven't felt this way in a long time, Tarrin."

"Neither have I," she admitted. "Travis . . ." She caught her bottom lip between her teeth for a few seconds then went on. "Travis and I were together for so long, I'm not sure I know how to do this anymore—you know, date after all these years."

Calum stared at her for a long moment before he reached out to cup her face. He rubbed his thumb along the ridge of her cheekbone. "It's not too hard." He held her gaze. "We can take as much time as you need to get used to the idea of dating." He chuckled. "That is, if you feel the same?"

His expression grew suddenly guarded, and Tarrin's heart fluttered. She drew a shaky, shallow breath. "I think I do. I mean—I know I do, but I'm . . ." She dropped her eyes toward the ground. "I'm so scared, Calum." She suddenly laughed. Her laughter sounded hollow—humorless. "And I'm not talking about being stalked by a serial killer either."

Calum grimaced. "I understand, and if I ever make you feel uncomfortable—"

She shook her head. "You don't," she added quickly. "I'm glad you're here. You don't know what it means to me to have you near through all of this."

His mouth twisted and his brow furrowed. "Please don't think if you didn't feel the same way that I wouldn't be here. I'll be here no matter your feelings, to help you through this."

"I know that. That's why it means so much to me."

He glanced down and nodded before he reached for her hand. They strolled toward the stables. Tarrin smiled when she saw Lexie bouncing up and down near the stalls. "This one! I want this one, see?"

Lexie's enthusiasm was contagious, and Tarrin laughed. "I haven't seen her talk this much in a long time. It's nice to see her smiling again."

"Calum! Mama! See?" Lexie called.

Calum winked at Tarrin when he called back, "He's all yours."

☙

It wasn't hard to keep her in sight, and when her mount

cantered ahead of the little group, he nudged his horse, increasing the animal's gait in order to keep her in his line of vision. Tarrin laughed, and the 'little princess' squealed in delight. Her eyes sparkled with excitement. He could tell Tarrin was nervous sitting atop the large animal. Her arms were wrapped tightly about Lexie, but the rush of the new experience left her face flushed—exhilarated. What an ideal time to enact his arrangement. What an experience it would be to watch her flushed, excited face suddenly plunge into lines of fear and despair. It would be easy to separate her and Lexie from the group. He laughed.

He loved watching her. He loved the way her hair whipped about her face, and the way her golden locks shimmered in the sunlight. He loved the way her eyes lit with pleasure. He smirked. It was amusing to him that she could so easily let go of reality—that she could forget him so effortlessly. Didn't she realize the danger she was in?

He suddenly groaned when his emotions quickly turned. Didn't she realize how close he was to her? Couldn't she sense him nearby? Why had she so easily forgotten him and the danger he posed? He frowned and ducked his head to hide his emotions. His brows furrowed, and he breathed in, deep and evenly. She'd forgotten him, but soon, very soon, he would graciously help her remember.

She would beg for mercy. She would plead for her life, and he would make her grovel. Killing the kid left a bitter taste in his mouth, but that would only add to Tarrin's grief. How could she abandon her fear of him so easily?

He raised his head slowly, plastering a smile on his face. Tarrin's laughter floated across him like a soothing balm. He would miss her laughter and her smile. He closed his eyes better to remember the sound. He would reflect on her smiling face and remember her laugh in the dark hours of his life. She would be his forever. No other victim touched his heart the way Tarrin Grace had.

☙

"Faster, Mama! Let's go faster!" Lexie tapped Tarrin's arm.

"Okay, hang on," Tarrin replied.

The horse rocked gently underneath her and water sprayed against her legs as the animal galloped through the surf. The misty air brushed across her face, and her heart beat excitedly when she reined the beautiful horse to a slow walk. She glanced back and laughed when Calum and Jake's horses caught up. She grinned when Jake's wild, excited eyes met hers.

"Pretty good riding," Tarrin called to him.

"You too, Mom."

Calum's horse drew level with theirs, and his gaze raked across Tarrin's wind-chapped cheeks and disheveled hair. "So what do think?" he asked.

"I loooove it!" Lexie jumped in, hugging her new doll against her chest. Tarrin caught Calum's knowing glance.

He chuckled then looked back toward the rest of the group. A few other riders had joined their small party. He had been quick to befriend two older, white-haired sisters and a middle-aged hippie type, who was the last to join their riding group. Macin rode with the others, but he soon separated from the group and caught up with Calum and Tarrin.

"Hey! You guys go fast," he breathed and reined in his horse near Calum's.

"I rode horses with my scout troop all the time before we moved," Jake answered.

Calum pointed ahead. "Why don't we go farther up toward those stacks in the distance? The tides out, and we'll get a good look at a few tide pools. What do you think?"

"Oh, yes," Tarrin answered, and Lexie's exclamation of approval joined hers.

Calum nudged his horse into a quick canter, and Tarrin's mount eagerly followed. Jake and Macin hung back, and she could hear their friendly banter. She was glad her children were having such a magnificent time. She was thoroughly enjoying herself. The Pacific Coast was as beautiful as she imagined it would be, and she delighted in all the new experiences this day had brought for both her and her children. She wished Erin were here to enjoy the day as well, but she couldn't wait to come back with her sister. She suddenly wondered what Erin would have to say about the changes the day had brought about in her relationship with Calum.

She studied Calum's back as she followed him. She loved the way his thick muscles bulged beneath his t-shirt, and his dark, damp hair glistened in the sun. He was undoubtedly a very handsome man, and the thought of his brief kiss left her feeling volatile. She was grateful their lives had touched, and she hoped she could find the strength to follow her heart.

She didn't want the pain of Travis's betrayal and unfaithfulness to jade the way she felt about Calum. Her feelings for him were genuine, but did she really have the strength to let go of the ghosts of her past and move forward into a future with Calum? Could she learn to trust and love again? He turned just then and caught her eye.

Her heart skipped erratically, and she blushed. She hoped she could learn to let go of her pain and trust in others once again. It would not be easy, but she felt more hopeful than she had in a very long time, and she clung to that hope.

"Here we are," Calum called, reigning in his horse.

He came to a stop near a black, jagged rock and Tarrin slowed her horse just as he dismounted. He ambled toward her to help lift Lexie down off the large animal. Setting the little girl onto the sand, he reached for Tarrin's waist, assisting her from the horse. He kept his hands against her hip for a moment longer than necessary, and his eyes bore into hers. She blushed a little before turning away, then took a step back to take in the view ahead. Craggy monoliths rose toward blue sky. Gnarled trees grew along the ridges, and mist rose like a curtain as waves crashed against the surface of a weathered cliff in the distance.

"This is beautiful," she gasped.

"The tide is out now, but soon this whole area will be underwater. Do you want to see the tide pools before we eat?" he asked.

"I'm starving!" Macin's voice broke through their conversation when he and Jake drew near.

Jake slid off his horse, and Calum tethered the animals to a large driftwood log. He removed their picnic lunch from the saddle bags. "Where's the rest of the group?" he asked.

"Scattered along back there," Macin answered. "A couple of people stopped to collect shells and some sand dollars, and a couple more people took the trail up the dunes," he finished.

Calum glanced at his watch, and he looked to Tarrin. "Do you and Lex want to go up the beach, while I get lunch ready? I'll meet you up there in just a minute."

Tarrin shrugged. "Sure," she replied.

"I'll be right behind you," he told her as he pulled Macin's worn football from the pack. "Hey, go long!" he called and motioned toward Jake. Jake's smile broadened and he ran into the water when Calum hurled the ball toward a cresting wave.

When Macin ran after Jake, Tarrin smiled down at Lexie. "Well, it looks like it's just you and me. Let's go on up and see what we can find." She grinned.

Lexie nodded, and Calum waved. "Keep a good eye out, Lexie. There should be sand dollars along that stretch, and I've found a few good-sized agates along there too."

"Oh! Sand dollars!" Lexie turned and ran ahead.

Tarrin waved before she turned to follow her daughter up the sandy coastline. She walked around a few jagged, black stones covered in streams of green kelp. She was amazed at the washed up plants.

"Look at these." She held up the round end of a strand of kelp.

"What is it?" the little girl asked, poking the plant tentatively.

"It's called kelp. Huge kelp forests grow in the ocean," she explained.

"Look at this one, Mama," Lexie exclaimed and held up a shorter plant with small, round bladder-type bulbs. Green leaves grew out from the top of the bladders, and Lexie laughed. "They look like little people with crazy hair." The little girl giggled. "Oh!" Dropping the plant back onto the sand, she ran toward another weathered rock. "Look, Mom!"

"Those are barnacles. Be careful, Lexie," Tarrin cautioned when Lexie climbed the rock to get a better look.

"These are neat. Can we go up there?"

Lexie pointed toward a sandy cove created by jagged cliffs. Large, driftwood logs were scattered haphazardly, and short, shrubby plants grew along the edge of the rock face. A narrow stream ran through the cove and disappeared as it emptied into the ocean. She could hear the soft music of trickling water beyond the roar of breaking waves, and she caught sight of a small waterfall along the edge of the precipice. Tarrin nodded her approval, feeling eager to continue exploring the coastline. A few beach-goers waved at Lexie and Tarrin when they passed, and Tarrin's smiled a quick greeting before eagerly following her daughter.

"It's beautiful, isn't it?" she commented, reaching for the little girl's hand.

They worked their way into the cove. The soft sand was difficult to walk in. Tarrin laughed when she stumbled more than once. They reached the bay and she sat on a sun-warmed, driftwood log. She could hear the hypnotizing sound of surf behind her and she gazed up at the high, mossy ridges surrounding them. A gull soared lazily on the air as she stared up toward the deep blue sky, relaxing.

Lexie ran farther ahead. Tarrin sat up straighter when her daughter disappeared behind a thicket of snowberry shrubs. "Be careful, Lexie!" she called. "Stay where I can see you." Lexie didn't answer, and after another moment passed, Tarrin stood.

"Lex?"

Still there was no answer, and Tarrin's heart picked up pace. She inhaled sharply when a cluster of small birds darted out from the vegetation growing near the base of the cliffs. Alarmed, she stepped across the log she had been sitting on.

"Lexie?" she called.

Fear rushed to the surface. How could she have let her daughter out of her sight? Especially with all that had happened? Her heart hammered in her chest. Tarrin's feet suddenly felt like lead, but she rushed toward the bushes in the distance.

"Lexie!"

"There you are!" Calum's voice called from behind Tarrin, and Tarrin spun around to see him walking toward her.

She turned and faced the wall of tall bushes again, then jumped when Lexie's voice sounded nearby. "Calum!"

The girl darted out from the foliage and ran toward him. Tarrin let out a pent-up breath. "Oh," she exclaimed weakly. She leaned over, resting her hands on her knees for a moment while the fear passed. Lexie was fine. She took a moment to breathe deep before she stood and moved to join them.

"Lexie," she spoke when she drew close, "why didn't you answer me when I called?"

Lexie paused and glanced at her mother quizzically. "I didn't hear you. I found a path through the cliffs, Mama. Come and see!" She grabbed Calum's hand and pulled him and Tarrin toward the cliff face.

"Lexie, you can't wander off like that. Please, don't ever do that again," Tarrin scolded.

Calum studied her carefully. "Are you okay?" he whispered.

"I didn't know, Mama. I'm sorry." Lexie's smile faded.

"I'm fine," Tarrin breathed. "She just disappeared for a minute. It scared me." She turned her attention to Lexie. "You found a path?"

"Mmm-hmm! It's really pretty looking."

"There is a path up there." Calum explained. "It's a trail that comes down off that ridge." He pointed ahead. "We can circle back that way. It'll take us right back to the horses." He grasped Tarrin's hand, threading her fingers between his. "It's an easy hike. It takes you through a patch of forest on the other side of these stones."

Tarrin nodded. "Sure, that sounds like fun."

Calum pulled her toward the trail, while Lexie ran on ahead. "Stay close," he cautioned, and Lexie paused.

She waited for them to catch up then grasped Tarrin's free hand to give it a gentle tug. "Come on, Mama!"

"Hey, Mom! Lexie! Wait up!"

"Uncle Cal!"

Jake and Macin appeared around the bend on the beach below, and Tarrin turned to greet them with a smile. "Hi, you two."

"I thought you boys were eating," Calum spoke. "We were just on our way back. I was going to show Tarrin the ridge loop," he explained.

"We want to see the tide pools. I was taking Jake," Macin replied.

"Yeah, Mom, can we go? Come with us," her son suggested.

Tarrin glanced at Calum, and he shrugged. "Why not? We can take this trail on the way back. You didn't eat all the food did you?" he teased Jake, ruffling his wet hair.

"Sure did." Jake patted his tummy. He laughed then ran on ahead with Macin.

"Well, I suppose lunch can wait. It's a fairly short hike to the tide pools. Do you mind?" Calum turned to address Tarrin.

"No, not at all," she replied. "I'd love to see them."

He grasped her hand once again, squeezing her fingers gently, as they followed Jake and Macin. Lexie ran after her brother, giggling.

CHAPTER *Fourteen*

*H*e swore quietly and cursed his bad luck. He'd nearly cornered them. The cove would have been the perfect place. It would have taken but a moment to get them into the woods alone. If he had only acted sooner. His hands clenched. He would not fail again. Failure never set well with him, and he refused to fail now. Tarrin Grace would die—today. The wind caught her hair and sent it spiraling around her expressive face. It was just a matter of time.

℗

"This was fun. Thank you." Tarrin spoke as she patted the white horse. The animal snorted and nudged Tarrin's hand. It pawed the newly strewn hay spread across the stall.

Calum nodded while he stroked the animal's nose. "It was fun, wasn't it?" He caressed the horse for another minute before he turned toward Tarrin. "I was wondering," he began slowly. "Do you want to pack up the car and head up to North Jetty? We can see the shipping channels, and Westport is just across the bay. I was thinking we could dig for clams and bake a few for dinner while we watch the sunset, or we could visit the lighthouse."

Her eyes lit. She always wanted to visit a lighthouse, and a clam bake sounded wonderful. She also couldn't deny the fact that she was very eager to spend more time with Calum. She didn't want to see the day end. She didn't want to go back and face reality. For just a moment, life felt normal—wonderful—but soon it would be over. "I like that idea," she replied, hoping to prolong the day.

They took their time walking back toward Calum's vehicle. Tarrin's lips turned up into a small smile when the cool, pacific breeze brushed across her face. Colorful kites floated along the coastline, and she sighed contentedly just as Lexie tugged on her hand. Tarrin glanced down, curious.

Her daughter's face contorted, and Lexie whispered, "I have to use the bathroom."

Tarrin glanced around the open dunes and beach. Lexie danced as she walked, and Tarrin suppressed a smile. "Calum, is there a restroom near here?" she asked.

Calum caught sight of Lexie's twisted features as the little girl squirmed uncomfortably. He smiled knowingly, and pointed up the dunes. "Follow that trail there, and at the end, near the road, is an outhouse. I'll go on ahead with the boys, and we'll get packed up. We'll pick you two up on our way off the beach. It should only take a minute or a two."

Tarrin followed the sandy path and Lexie pulled on her hand anxiously. "Hurry, Mama! I can't hold it!"

She and Lexie raced up the trail. She caught a brief glimpse of Calum and the boys on the beach below before they crossed over the crest of a small hill. Tarrin caught sight of the dirt road through the thick brush, and she could see the outhouse ahead. She hoped there wasn't a line, and she breathed a sigh of relief when she noticed the rest area was deserted. Lexie pulled Tarrin forward, and their feet crunched on the sand-covered cement as she darted for a stall.

"That was close," Lexie exclaimed.

Tarrin chuckled and gazed up at the restroom's cement ceiling. She studied the intricate pattern of a small spider web in the corner while she waited for the little girl to finish. Lexie hummed a nameless tune, and Tarrin's thoughts turned to Calum. Butterflies kicked up in her stomach, and a smile touched her lips while she waited patiently in the dim bathroom. After a moment, she heard footsteps approaching the restroom, and she jumped, startled, when the main door suddenly flung wide with a raucous bang. Her head shot up just as Zack entered the room. His expression looked frantic and Tarrin's breath caught in her lungs.

"*Zack*?!" she exclaimed. Her eyes widened and her mouth fell open.

"Tarrin, thank goodness! Where's Lexie?" he asked.

Tarrin spun around when Lexie stepped from the stall. The little girl gasped and her eyes opened wide. She pulled her doll in tightly against her chest and watched Zack warily while Tarrin's gaze swung back to his.

"Zack, what are you doing here?" she asked.

"Tarrin! Lexie! Come on! I'll explain in a minute."

He rushed forward and grasped her upper arm. Tarrin shuddered when his cold fingers pressed into her skin, and she jerked out of his hold. Lexie ran forward and buried her face against Tarrin's leg. "What's going on?" Tarrin asked, her voice rising in alarm.

"It's Calum! We have to get you out of here. Now! I'm just lucky I found you soon enough. He killed Edna Cope, Tarrin. We found her body this morning. That's how he had your key. His prints were all over the scene. Frank Sloan told us where to find you," he rushed to explain.

"What?" she breathed. "Edna's dead? No! It can't . . . It can't be. H-how did you find us?"

"I saw you, back near the horse stalls, and I followed."

"Zack . . ."

He groaned. "Tarrin, I know it's hard to believe, but you have to trust me! Do you think his own father would have told me where to find you, if it weren't true?"

Tarrin's lips parted and she could feel the blood drain from her face. "No." Her legs felt weak. "Jake," she whispered her son's name. "Jake is with him." She felt as if she were in a daze. *Not Calum! It can't' be!* But if it were . . . She needed to get Jake.

"Don't worry about Jake," Zack replied. "I have a plain-clothed officer going in after the boy. You and Lexie need to come with me. Now! It's not safe for you until he's apprehended."

"No! I can't leave my son!"

Tarrin could feel Lexie's trembling body against her leg.

"Tarrin, if he sees me, what do you think he's going to do to your son? My men are going in after him. My job is to get you and Lexie to safety. Now come on! He was heading this way, and until my officers have a clear shot at apprehending him, he can't know we're here or your boy is dead, got it? He'll take no chances. Follow me."

He left the restroom, peering around the door. "His car is coming up the road. Go into those trees. Quick! If he sees us, he'll bolt with your kid. We can't take that risk."

No, no, no, no! Tarrin's mind screamed while she followed Zack's instructions. She pulled Lexie's arms from around her leg. Grasping her hand, they ran from the restroom. Zack followed close behind. She could hear Calum's car as he pulled into the parking lot. The vehicle's tires sounded against the pea-sized gravel, and Tarrin moaned when she ducked into the bushes. Brambles and twigs scratched at her tender, bare skin, and she held her breath.

Zack raised a finger to his lips, and gazed firmly into Lexie's terrified expression. "Follow me," he whispered, his voice nearly inaudible.

He turned and weaved his way soundlessly through a stand of short, squatty trees, and with an aching heart, Tarrin turned to follow. If Calum were the killer, how could she leave her son behind? She had trusted Calum. Why had she trusted him? Her heart beat frantically while she followed Zack. Her feet snapped several twigs underfoot and he turned once with a finger to his lips. She nodded, swallowing hard. Her grip on Lexie tightened when they stumbled into the thicker foliage, and he led her toward a small grove of pines in the distance, just beyond the border of the dunes.

Lexie's hand trembled in hers. Calum wouldn't hurt Jake, would he? How could she let herself fall in love with a cold-blooded killer? Was he really a killer? Tarrin bit back a sob as her feet tangled in the understory. They neared the border of trees, and Zack ran ahead at a near neck-breaking pace.

Tarrin caught Lexie up into her arms while she followed him into the woods, and Lexie's arms tightened painfully around Tarrin's neck when they finally slowed. Zack turned to face them, and Tarrin struggled to loosen Lexie's strangling hold. Her daughter whimpered against her neck when Zack moved closer, and Tarrin glanced toward him, her expression frantic.

"Zack," she spoke breathlessly. "What now? I can't just leave Jake!"

Lexie sobbed again and her small body trembled. "It's him. It's him, Mama," she whispered against Tarrin's neck.

Zack's serious expression faltered then, and a slow smile stretched across his face. He chuckled.

Momentarily confused, Tarrin's eyes shot to his. He watched her, his expression amused, and her breath caught in her throat. Her eyes slowly widened in sudden realization, and she studied him carefully, feeling stunned.

"Zack?" The hair on her arms stood on end. "It's *you?*" she asked, her voice barely a whisper. He regarded her silently as reality set in. "It is you! Not Calum. You're the murderer?" Her arms tightened instinctively about her daughter and she stumbled back.

"This was almost too easy," he chuckled. "Yes, Tarrin. It's me. You see, it's *always* been me," he exclaimed calmly.

"H-how? How could you? Y-you're the police! You're the detective!" she stuttered, feeling physically ill. "People trust you with their lives! You're supposed to be the *good* guy. I trusted you!" she yelled.

"And that is the beauty of it." He shrugged. "I mean really, think about it. Who defines good or bad? There really is no black or white—good or bad. We are all good, and we are all bad, and who is to say what's right? We're all just people, Tarrin, and in the end—" He shrugged again. "We all just fade to gray."

Tarrin inhaled sharply, shaking her head. "No!" she spoke. "No, we don't. I trusted you!"

Zack cocked his head to the side. "You don't get it?" His mouth twisted. "Here," he took a step toward her, "have a seat. Let me explain." He pointed toward a stump. When Tarrin continued to stand, his brow creased. "I said to sit," he repeated, pulling a knife from his belt.

Oℬ

Calum paced in front of the rest area. A few beach goers brushed past him while he waited impatiently for Tarrin and Lexie to return. He could hear a couple of teenage girls laughing from inside the restroom, and his apprehension increased. What was taking Tarrin and Lexie so long? He tapped his foot nervously and tried to smile when Jake slid from the car.

"Wow, where are they? They're taking a really long time," the boy spoke.

Calum turned back toward the door when the pair of teenage girls stumbled out of the building. Moving toward them, he interrupted their giggling conversation. "Is there a woman and a little girl in there?" he asked.

The girls eyed him coyly and the taller of the two shook her head. Her friend giggled annoyingly and smiled. "There's no one else in there," she answered before they turned and walked back down the road toward the beach.

Calum's nerves suddenly shot to life. He walked to the door and knocked. When he heard no answer, he swung the door open wide. The room was empty. He could see no sign that Lexie and Tarrin had been in there.

"Aren't they here?" Jake asked, concerned.

Calum could feel his frustration grow. "I don't know. I told your mom I would pick her up here. Maybe they headed back down to the beach."

He strode back toward his vehicle and pulled his phone from the glove compartment. He scowled when he saw Tarrin's

196

phone sitting next to his. "There goes that idea."

"What's up, Uncle Cal?" Macin asked, setting aside his game console.

Calum shook his head. "They're not here."

"Where're they at?" Macin asked.

Jake took a step closer, and he stared toward Calum with worried-filled eyes. "Do you think they're okay?" he asked.

Calum could see the panic building in Jake's expression, and he ruffled the boy's hair. "I'm sure they're fine," he replied, attempting to keep his tone light.

Where are they? He didn't think Tarrin would go back to the beach, especially when they agreed to meet at the rest area. Calum knew she wouldn't just wander off. He glanced around, studying the wall of trees and shrubby dogwood surrounding the area. He called her name, but heard no reply. What had he been thinking? With the obvious danger Tarrin faced, what had possessed him to send her on alone? The thought caused a sudden wave of guilt.

"Mom? Lex?" Jake called.

They listened for a moment. The sound of a raven was the only reply, and Jake glanced at Calum. Fear filled the young boy's eyes. Calum frowned. He rubbed his temples as he thought about his options. He needed to find Tarrin and Lexie immediately.

"Macin, I want you and Jake to take Tarrin's phone with you and run back to the beach. Look for Tarrin and Lexie. If you find them, call me right away." He placed Tarrin's phone into Macin's palm as the boy slid from the car.

Calum glanced at Jake, who was standing on the edge of the road. The boy looked worried, and he searched the dunes and forest with frightened eyes. "Macin," Calum whispered, "be careful. Don't talk to anyone. She could be in trouble. I want you and Jake to stay on the beach until I call you. Stay close to the crowds and scream for help if you need to." He finished as he reached into the glove compartment once more.

He fished a semi-automatic pistol from the compartment then removed the gun from the holster.

Macin's face paled.

"I keep the gun for protection." Calum caught the boy's eye. He checked the gun's safety before he tucked it in the back of his pants.

"Do you think the murderer got them?" Macin whispered, and he glanced at Jake, worried.

"No, but we can't take chances. Don't let Jake out of your sight. Macin, promise me you'll stay with the crowd. I'm going to search the dunes and the forest. You keep that phone close, kid."

"Sure," Macin spoke. "Jake?"

Jake spun around, his pale face twisted in fear. "Huh?"

"Come on." Macin waved toward the road.

Calum forced a small smile when he caught Jake's eye, and the boy frowned as he turned to follow Macin down the dirt road, back toward the beach. Calum waited until they reached the edge of beach and disappeared into the crowd. He closed his eyes and desperately hoped they would stay safe.

ᐸ

Tarrin felt ill at the sight of the steel blade. The blood drained from her face and her knees grew weak. Lexie shivered in her aching arms. With a trembling breath Tarrin sat on the stump. She studied Zack carefully. He laughed with obvious delight, and Tarrin moaned.

"Why are you doing this?" she asked, her voice rising.

"Temper, temper," he taunted. "It's a long story. Let me explain. See, unlike you, I'm afraid to say, I didn't have a *charmed* childhood. I grew up in a cold, dirty, flea-ridden apartment. Every night I came home to a mom who was strung out on California cornflakes or crazy on meth.

"I spent nearly every night huddled under dirty, moth-eaten blankets, trying to escape the rain—the cold. I rummaged for scraps of food in dumpsters. I hated her. I hated that life. Eventually the state took me away, and I was shoved into one useless foster home after the next. I hated them! I hated them all, but I plastered a grin on my face and I worked hard to make a future for myself." He paused.

Tarrin's breaths were shallow, and she watched him in silence. She squeezed Lexie tighter against her. How was she going to protect her daughter? "Zack, please?"

He held a hand up to silence her. "Shut up! I like this part. Let me finish."

Tarrin felt ill.

He smirked and went on. "When I finally graduated, I went home. She wanted nothing to do with me. My own mother wanted *nothing* to do with me. She told me she was ashamed I was her son. She said I caused her nothing but grief. She told me I was useless and that I would always be a failure." His face grew ragged, and rage twisted his handsome features. "*Me*! She told *me* that *I* was useless! That *I* caused *her* nothing but grief." He pinched the bridge of his nose, and laughed humorlessly.

Tarrin licked her dry lips. "I'm sorry, Zack," she croaked. How was she going to get her daughter away from this man?

Lexie whimpered, and Tarrin could feel the little girl's warm tears running down her neck. She closed her eyes for a brief moment and prayed for help.

"I *hated* her. So I left. I never went back. I worked my way through college," Zack went on calmly. "I went hungry. I wore ragged clothes—shoes with holes in the soles—just so I could make ends meet. Eventually, I landed a job on the force. Homicides." He shrugged. "They *intrigued* me." He smiled. "I loved the thrill of solving murders."

"Zack?" Tarrin's voice trembled.

"I told you to shut up. I'm at the best part," he spoke calmly. "So, one day, I met this girl. Lindsey, I think. I don't remember. I found her at a nightclub. She was beautiful. Everything I ever wanted. But it didn't take long for me to realize she was just as shallow, just as worthless . . ." He sighed. "I convinced her to go home with me. We got into an argument. I honestly don't even remember what we were fighting about. So I stopped in the woods on the way home."

Tarrin closed her eyes, and she covered Lexie's ears with her hands while Zack finished. "I didn't mean to kill her. I was just so angry. I could hardly control the rage I felt. She was so much like my mother!" His voice rose angrily, and Tarrin winced when he swore and kicked at a fallen log near his feet. Within moments he calmed, and another smile spread slowly across his face. "But—" He laughed suddenly. "But, you see, the next day I was called in with my unit to investigate *my* murder." He shook his head. "How ironic, isn't it?" He spread his hands wide. "It was in that moment, I realized my path to the top." He chuckled with pleasure, and the derisive sound filled the thicket.

Tarrin cringed. "That's awful," she whispered.

"I killed four women within a month. They named me the Nightclub Killer," he grinned. "And I was right on *his* tail. Eventually, I knew I needed to have a fall guy if I was going to solve the serial killings, so I picked a guy. Just some random fool I'd met on the streets, and then I planted evidence at the scene. It was as easy as that. I solved the murders. I was a hero.

"It was an amazing feeling. I was a nobody, and then suddenly I was everybody's favorite guy." He shrugged. "I've solved nearly sixteen murders. Three were serial cases." He grinned. "All mine, of course. I get such a kick out of solving my own murders." He raked a hand through his hair. "In Seattle, I've been named . . . let's see—the Dock-Side Murderer. Oh, and the Lady-Cop Killer. I lost a couple of good, female detectives with that one," he sighed, and Tarrin's stomach turned.

She needed to get away from him, but how? Her breathing grew ragged, and her heart thundered painfully against her ribs as he continued in a low voice.

"I'm currently known as the Happy Hour Slasher." His eyes filled with humor. "I personally like that one. It's like a *game*—an exciting, addicting game." He smiled a little, but his brow furrowed. "But," he grew serious, "they've all been the same. I've made it to the top because I'm good at what I do. And I *always* get my man, but you were different, Tarrin. When Lexie caught me, I had to do something. I've worked too hard to build my new life, and I wasn't about to let some snot-nosed brat get in the way. But then I met you and my life took on new meaning." He chuckled, and Tarrin felt numb with fear.

"I didn't want to kill you, Tarrin. Really. I just wanted to scare you. I thought you would turn to me for comfort. I thought you would trust me to protect you. But, Sloan . . ." He shook his head. "Sloan was the perfect fall guy. It was providence. Our lives are so parallel. His childhood and mine—so similar. We both overcame terrible odds. How fitting he should take the fall, but instead of turning to me . . ." Zack's face contorted suddenly and anger twisted his handsome features.

Tarrin's heart beat frantically, and her body tensed. He was insane.

"Instead of turning to me, you fell right into his arms." He raked his hand through his thick, blond hair again then pointed accusingly toward Tarrin. "I tried to warn you! You didn't listen. You wouldn't even give me a chance. I may have even spared the girl. I don't like killing kids, Tarrin. I've never killed a child. Only the real psychopaths kill kids, and I might have spared her. I waited for her to talk. She didn't."

She kept her eyes on his, feeling like a caged animal. Desperation left her weak. "I'm sorry, Zack. Really, I am. Lexie won't say a word. We won't say anything," she whispered. She searched for the right words to reason with him. Zack was a monster. What could she possibly say to spare her daughter? "We . . . we can start over. You and I. Just spare Lexie. Give us another chance, Zack," she begged.

His eyes softened momentarily. "I'm sorry, Tarrin. Really, I am," he spoke, stepping toward her. "This has to be. This has to end now."

Tarrin shot to her feet, pulling Lexie with her. The girl cried out in alarm and wrapped her arms ever-tighter against her mother's neck.

"Don't run, Tarrin," he murmured. "I'll make it painless—quick."

Tarrin inhaled deeply, and she tried to set Lexie on her feet. "Please? Just let Lexie go. We'll go off together. Just you and me," she begged. Her voice quaked, and she tried to force some strength into her words. "We can be together if you'll just spare Lexie."

He paused his slow advance toward her. Sighing, he laid his head back to glance at the top of the trees. "If she runs, Tarrin, she dies first. I don't want to do that to you. I was angry for a while. I thought I wanted to kill her first to make you suffer, but I love you too much to hurt you that way."

Tarrin forced back a wave of sudden nausea. *Please* . . . She yanked Lexie's arms from around her neck. Setting her on her feet, she pushed her daughter behind her. "Zack, please," Tarrin beseeched, and his eyes lit with pleasure.

Anger coursed through her veins when she realized he enjoyed her pleading, and she nudged Lexie farther back with her foot. She prayed her daughter would run, but Lexie's hand clung desperately to her leg.

He laughed, and Tarrin's eyes narrowed to slits. *Stall him,* a voice suddenly pierced her mind. What could she do? How could she stall his evil intent?

"H-how did you find me here?" she asked. "Did you hurt Erin?" The air left her body in a rush. Her heart ached at the thought of her sister—her best friend. *Erin* . . .

His eyes narrowed. "Of course not. I have no reason to

harm Erin, and it wasn't hard to keep tabs on you. I mean, really, how dumb do you think I am? I followed you everywhere— *everywhere*." He smirked. "It was easy. Besides, being in my position does have its advantages. You see, I'm *expected* around a crime scene. Nobody questions that, day or night. So following you wasn't too bad. I've actually never done it before, and I have to admit, I had fun.

"The first night was too easy. I thought you might be watching the woods. So I came back and wandered through the trees. I just wanted to make you nervous. I was watching the house, and then that punk Sloan showed up. I left and came back later that night. That was when I set up the wire and the light.

"I knew then, when I saw Sloan—I had my perfect fall guy. And I got lucky with the photo. I'd climbed the tree to get a better idea of the house's layout. I didn't get much of an opportunity to explore during the initial investigation. That's when I saw you standing at the window. You were beautiful. The moment couldn't have been better."

"How did . . . how did you find me on the jogging trail?" Tarrin asked. She suddenly realized he enjoyed bragging. The thought caused her stomach to churn, but if she could just keep him talking, maybe she could find a way to escape. Maybe she could find a way to save her precious daughter.

He laughed again. "Aw, the mourning dove and photos on the trail. Now that was good work if I say so myself. I liked the symbolism. White feathers—you and Lexie—so pure and innocent. Absolute genius. Plus, a little wash out hair dye, spray-on tanner— I was a new man. I was already in my sweat suit, so that worked out. I planned on leaving the bird and feathers on your back lawn, but then I saw you leave the house, so I followed. I passed you on the trail, and then I waited. I trapped the bird the night before." He shrugged. "I hid it under my jogging suit. I tossed the bird and scattered the photos right before you came around the bend. I watched when you found it, Tarrin. It was exquisite." He laughed.

"Then I headed out, back to my apartment. I washed up and came back to be with you."

"And Edna? Did you kill her too?" The thought made Tarrin nauseated and her knees nearly gave out. Lexie whimpered behind her, still clinging to her leg.

He grimaced. "I did. That was one feisty woman. I only wanted the keys to your house." He shrugged. "I didn't mean to kill the old bat, but she woke up." He shook his head. "And today— well, it wasn't too hard. A cheap hair piece, a couple of fake face piercings, and I blended right in."

Tarrin's mouth popped open and she gasped. "You were in the group with the horses. Y-you were the hippie," she realized.

He laughed and nodded slowly. His eyebrows rose with humor. "I was everywhere, Tarrin. And I nearly caught you at the cove too. If that bumbling idiot Sloan hadn't shown up right then. But this works rather well, don't you think? Tarrin," he paused. "It's time."

◌ß

The scene before him was just as perfect as he imagined. Tarrin's face was like a painting—a various palette of emotions. Fear made her features pale, but her vivacious eyes were wide and wild, and her lips were set in a determined, firm line. Her knuckles bleached white as she balled her hands into fists. She leaned forward and poised on the balls of her feet, ready to strike. She would die trying to protect her daughter.

He wasn't looking forward to killing the girl. He'd thought about the most humane way to do it. Maybe he'd smother her. He sighed and cringed a little. But Tarrin . . . Tarrin belonged to him now, and the thought made him smile.

Tarrin glared and her eyes flashed. "You aren't going to touch her," she spoke between clenched teeth.

"I don't *want* to kill the girl. The idea was never a pleasant one. I leave the killing of babies to the real crazies, but I have no choice, Tarrin. You understand?" he asked.

CHAPTER *Fifteen*

arrin's heart beat erratically, and blood pounded in her ears. Her stomach turned when she glanced down toward her precious little girl. Her gaze shot to Zack's once again before she looked back toward Lexie.

"Then," her voice trembled. "Just let me hug her. Let me hold her," she begged.

Zack paused, and his hands fell to his side. He sighed. "Of course, Tarrin," he said.

Tarrin's eyes widened. Was he playing another game? Cautiously, she studied Zack before she knelt in front of Lexie. The little girl's frightened gaze remained fixed on Zack, and she sobbed quietly. "Lexie," Tarrin pulled her trembling daughter into her arms.

Lexie breathed hard and fast. "Mama?" she asked with a quaking, small voice.

Tarrin buried her face against Lexie's neck. Her body shook and she felt as though she would collapse at any moment, but she pressed her mouth against Lexie's ear. "Lexie, Mama needs you to be brave."

"No," the little girl cried, hugging her antique doll tightly. "No!"

Tarrin forced back tears of her own. Now was not the time to give into her overwhelming fears. She needed to stay calm and in control. She had to get her daughter to safety first, then she would fight. She would not go down without a fierce struggle.

"Lexie," Tarrin whispered in her daughter's ear. She continued to watch Zack. "You need to take Poppy and run. Go find help. You need to run. Don't stop until you find help for mommy."

Lexie shook her head.

"Lexie, please. *Please* go," Tarrin begged. Her voice cracked.

What sort of burden was she placing on her young daughter? The thought nearly made Tarrin scream. *Please help us,* she prayed desperately. *Help save my daughter.* Tarrin choked on a silent sob when she pulled Lexie in for what she could only hope would not be their last embrace. She caught Zack's maniacal smile over the top of Lexie's messy, blond curls. She kissed her daughter's soft cheek. She could taste the salt of Lexie's tears, and she struggled with the fierce longing to keep her close.

Tarrin forced her arms to loosen, and she pulled Lexie away, placing her on the ground. As she did, she reached for a long stick laying in the undergrowth.

Zack laughed, his tone mocking. "You're going fight?" he asked.

Tarrin stepped in front of her daughter. "You won't touch her," she returned.

"Don't be afraid, Tarrin," Zack spoke. "It will be over soon."

Tarrin swallowed hard and her hands tightened against the stick. Birds called from within the dense trees. Their joyous songs mocked her dire situation. She would fight. He was not going to do this to her. He was not going to hurt her daughter.

"It won't be over soon if I can help it," she spoke.

Her voice trembled with fury, and she gritted her teeth in anticipation. All her fears suddenly vanished, and in its place was pure determination. She would fight with all the strength she possessed, and she willed her mind to find the courage she needed to overcome him and survive.

"You won't win," she told him.

"Won't I?" He smiled derisively.

☙

Calum's gaze swept the vast, wind-swept dunes. He stood next to a tall Oregon ash. The gentle breeze rustled the leaves, and he closed his eyes, breathing in the spicy scent of resin. Something was very wrong. Tarrin wouldn't have stayed missing this long. They would have found one another by now. His nerves felt stretched, and he could feel his anxiety growing as the minutes passed. Where were they? He had to find them. If the murderer had somehow followed them . . . If he somehow managed to find Lexie and Tarrin alone . . . The thought made him groan. What had he been thinking? He should have stayed with them. He groaned and placed a hand against his forehead, then jumped slightly when his cell phone rang. Reaching for his phone, he recognized Frank's familiar number and he rushed to answer the call.

"Calum!" Frank's voice sounded in the phone, and Calum immediately heard the alarm in his father's voice. "Thank heavens! I've been trying to reach you or Tarrin for the last hour."

"What do you mean? What's happened?" Calum asked.

"It's Marzollo!" Frank spoke. "Marzollo is the killer."

"What?"

The air left Calum's lungs in a rush, and his blood turned cold as Frank continued. "The FBI and the Seattle PD have been following Marzollo for months, but he . . . Son, he killed Edna Cope. They found her body this morning. Marzollo left solid evidence behind this time. It's him."

"No," Calum exclaimed. "Dad," his voice cracked. "If its Marzollo, then where *is* he? Do they have him detained?"

A sudden sense of dread filled Calum, and he closed his eyes when Frank answered, "No, Calum. He's gone. They can't find him."

"Dad, Tarrin's gone. Tarrin and Lexie. I can't find them anywhere. We separated, only for moment, but I lost them. I sent the boys back to the beach to look for her, but . . ." Nausea churned in Calum's gut, and he swore loudly. "If they knew Marzollo was their killer, why weren't they watching him!?" he suddenly exploded. "Why did they let him near Tarrin to begin with?"

"Son, they were watching him. It's just now they've really discovered he was behind the murders. The guys from Internal

Affairs had nothing solid to link him to any of the cases. Just a gut-feeling. But now—"

Calum cut in. "I need to find Tarrin and Lexie. I need to find them now!"

"Calum," Frank spoke firmly. "There are officers and agents headed your way now. They think Marzollo followed you there. You need to find those girls." His voice faltered. "Because . . . Because, if he has them . . . Son, it won't end well."

⸸

Tarrin studied Zack. His eyes bore into hers, but she swallowed her fear. She knew she needed to act now, and with all the strength she could gather, she spun around, and shoved Lexie toward a wall of ferns growing nearby. "Lexie, run! Now! Run!" Tarrin screamed. "*Run!*"

Lexie cried out, but to Tarrin's relief the little girl darted into the mix of ferns and shrubs, and immediately, the dense foliage swallowed her from view.

"Run!" Tarrin screamed.

"No!" Zack bellowed. He rushed toward her—toward the spot where Lexie had disappeared. "No!"

Tarrin whirled to face him—to block his chase—and with the stick clasped firmly in her hands, she swung with all her strength. He winced and swore when the sharp stick glanced off his shoulder. He paused in his advance to chase Lexie, and Tarrin could clearly read the murderous intent in his gaze. If death were inevitable, then she desperately hoped it would be swift and painless. With bated breath Tarrin swung the stick again, but with snake-like reflexes Zack caught the end in his hand. With a quick jerk, he pulled her poor excuse for a weapon from her grasp.

Stumbling back, Tarrin cried out. Her arms flailed when she tripped on a jagged rock, hidden beneath the forest understory, and she struggled to keep her balance when Zack lunged for her, knocking her into the shrubs nearby. His strong hands encircled her forearms and she struggled against him, oblivious to the sharp thorns tearing at her bare skin as he shoved her toward the ground. She screamed when his thick arms encircled her waist.

"No! Please?" she pleaded, fighting against his crushing grip. She screamed again, hoping she could alert someone to her presence, but the sound was cut short when his hand covered her mouth. She twisted her head savagely. When his fingers neared her mouth again, she bit down hard. Zack swore and squeezed her tightly. Tarrin felt her ribs crack. She cried out in pain.

"Keep fighting! It only makes this more fun," he ground out. "You're going to die, Tarrin. And so will Lexie."

His words pierced her heart. His breath felt hot and sticky against her balmy neck. Knowing she couldn't pull free of his hold, she pushed herself in tighter against him then spun around in his arms to face him. She dug her nails into his face. He yelped in pain. His arms dropped from around her, and he stumbled back. Tarrin turned to flee, but she fell to the ground when he kicked her legs out from underneath her. Her shins burned where his foot caught her leg and she gritted her teeth against the pain. He advanced toward her, and she cried out when he grasped a handful of her hair.

His breath brushed across her face when he brandished the knife. Her scream caught in her throat. Panic constricted her chest, squeezing the air from her lungs. She closed her eyes. *I'm going to die.*

The world grew silent as Tarrin pictured her children. She could feel their arms around her, smell their sweet scent, and tears spilled from the corner of her eyes. Zack's mouth pressed against her ear and her body grew limp when he whispered, "I'm sorry, Tarrin. I love you." She felt the cold touch of steel against her throat.

Suddenly, the sound of gunfire echoed through the trees. Zack's scream of pain ripped the stillness, and Tarrin's eyes popped open. Stunned, she stared as he stumbled backward and fell to the ground. He grasped his shoulder and his wild eyes met hers when blood seeped between his fingers.

"Tarrin, run! Get out of there!" Calum's familiar voice spurred Tarrin to action, and she jumped to her feet.

"No!" Zack bellowed, rolling toward her.

His hand circled her ankle in a vice-like grip, and with a gasp, she fell to the ground once more. She spun onto her back and kicked. She caught him in the stomach with the heel of her shoe just as a second shot ripped through the air, the bullet catching Zack in the thigh. He yelled, rolling away. Within moments Calum surged into the trees, and Zack slumped on the ground. Blood ran from Zack's shoulder and leg, dripping onto the forest understory—soaking into the earth. Tarrin jumped to her feet.

"Why?" Zack whispered. His pale face rose toward hers.

Tarrin raised a hand toward the base of her throat and shook her head, then cried out with relief when Calum grasped her arm. He kept his gun trained on Zack.

"Lexie! Where's Lexie?" Tarrin cried.

"She's fine," Calum replied hoarsely, pulling her against him and pressing his lips to her temple for just a brief moment. Then to Zack, he spoke, "Don't you move a muscle. I'll kill you right where you sit." His voice trembled with rage.

Zack sat rigid and unmoving on the ground. He sneered at Calum. "You think you won?" he asked. He spat into the dirt just as his hand shot behind his back and came forward again in a blur of motion.

"Calum!" Tarrin screamed when she caught sight of the flash of metal in Zack's hand. A shot echoed deafeningly, and she felt Calum's arms encircle her, knocking her to the ground. His weight pressed against her body and her ears rang, muffling the sounds around her. Stars swam in her vision and she gasped, trying to catch her breath. She didn't know how long she lay there. Time seemed to stand still. The lines of reality faded.

"Tarrin," she heard Calum's voice near her ear. "Tarrin!"

Dazed and disoriented she lay still on the ground. She felt Calum's weight roll off her. A flurry of motion nearby kicked up dirt and debris and she slowly realized a dozen or more men suddenly surrounded her. Policemen rushed around them, encircling her, Calum, and Zack. She could hear Zack's loud protests as the ringing in her ears finally subsided.

"He shot me! That man shot me!" Zack screamed, and the sound pounded against Tarrin's skull.

"Tarrin!" She felt Calum grip her shoulders, pulling her from the ground. "Are you hurt?"

"Calum," she spoke his name. "He shot at you!"

"I'm fine, Tarrin." Calum grasped her hand.

"Drop your weapon!" An officer demanded of Calum as Tarrin stumbled to her feet.

Calum let Tarrin go, then dropped the gun he still held in his hand. He raised both hands into the air and remained silent when an officer forced him to the ground. Tarrin felt as if she were in a daze—a dream—and she watched, stunned—helpless—while officers cuffed both Calum and Zack. Zack's loud protests filled the forest. Blood covered the right side of his body and he groaned in pain.

Sirens in the distance grew to a deafening clamor as Tarrin stood frozen. When an officer touched her shoulder, she jumped.

"Are you injured?" the officer asked, his voice terse.

Tarrin shook her head. "No. No!" she turned to face Calum. "Please, don't arrest him. He saved my life! And Lexie?" A sob burst from her lips. "Jake? Where are my children?"

"It's okay, Tarrin." Calum spoke while an officer assisted him to his feet. "They're fine. I promise. They're safe. A couple of hikers found Lexie on the dunes. Frank called to tell me about Zack so I knew you were in trouble. I headed toward the woods, hoping to find you, and that's when I saw Lexie running through the trees. She was trying to find help. She told me where to find you, and the hikers took Lexie back to the rest area." He cringed when the officer tightened the cuffs against his wrists.

"Jake?" Tarrin's voice trembled.

"He's safe, Tarrin. I sent him and Macin back to the beach."

"The beach?" Tarrin murmured just as a crew of E.M.T's rushed into the area. Tarrin turned toward the officer who stood nearby. "I have to find my kids! And Calum?" She faced Calum once again. "He saved me." Her eyes shot back to the policeman. "You have to believe me. Zack—Lieutenant Marzollo—he's the serial killer in Seattle."

Another officer approached while the emergency crew lifted Zack onto a stretcher. The officer touched Tarrin's shoulders, and Tarrin stared in horror while they transported Zack past her followed by a team of SWAT agents.

"Ma'am, I'm Detective Jameson." He flashed his badge. "I need to—"

"Please?" She turned to face the detective, cutting him off. "Zack Marzollo killed them all—all those women. He tried to frame Calum. And, my kids . . . I have to find Jake and Lexie!"

"We understand," the man replied. "We do. You're children are safe."

"Zack?" Tarrin whispered, trying to shake off the hazy fog gripping her mind.

"I know. We've been following Zack Marzollo for some time. He came under suspicion a few months ago, and we've been keeping an eye on him ever since—"

"Not close enough," Calum murmured. The policeman holding Calum gave him a little jerk, and Calum scowled.

The detective speaking with Tarrin grimaced. "No, it's apparent we should have been watching closer. We've had a few officers on his team keeping an eye on him, trying to track his movements, but it hasn't been easy," he explained. "You need to understand, it's difficult when one of our own comes under suspicion. But know we will do everything we can to uncover the rest of Marzollo's crimes."

"So why are you arresting Calum?" Tarrin asked, her voice shaking.

"We have to follow protocol. Anytime there's a shooting, we need to take those involved into custody." He nodded his head toward Calum. "Do you understand?"

Tarrin shook her head. "No."

"I understand," Calum spoke. "Tarrin, don't worry about me. Go find Jake and Lexie."

"But?"

"Like I said. You're kids are fine," the man spoke. "Frank Sloan has been relaying information. He told us the boys were at the beach. Some of my men have the children."

"You have Jake and Lexie? Macin?" Tarrin whispered.

The detective nodded. "They're safe."

Waves of relief washed over her body leaving her weak and her knees nearly gave out. Her children were safe. Lexie made it to safety. She had found Calum. She found help, and she had saved Tarrin's life. Tarrin closed her eyes, and she could hear Calum sigh.

"Tarrin," Calum spoke.

Tarrin opened her eyes, and she swayed a little on unsteady legs. Detective Jameson grasped her arm, steadying her. "I think maybe you better sit down."

"I'm fine." Tarrin pushed his hand away. "I need to see my children."

The detective nodded toward a couple of men standing nearby. "Take these two down to the road."

Tarrin followed as two men escorted her and Calum from the woods, and when they neared the rest area, Tarrin cried out when she caught sight of Lexie's familiar pink shirt among the multitude of people. Jake stood near his sister, and Tarrin rushed ahead on trembling legs.

"Jake! Lexie!" She screamed their names and nearly collapsed when her children pushed from the crowd and ran her way. She caught them against her. Falling to her knees, she sobbed.

Her children were safe.

◌੪

With Lexie and Jake in her arms, an officer led them toward a waiting ambulance and Tarrin eyed the emergency vehicle warily. She knew she and Calum would be separated soon, and she moved to be near him.

"Thank you," she whispered, her voice trembling. Her gaze fell to her feet. "Forgive me for doubting you. Z-Zack said you'd killed Edna, and . . ." How could she make him understand why she had ever doubted him? "I shouldn't have followed him, but he was so sincere. I trusted him, and I'm *so* very sorry."

Frowning, Calum nodded. "There's nothing to forgive. Like you said, you were supposed to be able to trust Lieutenant Marzollo, Tarrin. I can't blame you for doubting, but I hope you can trust me because I'll always be here when you need me."

Tarrin's heart fell and her tortured eyes met his. She could read the hurt in his expression, and she wondered if he really would forgive her in time. "Thank you," she murmured again.

"Ma'am," another officer spoke loudly and Tarrin tore her gaze from Calum's. "I need to escort you and your children back to Seattle."

Tarrin nodded before she turned back to Calum. "You saved my life."

He smiled wearily. "Anytime."

"I'll see you later?"

He nodded slowly then grimaced when the officer escorting him pushed him forward toward a waiting police car. Her heart ached when the policeman lowered him inside the vehicle, and she forced back the tears hovering near the surface. Macin stood nearby, and she moved to his side. The boy wiped the tears from his eyes as Tarrin placed her arms around his shoulder.

"He'll be okay. They know he did what he did to save me."

She did her best to comfort the boy.

"Mama, I want Calum to stay with us," Lexie murmured.

Tarrin felt Lexie's small fingers tighten against her own. The policeman shut the door, and Tarrin reached over to pull Macin into her embrace. He didn't resist and she kissed the top of his head.

"Me too," Tarrin whispered when she caught Calum's eye through the window.

"Why are they arresting him, Mom?" Jake asked stepping closer to Tarrin.

"It's just protocol," Tarrin told the children. "They know Zack was behind the murders."

"He isn't under arrest?" Macin asked.

"No," Detective Jamison suddenly spoke from behind them. "He's just being detained while we finish up our investigation." Tarrin and the children turned to face him, and he smiled. "Come on. Let's get you home."

Tarrin nodded, and Lexie looked up to face her. "Are we all safe now, Mama?"

Tarrin closed her eyes, and a small smile touched her mouth. Tears clouded her vision. "Yes," she whispered through trembling lips. "We're all safe now, Lexie."

∽

Tarrin eyed the swollen clouds overhead. A few rain drops fell onto her upturned face and she shivered. She could scarcely believe it was the end of November, but she and her children were enjoying their Thanksgiving Day break from school and work. The weatherman had predicted snow later in the evening. Tarrin grinned, remembering Jake's excitement.

It didn't snow very often in Seattle, and he and Macin had been preparing all morning for a winter adventure. Lexie had tagged along as the boys pulled dust-covered sleds from the small garage and gathered winter gloves and hats. Tarrin hoped they wouldn't be too disappointed if it didn't snow very much. She smiled a little and looked at her watch. Erin and Sarah had plans later in the afternoon, and Tarrin knew it was time to return from her walk.

She glanced around the crowded dock as she turned from the water. Several people mingled in the ever thickening haze, and she suppressed a shudder. It had been three months since Zack Marzollo's initial trial, but she still felt nervous from time to time. She was certain the terror she and her children lived through during those awful days would last a lifetime, but they were doing their best to cope. They had all made great strides toward healing.

She and her children continued therapy, but the past few months hadn't been easy, especially considering they had all been required to testify during Zack's lengthy trial. It had been heart-wrenching to hear Lexie recount happening upon Zack in the act of murder. The details of that day had finally returned, and Tarrin listened with horror and grief as her young daughter tearfully recalled the event.

Tarrin's parents also came up for the trial. They'd stayed a few weeks in Washington helping shield Tarrin and the kids from the frenzy of press and media. It had been nice to spend some time with them. She had missed the comfort of their presence. She enjoyed their visit immensely, but they left disgruntled and angry when they couldn't convince Tarrin or Erin to return to Colorado. Tarrin toyed with the idea of leaving, but after wrestling with her fears and anxiety, she'd finally decided to stay. She knew she'd made the right choice remaining in Washington, despite those difficult weeks. Living in the little house had been frightening at first. Tarrin knew Zack was behind bars where he belonged, but she had awakened many nights, drenched in sweat and trembling from nightmares. Over time, however, their lives had fallen into a comfortable pattern, and the anxiety was slowly dulling.

The children had started school, and Jake and Lexie were

staying busy with new friends both there and within the close-knit neighborhood. Tarrin remained employed at Sloan International, but she and Calum, though they stayed very good friends, had drawn apart. He still teased her over botched calls, and they had lunched together several times, but she knew Calum had been hurt when she believed Zack so easily. He never let on that it bothered him, but she knew he'd still been wounded.

He distanced himself from her. Was it because he hadn't forgiven her or was it something else entirely? There had been moments over the course of the last few months when Tarrin caught a glimpse of something more flash in his eye when he glanced her way or touched her hand, but nothing ever came of it. Every time she found his gaze on her, her heart accelerated. She found herself yearning for the closeness they once shared, if only for a few days.

Jackie returned home in October, and Calum had moved back into the heart of the city. Tarrin still saw him nearly every day at work and once in a while at the community center, but still, she missed him. Thoughts of Calum left her feeling rather discouraged as she climbed the steep hill that led home, but she did her best to shake off her melancholy.

She could see Jake and Macin playing ball in the front yard, and she smiled when they waved. She forced her mind away from painful thoughts and returned their greeting. Lexie jumped from the porch with a wide smile, clutching Poppy the doll in her hands as she raced down the walk to meet her. It felt good to be home.

Oᔕ

Calum cringed when the door squeaked, and he smiled awkwardly as he walked into the crowded classroom. Tarrin paused for a brief moment while he took his seat at the back of the room next to Frank. He nodded, and Tarrin resumed her lesson on *Eating Healthy on a Budget*. Calum smiled a little. His dad had wasted no time calling Tarrin to volunteer her time at the community center, and he couldn't help but feel grateful she had accepted Frank's proposal. He enjoyed her classes, and it gave him a good excuse to see her. He sighed, then leaned back in his chair to listen to her soft, familiar voice just as Frank cleared his throat. When Calum didn't respond, the old man jabbed his elbow into his side.

Startled, Calum jumped then winced. He turned to face his dad, and Frank grinned, unrepentant. "So have you decided yet?"

Calum's eyebrows furrowed, and Frank nodded toward Tarrin. Her back faced them while she wrote on the large whiteboard at the front of the room. He glanced back toward the older man and whispered, "Decided what?"

"Oh, don't give me that. I've known you for years, Calum, and considering how old you are, you know that's been a while." Frank chuckled.

"I don't know what you mean," Calum whispered.

He knew exactly what Frank meant, but he wasn't willing to admit it openly. If anything, his feelings for Tarrin Grace had only deepened, but ever since the beach, he was hesitant to pursue a relationship. He knew Tarrin had been deeply hurt by her ex-husband, and her trust in Zack Marzollo had been sorely misplaced. He didn't want to put any undue pressure on her while she recovered, and so he had forced himself to bury his feelings for her and back away.

Hiding his feelings for Tarrin wasn't easy, either. In fact he'd had a very difficult time over the past couple of months. He wanted to tell her how he felt, but he hesitated. If she didn't feel the same. . . The thought left him feeling discouraged. He wasn't sure he could handle her rejection if he were to lay it all on the line and expose his heart.

"You don't know what I mean?" Frank's gravelly voice cut into Calum's thoughts.

The old man harrumphed loudly, and Tarrin glanced their way. Calum quickly looked down at his lap to avoid her stare and whispered, "What do you want me to do? I'm trying to give her time. She needs time to heal."

"Oh, and I suppose you know exactly how much time she needs, huh? That's very considerate of you to decide that for her."

"That's . . . You know that's not what I meant," Calum stuttered.

"Isn't it?"

"No!" He spoke louder than he'd intended, and he groaned when several eyes turned his way. He caught Tarrin's curious look before she went on with her lesson. Frank chuckled, and Calum exhaled before he whispered, "I just don't want to rush her."

"Uh-huh."

"I don't want her to think . . ." He paused. "Besides, she's been out with some guy from the office. I don't want to get in the way."

"Well, what do you want her to do, son? If you want that woman, you have to fight for her. Win her heart! If you ask me, you'll probably find you have it easier than you deserve," his father spoke bluntly.

Calum's eyes shot to the old man's, and Frank grinned. Calum shrugged. "I just—"

"Don't want to get hurt," Frank cut in. "You know that's a chance we all take. *Or* you can just exist under that rock you're hiding beneath. The choice is yours."

Calum raised his eyes toward Tarrin. "I'm not hiding under a rock," he muttered.

He knew he loved Tarrin. He did want what was best for her, but maybe Frank was right. What right did he have to decide what that was?

"If you want my opinion—and I'm going to give it to you whether you want it or not," Frank added. "You'll buck-up and ask that girl to dinner. In fact, invite her over to our place. We'll enjoy some of Kathy's famous meat loaf."

Calum laughed and watched Tarrin from beneath lowered

lashes.

"Or," Frank continued, and Calum groaned again. "I suppose I can just ask—" His gaze traveled around the room before he pointed at a man sitting close to the front. "*That guy* to invite her over. I've seen them chatting after class. I think he likes her."

Calum rolled his eyes, and the old man's shaggy eyebrows wiggled up and down. "Fine," Calum spoke. "You win. I . . . I'll ask her after class."

Frank smiled, pleased with himself.

The class went by quickly, and Calum stood when people began shuffling from the room. He caught sight of Tarrin bent over a stack of books, and Frank nudged him none-too-gently. Calum shook his head, exhaling, then pushed his way through the crowd of people to reach her. His heart beat fast when she raised her eyes to his and a smile lit her attractive features.

"Calum!" she spoke his name happily, and his words caught in his throat.

He swallowed hard and returned her smile. "Umm . . . hi." His voice sounded strained, and he forced himself to relax. "I enjoyed your class today," he spoke.

She nodded. "Thanks! How was your Thanksgiving?"

"Good. It was nice to have Jackie home, and Mary made an absolute feast. I'm going to have leftovers until next year."

Tarrin chuckled. "Mary brought me some left over pie. It was amazing," she replied, lifting her books into her arms.

She dropped a chart, and Calum reached out to catch it. "Here, let me." He reached for the stack of books.

"Thanks. Those actually need to go back to the center's library."

"No problem." He inhaled before he went on. "Listen, I was wondering . . . Frank invited me over for dinner, and I was wondering if you'd care to join me."

Her mouth twisted thoughtfully, and his heart froze. Why

did she make him feel like a stumbling teenager vying for his very first date? He gritted his teeth and waited for her rejection.

"What time?" she questioned.

He breathed again. "I didn't ask," he admitted, feeling ever-more awkward.

Tarrin laughed. "Well, no matter. I'd love to."

He grinned. "Great. I'll ask the time and give you a quick call. And I'll . . . uh . . . get these back where they belong." He nodded toward the stack of library materials in his arms. "I'll see you later."

ᙦ

Tarrin glanced at the clock as she entered the kitchen. She brought a hand to her stomach to quell the butterflies. Calum would be there soon and she was feeling eager for her dinner date. She stepped to the table, then turned when she heard Jake laugh. She peered around the corner, and a smile touched her lips.

"Well hello, Macin," she replied when she caught sight of Macin and Jake playing a board game with Lexie. "When did you get here?"

Macin waved and grinned. "Just a few minutes ago. Mom said she'd strangle me if I didn't disappear, so I came by. Hope you don't mind."

Tarrin laughed pleasantly. "You know you're always welcome," she replied, then faced Jake and Lexie. "Will you two be good for Aunt Erin?" She eyed her children meaningfully.

"Sure," Jake replied. "Where is she?"

"Upstairs. She's studying for finals, so try not to disturb her too much."

"Can I come with you, Mama?" Lexie asked. "I want to see Calum too."

Tarrin shook her head. "Not today."

Macin grinned. "It's about time he asked you out. I heard

Mom telling Grandma Mary that he's been madly in love with you for ages, he's just a coward."

Jake snorted and burst into laughter. Tarrin blushed, but had to force back a happy grin, and she jumped when a loud knock sounded on the old wooden door. She spun around and nearly tripped over the rug. She scrambled to regain her balance while the boys continued to snicker, and Tarrin shook her head, feeling exasperated. She composed her skirt before taking a deep breath. Calum knocked again and she opened the door.

"Hi," she greeted him. Her voice trembled slightly.

He stepped into the house and nodded cordially. "Hello."

When he smiled, Tarrin's heart lurched as she remembered Macin's words. The boys giggled again, and she cast them a warning glance. With sheepish grins, they turned back to their game while Lexie stood and ran into Calum's arms. He caught her up with a chuckle before replying, "How are you today?"

"Good," Lexie murmured.

He squeezed the little girl gently before setting her on her feet.

"Be a good girl. Don't bother Aunt Erin unless you really need something. Just ask Jake to help you," Tarrin reminded her.

"Mmm-hmm," the little girl nodded somberly.

"Have her home by midnight, mister!" Macin teased.

Calum chuckled, catching Tarrin's eye just as Jake snorted once again. Her son laughed aloud, and Tarrin's lips quirked. Jake was slowly accepting the fact she was dating again, and the thought pleased her. She knew they had made great strides as a family.

"Just wait, kid." Calum winked, and the boys continued to giggle.

Calum shook his head while he ushered her out the door, and Tarrin inhaled the crisp, fragrant air when they walked across the thin blanket of snow. They walked to Calum's car, parked on the curb. Despite the chilly air, Tarrin's palms were balmy, and she took a deep, calming breath when he held her door. She slid into the warm interior.

It took only moments to reach Frank and Kathy's familiar house, and they greeted Calum and Tarrin with wide smiles. The kitchen smelled amazing, and Tarrin's mouth watered. The beautifully laid setting was filled with bowls of steaming food and warm rolls.

Calum directed her to a chair then moved to sit opposite her. "This looks wonderful," he told Kathy.

"Yes, it does," Tarrin added.

"Oh, well, thank you, but do you know," Kathy paused, glancing toward her husband with a slow, conspirator's grin, "Frank and I have already eaten."

Tarrin's eyebrows rose, confused, and she cast a quick look at Calum. He raised a hand to rub his forehead. "Is that so?" he asked. His eyes shot to Frank's.

Frank patted his ample waistline. "Sure is so. Why don't you two go on and enjoy this wonderful meal, while my sweetheart and I burn off some calories. Care for a walk, dear?"

"That sounds wonderful. You two enjoy." Kathy reached for her purse hanging from the rack near the door, and Tarrin stared as Frank helped his wife shrug into her jacket.

They waved when they reached the door, and Frank winked before stepping out. Tarrin's gaze met Calum's, and he chuckled. "That sneaky old man."

"What was that all about?" Tarrin asked with a smile.

"I have a pretty good guess."

"What?" Tarrin asked. Her heart picked up pace.

Calum suddenly sobered, and his expression grew serious. "I think you and I need to talk," he stated matter-of-factly.

Tarrin bit her lower lip while she waited for him to continue.

"Tarrin." He exhaled slowly. "Look, I'm just going to say it. Tarrin," he paused, then went on. "I care about you—deeply," he said.

Tarrin's face reflected her surprise. Had she really just heard him speak those words?

His expression grew wary. "I realize this is a bit sudden, considering I've been a bit of a . . . well, as Jackie would put it—a *jerk*, lately. I wanted to give you time—space—after everything that had happened. So, I was kind of hoping you would give me another try. These last couple of months, I never stopped caring about you."

Tarrin lowered her eyes and stared toward her empty plate. Did he mean what he was saying? Could she trust the sincerity in his eyes? Her heart told her yes, but could she finally trust her heart? Trust and faith was something she had learned a lot about, and deep down she believed Calum to be sincere. His words were everything she hoped to hear and more. She closed her eyes briefly.

"Calum, I feel the same way . . . ." She paused, and his mouth twisted into a slight grimace.

"But?" he whispered.

She bit her lower lip. "I care deeply for you too, and I've missed you. I mean, you've been there, but—"

"But I haven't, and I'm sorry," he murmured. "Frank was kind enough to point that out today. I had no business waiting like this. I held back because I thought it was best for you, but I was wrong. I've missed you too. We can take things slow. I don't want to rush this. I can wait as long as you need."

Tarrin's stomach filled with butterflies, and she smiled. "You know I can't help being glad the kids and I moved here, despite what we've gone through, because—" She inhaled. "I care very deeply for you too," she whispered.

He regarded her carefully then leaned across the table to kiss her. His lips brushed across hers gently—as if testing her response. She returned his kiss, although a little awkwardly, across the table, and he chuckled when he pulled back. He took her hand in his. His thumb traced patterns along her skin and she shivered pleasantly.

"Well," he exhaled. "To be honest, eating is the last thing on my mind right now, but I'd hate to see all this food go to waste."

Tarrin couldn't help the laughter that burst from her lips. "And the table . . ."

"Yeah, there's that," he laughed with her. His brow rose. "On second thought, I'm not very hungry, and they have a pretty comfy couch."

Tarrin felt the blush rise in her cheeks. "No," she breathed, but smiled. "I'm not wasting Kathy's hard work."

They shared the meal Kathy had prepared while they laughed and talked. She had missed him more than she'd thought, and as she gazed at him across the table, she felt intensely happy. The past few months seemed to melt away. When they finished, they washed their dishes and cleared the table.

Rather than drive back to Tarrin's house, they took the opportunity to walk together. When their feet crunched on the quickly disappearing layer of snow, Tarrin remarked, "Jake and Macin are so disappointed we didn't get more."

"I saw the sleds. They might do better with water skis. This snow won't last long."

They reached Tarrin's house sooner than she wanted, and she sighed when he led her to the front porch. "Thank you for . . . for everything. The meal was wonderful," she said when she reached for the front door.

"I'll be sure to tell Kathy," he chuckled, then suddenly, he reached for her hand. Removing her fingers from the door knob, he curled his hand around hers.

"Tarrin," he whispered her name and placed his free hand against her hip. "I'm sorry. Really, I am. Forgive me, please? I should have never stayed away." He spoke, pulling her in against him.

Tarrin held her breath when his lips brushed against her ear. Closing her eyes for a moment, she savored the feel of his touch—the feel of his arms as they slid around her waist. She couldn't recall a time when she felt more alive. How she had missed him. She inhaled his familiar scent before she opened her eyes and stared into his.

"I understood. I shouldn't have thought . . . How could I have thought you were a murderer?" She ducked her head against his chest, and then shivered when his finger touched her chin, lifting her face toward his.

"It was never about that, Tarrin. Never. Zack tricked you. You had no reason to think he'd lie to you. I've been . . . scared. I'll admit it. I am a coward. But I never stopped caring about you. I just thought, that after everything you went through—after everything that happened . . . I worried if I pushed you, I'd lose you."

"I did need time, Calum," she confessed. "I did. It was better this way. I had so many feelings I needed to sort, especially concerning my marriage and the divorce with Travis. I'm in a better place now than I was. I've missed you, but I did worry that maybe . . . I worried I'd hurt you by believing Zack, even for a moment."

"You didn't," he answered, then laughed a little. "Okay, maybe a little, but I understood." He grinned. "Nobody wants to be branded a murderer."

Tarrin winced, but he pulled her closer. She could feel his warm breath against her forehead. Tenderly, he cupped her cheek.

"Tarrin," he whispered, "nothing else matters." His eyes held hers for several seconds before he went on. "I'm in love with you—very in love with you, Tarrin."

Tarrin inhaled sharply, and her heart hammered against her ribs. She closed her eyes briefly, savoring his words.

"Calum," she spoke his name. "I love you too."

Their eyes met in silent understanding, and his hand caressed her cheek. Her body trembled as he pressed his lips against hers. When their kiss deepened—the pain, grief, and uncertainty that had plagued her for so long melted under his touch. She inhaled, and tears burned her eyes while he kissed her face, her lips, and then the tip of her nose.

"I love you," she breathed once more.

"And I love you," Calum returned before catching her lips with his again.

Hope filled her soul, and their love chased the lingering shadows of doubt from her mind. When they drew apart, she laughed happily. He leaned his forehead against hers and inhaled deeply, then slowly lowered his hands from around her waist. A slow grin spread across his face, and he took a small step back.

"I . . . um . . . I think we might have an audience," he spoke, nodding toward the window.

A slat in the blinds dropped when Tarrin turned to look, and she sighed. "I think you're right. Would you like to come in?"

"I'd love to come in."

Reluctantly, Tarrin stepped into the house. Jake, Lexie, and Macin greeted them at the door and Lexie jumped into Calum's arms.

"Hi, princess." He hugged the little girl.

"Hi," Lexie murmured. She squeezed his neck before she placed her hands against his face.

Calum caught Tarrin's eye over the top of the little girl's head. A smile touched her lips.

"Can I come next time?" Lexie asked, leaning back to look into his eyes.

Calum laughed at the little girl's petulant expression, and he pinched her cheek gently. "Well, maybe if we beg your mom, we can all go out for ice cream tomorrow?"

"And the next day, and the next, and the next," Macin teased. He and Jake snickered, making kissing noises.

Tarrin gave the boys an exasperated glance, but her heart raced happily when Calum fixed his gaze on hers.

He looked at her for several moments, and she blushed under his intense stare.

"The kid has a point," he spoke. "But it isn't days I see when

I look into your eyes."

"Really?" Tarrin's lips twisted pleasantly. "What do you see?" she asked.

"Oh, *much* longer. What do you see?" he asked, grinning.

Tarrin hugged her stomach and looked deeply into his eyes. She could see her and the children's reflection in their dark, vibrant depths. She smiled and knew she truly loved him. Calum took a step forward. He touched her cheek gently, and with a joy she hadn't felt before, Tarrin leaned into his embrace.

"I see—a family," she whispered.

"So do I," he replied. "Family."

About The Author

*M*andi Tucker Slack currently resides in Santaquin, Utah with her husband and four children. She is a stay-at-home mom who loves spending time in the outdoors with her family. They love to camp, hike, fish, and rockhound in their spare time. She and her children are always on the look-out for a new adventure. Fade to Gray is Mandi's third novel.

Find Mandi on Facebook at www.facebook.com/MandiSlack/.

www.ingramcontent.com/pod-product-compliance
Lightning Source LLC
Chambersburg PA
CBHW020607180626
46810CB00007B/2678